What Readers Are Saying About Miss Match

"I found *Miss Match* at our library, and it was great timing. I got pretty close to finishing it in the middle of the night the first night I had it! I did finish it in the morning and took it to church for my best friend to read. I really, really loved it and am going to be looking for the sequel for sure! Thanks for the fun, clean read!"

—JENNESS W.

"I loved it. I can't wait until Erynn's next book comes out!"

—LAUREN L.

"*Miss Match* was great! I read a lot, and *Miss Match* ranks up there as one of my favorites. I hated to see it end. I went to Erynn's website to see when *Rematch* would be available to preorder. I have to know if Lauren meets or has already met her match! Erynn, keep up the good—no, make that great—work."

—SANDY S.

"I just finished reading *Miss Match*, and I absolutely loved it! I have read a ton of chick-lit novels, and this has got to be one of my favorites! I'm a twentysomething career girl and can so relate to Lauren's character (although what girl can't?), especially the crazy random thoughts that spout out of her mouth and, of course, her love for chocolate. This book has more meat than other chick-lit novels I've read and is even more in tune with the life of a twentysomething, where everyone and their uncle is getting married. *Miss Match* is a fantastic first novel. I can't wait for *Rematch*!"

—MICHELLE D.

"It's amazing! The characters are funny and believable. And I love Erynn's sense of humor!"

—KATELYN R.

Also by Erynn Mangum

A Lauren Holbrook Novel: *Miss Match*

a lauren holbrook novel|book 2

e r y n n   m a n g u m

REMATCH

NAVPRESS

www.thinkbooks.com

NavPress is the publishing ministry of The Navigators, an international Christian organization and leader in personal spiritual development. NavPress is committed to helping people grow spiritually and enjoy lives of meaning and hope through personal and group resources that are biblically rooted, culturally relevant, and highly practical.

For a free catalog go to www.NavPress.com
or call 1.800.366.7788 in the United States or 1.800.839.4769 in Canada.

© 2007 by Erynn Mangum

NAVPRESS and the NAVPRESS logo are registered trademarks of NavPress. Absence of ® in connection with marks of NavPress or other parties does not indicate an absence of registration of those marks.

ISBN-13: 978-1-60006-096-0
ISBN-10: 1-60006-096-X

Cover design by studiogearbox.com
Cover image by studiogearbox.com
Author photo by Portrait Innovations
Creative Team: Melanie Knox, Amy Parker, Kathy Mosier, Arvid Wallen, Kathy Guist

This novel is a work of fiction. Names, characters, places, and incidents are either the product of the author's imagination or are used fictitiously. Any resemblance to actual events, locales, organizations, or persons, living or dead, is entirely coincidental and beyond the intent of either the author or publisher.

All Scripture quotations in this publication are taken from the HOLY BIBLE: NEW INTERNATIONAL VERSION® (NIV®). Copyright © 1973, 1978, 1984 by International Bible Society. Used by permission of Zondervan Publishing House. All rights reserved.

Mangum, Erynn, 1985-
  Rematch : a Lauren Holbrook novel, book 2 / Erynn Mangum.
     p. cm.
  ISBN-13: 978-1-60006-096-0
  ISBN-10: 1-60006-096-X
  1. Dating (Social customs)--Fiction. I. Title.
  PS3613.A5373R46 2007
  813'.6--dc22
                              2007020196

Printed in the United States of America

3 4 5 6 7 8 9 10 / 11 10 09 08

To Cayce Louise Mangum. As completely gorgeous as you are on the outside, it's your inner beauty that is so captivating. I'm incredibly blessed to have a best friend who is also my sister. Our late-night conversations and movie dates are some of my favorite memories. I love you, Kiki!

Acknowledgments

To the One who holds my heart. Lord, I love so many things about You. I love how Your Word speaks to me just when I need it most. I love how You use the happy times to show me Your grace and the sad times to show me Your mercy. I love the way You comfort me when I'm feeling overwhelmed and the way You discipline me when I'm straying from You. Father, this book is all for You. I love You.

Thanks also to:

Mom, who is so willing to pour her time and energy into each one of her kids and their passions. You amaze me! Thank you so much for all the work you've put into this book and *Miss Match*. I love you!

Dad, who has always been able to make me laugh harder than anyone else. I'm so grateful for all the things you've taught me and for everything you've done to make this dream come true. I love you!

Bryant, who despite every reason I've given him to hate me is still one of the two best brothers in the world. You're awesome. God has blessed me so much with your friendship. Love you!

Caleb, who is one of the funniest guys I know. I absolutely love your sense of humor and the way you brighten a room when you walk in. You're amazing, and I love spending time with you. Love ya!

Cayce, my little sister, who is also my hero. I love how close we are;

I wouldn't trade it for the world. You never cease to amaze me—how you can be so tough when faced with a hard situation and so soft when someone is hurting. I love you!

Nama, my grandmother who consistently shows her grace and sweetness even in the midst of really hard times. I am so blessed to have a role model like you in my life. I love you!

My fabulous extended family: You guys have put up with a lot from me, and I love each of you so very much!

My wonderful friends: God has blessed me so much with you. You have made me laugh and helped me grow, and I love you for it!

NavPress, my amazing publisher, and specifically to Kate Epperson, Melanie Knox, Amy Parker, Kathy Mosier, Kate Berry, Danielle Douglas, Jessica Chappell, and Rebekah Guzman: You are all amazing women! I'm so grateful to know each of you; this book is much better because of you. Thank you so much for everything—I'm sorry if I bug you with all my constant e-mails!

David Terry for all the counsel and encouragement you've given me. Thank you so much!

The Christian Writers Guild for guiding me through this journey with incredible support. To my mentors, Terry White and Brandilyn Collins, who taught me more than they will ever know. Thank you so very, very much!

WebMD and Wikipedia—amazing online treasure troves.

And last, but definitely not least, two girls who formed my love of Jane Austen and coffee: Shannon Kay, who first introduced me to both *Pride and Prejudice* and Starbucks. Without you, darlin', I would be a much different person. God was so amazingly kind to bless me with a friend like you! I love you! And Kaitlin Bouloy, who would disappear with me for a full day watching Jane Austen classics and helping me eat a huge bag of candy and drink Frappucinos in the process. You are wonderful! I thank God so much for you. I love you!

Chapter One

I sling my backpack over my shoulder and march up the walk past the land-scaped grounds. The Colorado day is sunshiny; birds are chirping. The door squeaks slightly as I open it.

The lingering scent of coffee brushes my nostrils.

Starbucks seems fairly empty, but maybe this is just not a busy time of day.

I find the cash register hidden behind a gargantuan pile of those annoy-ingly breathy CDs they sell and tap my nails on the counter.

A kid about twenty, with scruffy red stuff masquerading as a beard and a serious wrinkle above his eyebrows, slinks in from the back.

"I'd like a Venti Mocha, extra mocha, with a triple shot of espresso and whipped cream, please," I say before he opens his mouth.

The wrinkle deepens. "We're out of coffee, ma'am," he mumbles.

I blink.

"I'd like a Venti Mocha," I begin again.

He holds up a hand, silencing me. "We're out of coffee, ma'am," he says louder. "The whole city is. We were supposed to get a shipment of coffee beans early this morning. The delivery guy who supplies this town accidentally drove his truck off a cliff late last night. I'm sorry, ma'am. Can I interest you in a vanilla creme?"

Shock starts at my toes, electrocutes my kneecaps, buzzes my heart, and finally kicks my brain.

I grip the counter until the veins in my knuckles turn neon magenta and try to control the shaking.

"Where did the truck crash?" I ask. My voice is sheer desperation.

"Why?"

"Maybe . . . maybe we could salvage some of the beans!"

The kid frowns; then the sheer brilliance of the plan must occur to him. His face brightens. "Yes!" he says. "That's it! Quick! Gather everyone you know! We'll need a lot of people!"

I shake off the lack-of-caffeine attack, straighten, and rush for the door. "I'll be back in fifteen minutes!"

———⊕———

"Laurie? Laurie!"

I jerk awake.

The sickening scent of lemongrass tea drifts to my nose. *Blegh!* Definitely not the smell I want to wake up to. Dad's concern-creased forehead hovers above my face. He shakes my shoulder and I blink.

"Honey, you fell asleep on the couch last night. You need to go to work soon."

I rub my face and shift to a sitting position, feeling the imprint of the sofa's fabric on my cheek.

Last night Ruby Palmer and Nick Amery tied the knot. I had this great idea that they should literally tie a knot, but Nick didn't go for it. It's sad how many people don't recognize a true sense of humor.

Ruby is my coworker, and she and Nick left last night for an amazing two-week honeymoon in the Caribbean. I begged Nick to let me carry their bags, but he said no.

My life is so unfair. You'd think Nick would realize that this is my one chance to meet Orlando Bloom on a pirate ship.

Hannah Curtis is another coworker of mine who's quickly ranking next to Brandon Knox as my best friend. Here's the thing about her:

1. She's beautiful. And it turns out it's not in the plastic, Barbie-like form of the word, but just absolutely gorgeous—both inside and out.

2. She recently became a Christian and is growing like crazy in her faith.

3. She can cook!

So I know that Hannah's fate will include marriage because nobody turns down a woman like that.

Confession: I'm really hoping *nobody* includes Brandon.

Second Confession (Judgment Day will be interesting, let me tell you): I'm kind of, sort of, maybe, possibly getting them to run into each other quite frequently. *Accidentally*, of course.

I am a matchmaker.

And since Brandon is always clueless and Hannah already has a small crush on him, this should be a cinch.

Well, "should be" isn't always as it should be.

For instance, last week we ran out of stamps at the photography studio. So, rather than be a good employee and a faithful servant, I told Brandon to go to the post office to get more while simultaneously asking Hannah to go there to mail some letters.

And we wouldn't want to waste precious gasoline during this shortage, right? As Zorro would say, "Of course no!"

Thus, they rode together.

Rather, they were *supposed* to ride together. But Hannah developed a brain and realized that Brandon could just take the letters himself and she could stay at the studio.

Crafty, that girl.

I have a feeling it will take more than just brownies to meld these two together.

Maybe a chocolate pie is in order.

—⊛—

I get to The Brandon Knox Photography Studio dressed in a skirt. Shocked?

Yeah, so am I. This is what happens when the coffeepot breaks after making only one and a half cups. Thus the cup from Merson's in my hand, filled to the brim with a mixture of coffee, cream, and sugar so powerful I nearly bowed to it on the drive over here.

Hannah looks up as I open the door.

"Morning, Laurie."

"Hey."

She takes my backpack and slides it into my cubbyhole for me. "So Ruby and Nick are married." She smiles sappily.

"Yeah."

"Thanks to us."

I choke on my coffee. "Thanks to who?"

"All right. You. But I helped!" She jabs her finger in my face.

"You helped. Where's Brandon?"

"In his office. He's getting crazy about finances, so watch out for him today."

I quirk an eyebrow. "Cranky?"

Hannah nods, her eyes big.

"Where is Ty?" I ask.

"He's already taking pictures. And Newton's on vacation." She looks behind me and grins. "Hey, I'll be right back."

She disappears into Studio One and shuts the door.

The bell over the door rings.

"Hey, Laur."

"Hi, Ryan." Figures. Drat that Hannah.

Ryan is a builder, and today he looks it. His hair curls ringlet style all over his head as if it hasn't seen a brush in a couple of weeks, even though I know for a fact that he brushed it for his sister Ruby's wedding. He wears faded, beat-up jeans and, even though it's summer, a long-sleeved flannel shirt.

Ryan's one of those guys whose wardrobe doesn't change whether it's nineteen or ninety degrees outside.

He looks around at the empty lobby and closed doors.

"Quiet here today. When was the last time that happened?"

"Before my conception." I smile at him. "What are you doing here?"

"Just came by to say hey. We're starting a new project today." He sighs. "I'm going to need a lot of prayer, Laur."

"What's the project?"

He groans as he says it. "Mrs. Galen."

I press my lips together. "Ah."

"Yeah." He rakes a hand through his hair. "She wanted me to meet the architect at her house. So I went over there. It's like *The Twilight Zone*, I swear!"

I nod. "I've been there."

"There's an elevator in her house!" he exclaims.

"I know."

"And those Venus flytrap things are everywhere. One tried to eat the side of my pants." He rubs his leg.

"There's a rumor going around that one of them ate Mrs. Galen's dog."

He makes a face. "That is gross."

"Not really. It was a Chihuahua. It's hard for me to get too emotional over the world losing another ankle biter."

He laughs. "It's good to see you, Laurie." His cute little fourth-grader on-the-monkey-bars smile appears, making his eyes sparkle. His eyes are just plain brown until he smiles. "So actually I did come here to ask you something."

"Shoot," I say.

"Want to go get lunch with me today?"

"Where?"

"Merson's?"

I snort. Unladylike, I know. "Did you have to ask?"

He grins again. "I heard somewhere that it was better to ask than just assume."

"Huh. Well, I learn something new every day."

"You look pretty, Laurie. I don't think I've ever seen you in a skirt outside of church."

I show him my coffee cup. "Our coffeemaker broke."

He frowns. "There's a connection here, I know it. . . ."

"I wasn't awake when I got dressed."

"Oh. Well, I like it." He turns toward the door. "I'll be here about twelve thirty."

"Okay. Have a good morning. Keep away from the man-eating plant. Closest one to the elevator."

He chuckles and leaves.

I sit in one of the chairs in front of Hannah's desk.

Hannah comes out of the studio, grinning. I shake my head. I will have to be put in a rest home many years before my time because of her. "How's Ryan?" She bats her eyelashes flirtatiously.

"And here I thought I was having a private conversation." I roll my eyes. "I'm not sure why. I never do here."

"The walls are wired. So lunch?"

"So breakfast?"

"So Merson's?"

"So Vizzini's?"

She sticks her tongue out, licks an envelope, seals it, and flaps it at me. "Altar in seven?"

What she means is this: Will you be getting married in seven months?

"In your dreams."

What I mean is this: Um . . . in her dreams.

She smiles at me in that "Gee, I'm sorry your whole life is dependent on a guy" smile, which I do not deserve. I am standing here holding coffee, aren't I? "Don't worry," she says, "it'll happen."

"Mmm."

She changes the subject. "How's Laney?"

"Big." My oldest sister, Laney, is eight months pregnant with the fully grown Jackson Five. Actually, it's just twins. She's big enough for the Five, though.

"Nothing new?"

"She picked the names."

Hannah looks up. "Great! So she told you whether they're boys or girls? What are the names?"

"Jamie and Sammie."

She starts laughing. "She didn't tell you the sex, did she?"

"No."

Mr. and Mrs. Gordon, along with their two kids, open the front door and troop in.

"Hi, Lau-rie," Mrs. Gordon singsongs. Mrs. Gordon is an opera singer and likes to remind people of that fact.

Mr. Gordon grunts something that could have been my name. Little Keithy, Boy Wonder, blows a snot bubble at me. Little Gina, Girl Einstein, sneers.

There are days when I hate my job.

"Oh, Laurie, I absolutely *love* your skirt," Mrs. Gordon raves. "Look, children! Doesn't she look simply *divine*?"

Mrs. Gordon is fairly large and has a penchant for speaking in italics and using her hands animatedly. Mr. Gordon, though, has never spoken anything in English to me and relies on grunts to get his point across. No wonder Keithy and Gina are such holy terrors. I drain my coffee as I follow them into Studio Two.

I wave good-bye to the Gordons at ten and turn to Hannah. She dimples.

"What?" I ask.

"Guess who called."

"Brad Pitt?"

She rolls her eyes. "Laur, if Brad Pitt had called, do you think I'd tell you? Do you think I'd still be here?"

"Um, no."

"Ruby called."

"From the Caribbean?" I ask. Then I frown. "Isn't it poor form to call your workplace on your honeymoon?"

Hannah shrugs. "Well, she did it anyway. Said to tell everyone they're on the cruise ship and having a great time."

I sit in one of the chairs. I love Ruby and Nick. I honestly do. But thinking about good friends on their honeymoon and what they might be doing . . . it's downright disturbing. Not good for healthy emotional growth, you understand.

Brandon comes out of his office waving a piece of paper at me.

"Have you seen this?" he asks.

"Nope."

He stops in front of me, frowning. "It's your paycheck from last December. You haven't seen it?"

"I didn't know what it was, Brandon." I take the paper.

"Look at how much you made!" he says loudly in my ear.

Brandon is similar to my sister Lexi in that he does not know the theory of distance in relation to sound. He cannot grasp the concept that when I am standing right next to him, he does not need to yell.

I look at the amount on the copied check.

"This is how much I always make, Brandon." I smile sweetly at him. "Does this mean I'm getting a raise?"

"Nope. Just wanted to show it to you." He grins evilly, and I smack his head with the paper. Hannah watches all this, laughing.

"Hannah, I need a companion who doesn't create conflict." I groan, rubbing my forehead.

"You could get a pet, I suppose," Hannah says. "Lucky is a good pal. And she keeps me in shape." She pats her abs. I've never actually seen Hannah's abs, but I have seen her arms and legs, and the girl is more toned than Hilary Swank.

Heck, if getting a dog did that for Hannah . . .

"Where'd you get Lucky?" I ask.

"The shelter. I saw an ad for boxer-cross puppies." Hannah frowns. "But Lucky's not big enough to be a boxer, so who knows?"

Brandon shakes his head. "Laurie, the last thing you need is something to be responsible for."

"You're great at compliments, you know?"

He winks and goes back into his office.

"The shelter, huh?" I ask.

"Have Ryan take you by on your way back from lunch," she says offhandedly, but I see the gleam in her eyes.

"Hannah, Darlin', there's only room for one matchmaker in this town, and you're looking at her." I stand and wave as my ten fifteen walks through the door.

A dog.

Dad might not go for a dog.

I couldn't keep it at my sister Lexi's, either, because Lexi has a dog. Muffin. A little terrier who attacks my ankles and has ruined three pairs of good shoes.

I would fear for my dog's life if I left him at Lexi's.

Or Laney's. Laney has three kids, and that's about as bad as a terrier.

Plus, I'm not even sure I want a dog. Maybe I'm not a dog person. Maybe I'm a bird person. I saw this study once about people's personalities tending toward one animal or another.

I wonder if you have to take a personality test before the shelter lets you adopt?

Chapter Two

Ryan picks me up a little after twelve thirty.

"Hey," he says to me, coming inside, swinging his keys around his index finger. "Hi, Hannah."

She smiles at him. "Ryan. Gee, are you two going to lunch together?"

I roll my eyes at Ryan and grab my backpack. "Good-bye, Hannah," I sing.

"Don't rush back now."

I climb into Ryan's truck. "I'm going to match Brandon and Hannah," I tell him matter-of-factly, buckling my seat belt.

Ryan turns the ignition and sighs. "Here we go again."

I take on a superhero tone. "Ryan. They need my help."

He humors me with a smile. "Look, Laur, they're both Christians; they're both mildly sane; I think they'll figure it out if they're meant to be together."

"You know, Brandon told me once he thought Hannah was pretty," I say. "Maybe I could sort of remind him of that. . . ."

"Stay out of it, Laurie."

"We could have dinner on Wednesday before Bible study."

"Laurie."

"I could make brownies. It worked for Nick and Ruby."

"Laurie!"

"What?"

He shakes his head. "Never mind. It doesn't do any good to tell you no."

I grin and rub his shoulder. "Well, at least you're learning."

He pulls the truck into a parking space in front of Merson's, the cutest little restaurant ever. It's owned by Shawn Merson, who won me over with great coffee and Dessert Heaven. He's the one man in the world other than Brandon who has refused me coffee.

It takes a very secure man to attempt that.

"Hi, Shawn!" I call as we walk in.

He waves. "Be right with you, Laurie. Hey, Ryan." He hands a curly-haired woman a piece of apple pie and takes his place behind the counter.

"Hi, Shawn," Ryan says, letting me go in front of him. Ryan's like that. Girls always go first. Ruby trained him well.

"So, Laurie, Ruby and Nick are married. Who's your next project?" Shawn grins.

Shawn knows about my skills because Merson's coffee and chocolate-covered strawberries have been used to soothe wounded hearts.

"Well," I start.

Ryan butts in. "Come on, Shawn. Help me out here and don't ask her."

"He likes to torture you, Ryan. Haven't you figured that out yet?" I turn back to Shawn, leaning over the counter. "Brandon and Hannah."

Shawn whistles. "Tough stuff, Laur."

"Yeah. Especially considering they're totally oblivious to each other."

Shawn's eyebrows crinkle. "And you still think they're going to be a couple?"

"They're right for each other, Shawn," I confide. "I can feel it."

He *tsks*. "Well, you've got the magical touch, so I won't argue. What can I get you?"

"I want a slice of your chocolate cheesecake," I say.

Ryan squeezes my shoulder. "Not feeling healthy today, I gather." He turns to Shawn. "A turkey sandwich, hold the mayo."

"And two coffees," I order.

Shawn chuckles. "Those are a given, Girl. Have a seat. I'll have it right out."

Ryan picks a table by the windows, and I sit. "I'm thinking about getting a dog," I tell him.

He blinks. "A dog?"

"Yeah. What do you think?"

"Dogs are a lot of work, you know."

I shrug. "I know. But Lucky gave Hannah abs, so I figure . . ."

Ryan shakes his head. "You're already beautiful, Laurie. And you have to exercise with the dog to get abs."

My cheeks heat suddenly, and I fiddle with my napkin. Ryan's so easy with compliments; it's hard to tell if he *means* them or if he is just a sweet boy.

How is it that I can clearly see other people's feelings but can never see Ryan's?

I clench my napkin in my lap, will the blushing to stop, and shrug. "I could start exercising."

Shawn sets the cheesecake, sandwich, and coffees down. "Have a good lunch, guys," he says, touching my shoulder.

Ryan smiles at me, takes one of my hands, and says a quick blessing.

I echo Ryan's "amen" and watch Shawn go back to the counter. "Shawn's a nice guy," I say, mostly to myself.

Ryan bites into his sandwich. "Mm-hmm."

"How old do you think he is?"

Ryan finishes chewing. "I don't know. Twenty-six. Twenty-seven."

"Hmm." I watch Shawn smile at a cute little girl and give her a cookie.

"Lau-rie . . ." Ryan says.

I hate it when he draws my name out like that.

"What?"

"Don't you even—"

"Oh, Ryan, why not? He's single; he's nice to look at; he's got a whole wall of desserts." I point to the glass-encased heaven.

"And just who would you arrange him with?"

"I don't know. I'm sure it will come to me, though."

Ryan shakes his head. "You're an amazing woman."

He doesn't say it admiringly, but I take it as a compliment anyway. "Thanks." I fork off a chunk of Oreo crust, chocolate-cheese filling, and whipped cream.

Mmm. I have decided where I am going to die.

"Maybe I'll marry Shawn," I say after swallowing.

Ryan grins at me. "Uh-huh."

"What? He needs to marry a woman who will appreciate him on all levels. And I definitely appreciate his culinary talents."

"Honey, he wouldn't have any desserts left to sell if he married you."

"Yeah, well. He could just sell sandwiches."

"And he's not a Christian."

"But that can change. Look at Hannah." I wave my fork at Ryan. "Too bad she's already matched. If she married Shawn, I could come visit her."

"And thereby get free desserts."

"Exactly." I smile at him. "See? You're getting it. One of these days you'll take over matchmaking, and I can just relax and watch movies."

"Considering the movies you watch, either option is dangerous."

"Hey!" I yell. "What's wrong with my movies?"

"How much time do I have?" he says. He ticks the points off on his fingers. "They're totally unrealistic, completely corny, filled with bad actors, and have too much kissing." He makes a face. "And then there's *Pride and Prejudice*—"

I hold up a hand. "If you're going to critique my all-time favorite movie, I'm afraid this is it, Buddy."

He picks up his mug and smiles at me. "Okay. I won't."

"Smart. So. Shawn."

"*So*," he mimics. "Leave it alone."

"But he's lonely," I beg.

Shawn pours me a refill. "Who's lonely?" he asks.

"You," I inform him.

"Yeah, lucky you," Ryan dressles over the rim of his mug.

Here's what I do: Make up words.

Dressle: (*v*) To say something intending to be funny.

Shawn sets the pot down and holds his hands up. "Whoa, Laurie. Okay, listen. It's entertaining to watch you do this to other people—"

"Thank you."

"But I'd rather not experience it myself."

"You have to admit you'd like a girlfriend," I say, jabbing him in the chest.

"Yeah, but so would everyone."

"Married people wouldn't."

Shawn looks at Ryan, pain etched on his face.

Ryan shakes his head. "Don't look at me, Pal. I'm powerless here."

"She's your girlfriend. Corral her, please."

"First," I start, "Ryan is not my boyfriend. Second—"

"He's not?" Shawn interrupts.

"I'm not?" Ryan asks.

I blink repeatedly at him. "You are?"

"He is?" Shawn asks.

"I think I am," Ryan says.

"You do?"

"He does," Shawn says.

"I do," Ryan says.

I press my lips together, trying not to laugh. Ryan's eyes twinkle dangerously. Shawn still looks from me to Ryan, confused.

"You know what?" Shawn says finally. "I think I'll just leave."

"Probably safest," Ryan says, looking at me.

Shawn leaves, mumbling something about womanly conversation.

Ryan still watches me, a smile flirting with his mouth. "So what's with this confusion, Laurie?"

"Ryan, we were pretending to date earlier. How was I supposed to know we switched to real dating?"

"You know, for being such an expert in other people's dating lives, you're basically a novice in your own." He sets his coffee on the table and takes one of my hands. "But that's one reason I like you."

"Because I'm clueless?" I say, guppies exploding in my stomach and the blush firing up again.

He tips his head as he studies me. "I was actually thinking *naive*, but I guess clueless works." He squeezes my fingers lightly and lets go, picking up his sandwich again.

I breathe and stab my cheesecake. "So blind date has been done," I say.

"What?"

"Brandon and Hannah. They've already watched Nick and Ruby do the blind-date thing. What's something else we could do?"

He swallows. "You switch subjects faster than a . . ." He shakes his head. "I leave analogies to you."

"And yet another compliment. My gracious, Ryan. Whatever is in that coffee must be good for you."

He smiles and then shakes his head again. "Do us all a favor. Leave Shawn alone. At least for a little while."

"Fine." I frown.

"So how's the memorization going?" he asks, taking another bite of his sandwich.

Ryan and I are having a contest as to who can memorize the most Bible verses that have the word *delight* in them. It's a favorite word of mine.

"I have six," I say proudly. "How about you?"

He immediately grins.

"No way!" I yell. "How many?"

"Nine."

"How do you do it?" I'm in awe. It takes a lot of work for me to memorize a verse—particularly if I want to remember it for more than a day or two.

He shrugs. "Most verses have a natural rhythm to them. I just sort of go with that."

"I guess we could make up little songs."

"I guess *you* could make up little songs," he revises.

"'Delight yourself in the Lord and he will give you the desires of your heart.'" I sing this to the tune of "John Jacob Jingleheimer Schmidt." Quite loudly, actually.

Ryan laughs and shakes his head. Shawn comes over and grabs my coffee cup.

"Hey!" I yell.

He doesn't even apologize. "You're done with the caffeine."

Ryan drops me off at the studio at two. "Want to come in?" I ask him.

"I need to get back to Mrs. Galen's." He makes a face.

I pat his arm. "Buck up, Cowboy. You'll live."

"Maybe."

"See you later." I open the door and climb out.

"Hey, Laurie," he says as I start to close the door.

"Yeah?"

"Want a ride for Wednesday night?"

"Free gas? Are you kidding? Absolutely."

He chuckles. "I'll pick you up at seven."

I close his truck door, wave, and walk through the glass door.

A yellow sticky note is on Hannah's desk. In Hannah's handwriting: *Went to lunch, Laurie.* In Brandon's handwriting underneath: *Get in my office, Laurie.*

I march down the hallway and slam open his door.

"You demanded; I came." I climb on his desk and sit cross-legged on top of it. "Thus the sorry life I lead."

He grins at me, leaning back in his chair. "Very funny."

"What's up?" I ask.

"I need to run some figures by you."

"Sure thing. Whose figure? Johnny Depp's?"

He sighs. "Why do I keep you around again?"

I spread my hands out. "That should be fairly obvious, Brandon. You love me."

"Right. So here are some *equations* I need you to look at."

I stare at the jumble of numbers on the page he gives me. "What is this?"

"Hannah's raise and how it would affect the budget."

"And you're showing me this because . . . ?"

"Because I think you should start learning the business of photography."

I blink at him. "Why?"

"Just in case you want to run this business one day."

I nearly fall off the desk, I laugh so hard.

"Maybe I should have shown Hannah instead."

"Yep, you should've." I cross my arms. "What happened to you thinking she was gorgeous?"

He blinks at the change of subject. "What?"

"Oh please. Remember the first time you saw her? You looked at her like you were an Eskimo and she was a cruise ship to Hawaii."

His face twists. "You have the weirdest examples, you know?"

I sock his shoulder. "Don't knock the talent, Kid. I just got complimented on my analogies not even an hour ago."

"By Ryan?" Brandon hums.

"You thought she was gorgeous," I say.

He clears his throat. "Well, she is."

"And now she's a Christian . . ."

"Mmm."

"Make that a gorgeous Christian."

He shakes his head, mouth open. "You are unbelievable," he says slowly. He closes his eyes. "Laurie Holbrook, I can't believe you!"

I lean back. "What?"

"You are trying to set me up with Hannah!" He jabs a finger in my face, and I swat it away.

I play evasive. "What are you talking about?"

He stares at me. "You are such a pathetic—"

"But personable," I interrupt.

"Persistent . . ."

"Pleasant," I add.

"Pain in the rear," Brandon finishes.

"And pretty," I supplement.

He smacks my shoulder. "Get out. Send Hannah in when she gets back."

I hop off his desk and salute. "Sir, yes, sir!" And close his door with a bang.

Man, I am good!

I climb into bed at exactly eleven o'clock and turn on my bedside lamp, pulling my Bible over. This past winter I read through Paul's letters to the churches and discovered a characteristic of God I had only heard references to: His sovereignty. I've now changed the pace a little bit and am reading through Psalms.

I pause on Psalm 42:2: "My soul thirsts for God, for the living God."

What does that look like, practically?

Chapter Three

Wednesday night Bible study takes place at Nick's house. Since he's on his honeymoon, he's letting Stephen Weatherby, our local med student/ guitarist, housesit and lead the study.

Ryan holds the door for me, and we walk into pandemonium.

Nick needs a bigger house, or we need to start meeting at a church.

Married Couple Numbers 4, 7, and 9 chat in the entry; Nikki and John, who will be married on Saturday, smile adoringly at each other on the staircase; and twenty-odd people fill the living room, kitchen, and hallway. I set the brownies I brought with me gingerly on the counter, praying for them to still be there after the study is over.

Ryan pushes me through the crowd, and I fall down next to Hannah, who must have gotten here yesterday to save us seats on the sofa.

"Hi, Laurie, long time no see."

"About two hours now. Have a nice dinner?"

Brandon joins us. I smile at him.

"Hey, guys," he says in a low voice, smiling. He stands in front of the three of us, hands in the pockets of his jeans. He's wearing a white T-shirt under a navy blue, short-sleeved, collared shirt. His straight dark hair is doing the flick-up thing because he apparently put some gel in it. He looks good.

This is an opportune moment. "Hey, Hannah, can you go check on the brownies and make sure they're still there?" I ask, smiling.

"Didn't you just put them there like thirty seconds ago?" she says.

"Yeah, but you never know. There're ten guys here without girlfriends. And the girl half of Married Couple Number 2 is experimenting with healthy foods. The boy half might have eaten them."

Brandon starts laughing. "I'll go, Laurie."

I must think quick. "I don't trust you alone with them," I say, shaking my head. "Hannah, please?"

"Fine." She stands.

Brandon puts a hand on her shoulder and leads her into the kitchen. Meanwhile, Hannah's seat is quickly filled by the engaged Nikki.

Oh no.

"So I must admit it," Ryan says, leaning close to my ear.

"Admit what?"

"You were right. About Brandon and Hannah."

I look at him and grin.

"And you can wipe that smirk off your face."

"Just wait until they get to the brownies."

He leans back, shaking his head. "You're something, Laurie."

I shrug. "I guess I'd rather be something than nothing."

"Slowly rotting their insides with chocolate," he mutters. "I hope you realize that by feeding this garbage to them, you are, in fact, shortening their life spans."

"Not true! Chocolate is an antioxidant," I say.

"Meaning?"

"Meaning that it can fight cancer, reduce heart disease, and even lower cholesterol," I say proudly. "Besides, studies have shown that chocolate lovers live longer."

He shakes his head. "It's disturbing how seriously you say all that."

Stephen Weatherby stands on his chair and waves his hands. "Hey! Hey! Hey!"

"Look, Fat Albert!" I point.

Ryan slaps a hand over his mouth, muffling the laugh.

"Let's get started! Find a seat, everyone!" Stephen yells.

People sort themselves out and plop down everywhere. I look around and finally find Brandon and Hannah on the stairs.

Sitting together. *Close* together. Mostly, I think, because there's one-half of Engaged Couple Number 8 smashed on the stair with them.

But together nonetheless.

I am beyond good!

Ryan pokes me in the ribs. "Just for that, you'll get a lesson on pride," he whispers.

I need to find someone who can't read my thoughts so easily.

"And I'm not going anywhere until you do," he says.

Rats. Sickening, I tell you.

Stephen sits down on his chair and whips his guitar into place. "Hey, everyone," he grins. "So Nick's on his honeymoon with his gorgeous bride . . ."

Someone whistles.

"Yeah, exactly. So be praying for their safety in the Caribbean. Meanwhile, we'll be meeting here next week as well, so be sure to come."

I look around, noting the number of married people.

Don't they know that a singles' Bible study is for singles? You'd think that would be self-explanatory, but maybe not.

Stephen keeps rattling off announcements.

Remember in corny movies the Sunlight Beam scene? It starts like this: Single Guy is looking around the room for the woman of his dreams, and, *boom!*, like all of nature is catering to this one woman, there she is — bathed in sunlight for the world to see, yet apparently not realizing it herself.

Single Guy then knows innately that this is *she*—the one of his dreams! Obviously, because otherwise the Sunlight Beam would have landed on someone fairer.

Well, I kid you not—in this exact moment I experience the Sunlight Beam scene!

I watch the song sheets make their way around the room and suddenly realize that the setting sun is shining directly through the windows and, *bam!*, landing smack on a pretty red-haired girl I have never seen before.

I elbow Ryan. He winces and leans closer.

"Who's that?" I whisper.

"Who?"

"The one bathed in sunlight."

He looks at me for a full ten seconds, one eyebrow cocked. Then, like he doesn't believe me, he turns to where I am discreetly pointing.

He blinks and shrugs. "I don't know."

"She's pretty."

"Leave it alone," he mutters.

"I wonder how old she is?"

"I swear, Laurie . . ." he says through the side of his mouth, smiling at Married Couple Number 2 on the floor in front of us as he takes the song sheets from them.

I lean against the cushions, watching her inconspicuously. She smiles at the married woman next to her, her hair slipping out from behind her ear.

Like I said, pretty.

I decide she is about five four and as such would be the perfect height. Her hair is red, and she has green eyes.

Green eyes are getting rare, just like natural blond hair. I once heard that in fifty years there won't be any more natural blonds. Thus, natural blonds are supposed to marry other natural blonds to prevent total annihilation.

The same follows for green eyes, right?

I elbow Ryan again.

He cringes and leans over again. "What?"

"Shawn has green eyes."

"So?"

Stephen rakes his pick down the guitar strings. *Twang.*

"Day by day, and with each passing moment . . ." everyone sings.

I smile at Ryan.

And thus it is set. Mystery Girl, She of Red Hair, will become a regular patron of Merson's and as such will have the daily opportunity to win Shawn's heart both with Christ and herself.

As Hannah would say, in seven months or less.

Ryan must have read my thoughts again because he closes his eyes and mumbles something under his breath.

I look at the song sheet and mostly sing it to Ryan.

"I've no cause for worry or for fear . . ."

Stephen is teaching. "Okay, everyone, flip to Mark. We're going to begin a study on the life of Christ."

The soft thopping of Bible pages fills the room for a moment. Stephen looks around. "Starting in chapter 1, verse 1: 'The beginning of the gospel about Jesus Christ, the Son of God.'"

He teaches for forty minutes on John the Baptist's preparation for Christ and then prays, finally dismissing us to the kitchen for my brownies. I'd been good and careful and made four batches. Starving single guys and all that.

I push through the crowd hacking into the brownies and grab two for Brandon and Hannah.

I turn around and nearly ram into She of Red Hair.

"Hi!" I say brightly. Maybe too brightly. Even cheerleaders have softer voices, I think.

Stephen stands next to me and sends me one of those "You're giving Turkish monks piggyback rides?" looks I get frequently.

She of Red Hair doesn't notice. "Hi." She smiles, her eyes crinkling into dark slits.

She is too cute!

"I'm Laurie!" I yell over the crowd.

"Hallie!"

"Hi! Nice to meet you! Did you get a brownie?"

"What?"

I squish between two guys, grab the knife from one of them, saw off a brownie, stick it on a napkin, squeeze back through, and jerk my head toward the living room. Hallie nods.

A moment later I hand her the brownie. "Sorry about that," I say. "Most guys here don't eat for weeks before coming."

She grins. "Got it." Takes the brownie. "Thank you. These look great."

"So, Hallie, where are you from?"

She finishes chewing. Swallows. "Mmm. San Diego."

"Oh. SeaWorld. Sunny."

She chuckles. I check off *nice laugh* on my mental list. "Yeah, that's the place," she says.

"What are you doing here?"

"My dad bought a business. I still live at home."

I shrug. "Hey, so do I. It's free."

"Exactly."

"Do you like coffee?"

"Are you kidding? I love coffee."

I point to the brownie. "And you like chocolate."

"No, I *love* chocolate."

I grin at her. "Then, Honey, I have the place for you!"

She screws up her face. "Last time someone said that to me, they tried to talk me into buying a car wash."

"Why? Are you a car washer?"

"No, actually I'm looking for a job right now. This person just drove by and saw me washing my mom's car."

"Odd."

"Yeah." She shakes her head. "Happens, I guess. So where is this place?"

"It's called Merson's. Best coffee and desserts in town."

"Merson's?"

I nod, smiling knowingly.

Hannah taps my shoulder. "Hey, Laurie." She smiles and puts out her hand toward my newest project. "I'm Hannah Curtis."

"Hallie Forbes."

They shake hands.

"Hey, Hannah, I saved two brownies for you and Brandon." I hand her the napkin-shrouded blobs.

She takes them, one eyebrow cocked. "Hmm."

"Oh, they're really good," Hallie says.

"I'm sure they are," Hannah says, not taking her eyes off me. She shakes her head slightly.

"It was nice meeting you, Hallie," she says. "Guess I'll go find Brandon."

"Guess you will. Bye, Hannah." I turn to Hallie, ignoring Hannah's stare. "So, Hallie, favorite candy bar?"

"Definitely Milky Ways."

I gasp. "We are kindred spirits!"

Chapter Four

Hannah sits at her desk principal-style as I come through the studio door Thursday morning.

"Hey there," I say, setting my backpack down.

She raises both eyebrows. "What is going on?"

"I work here, Hannah."

"You're trying to set Brandon and me up." She points at me. "Admit it."

I shake my head, mouth open in shock. "You're crazy! Why would I do something like that?"

"Because you're a sadistic matchmaker."

I frown. "That's a little harsh."

"Harsh or not, it's true. You forget that I walked through Ruby and Nick's setup with you. You can't do this to me."

I spread my hands innocently. "Do what to you?"

She rolls her eyes. "Fine, okay? Fine. You're not going to confess, and I know you're trying to set me up, so let's just both try to work here."

"You have to admit that he is pretty good-looking."

"Laurie!" Hannah stands and yells.

"I'm leaving, I'm leaving!"

I walk into Studio Two, still carrying my backpack. My cell phone rings.

"Wonderland. Alice here," I answer.

"Hi, Alice. It's the White Rabbit. What time is it?"

I smile. "What's up, Ry?"

"Not much. Mrs. Galen just declared all of us on a coffee break while she entertains some guests." He says this ruefully, and I can picture him rubbing his curly hair.

I'm not following. "That's bad?"

"Well, yeah. Now I can't leave until later."

"Why?"

"Because if we can't finish the installation of the sinks and new shower appliances in the guest bath, I can't turn the water back on."

"I'll take your word for it."

"Yeah. Anyway, just wanted to call and say hey. . . . Hey."

"Hi." I smile. "What exactly are you doing to her guest bath?"

"New tile, new fixtures, new mirrors. Today we're finishing the tile and replacing the fixtures. Hang on." I can hear him muffly talking to someone else. "Gotta go, Laur. Short visit."

"Okay. See you."

"Bye."

I walk back out to the lobby. Brandon stands in front of Hannah's desk, spinning a pen between his fingers while he talks.

He looks up and sees me. "Hi, Nutsy."

Don't ask. It's my nickname, sad to say.

"Hey." I walk over, push Hannah closer to the desk, and shove my backpack behind her in my cubbyhole.

"Was that Ryan?" Hannah asks, grinning evilly.

"Where?" I blink.

She sticks her tongue out at me.

"So what are you guys doing for lunch?" I ask, casually changing the subject.

"Bud's," Hannah states.

Brandon nods. "That or Vizzini's."

Bud's is a hamburger joint three shops down from the studio. Best hamburgers in the county, cooked in their own grease. Vizzini's is the town's favorite Italian restaurant.

"Can I come?" I ask.

Brandon shrugs. "You had to ask?"

"It's not like we had plans to go together or anything," Hannah says, her eyes snapping in Morse code to me, *Back off, Laurie Holbrook!*

Here's what's not in my dictionary: *Retreat.*

"So Vizzini's sounds good," I say. "Let's all go at twelve-ish. Does that work for you two?"

Brandon shrugs again. He's like Ryan in the sense that as long as he's fed, he's happy. Very odd, single guys.

Hannah checks the calendar on her desk. "I guess it works."

"Good."

Brandon squints out the windows. "Laur, the Newmans are here."

———❖———

At twelve o'clock I arrange three-year-old Shelby's legs for the thirtieth time. "Okay, stay right there."

"Okay!" she chirps.

I scoot around the camera and wave at her. "Say vanilla ice cream with cherries on top!"

Shelby blinks. "Banilla I-ceam wif chweeys on twop."

Click! goes the camera.

I wave good-bye to Shelby and her mom just as Brandon comes out of his office. "Ready, Laurie?" he calls.

"Yep. Just got to get my backpack."

Hannah stands. "Whose car?"

"I need to get gas," I announce. "Let's take two cars and you can get us a table."

Hannah looks at the ceiling and shakes her head.

What can I say? I'm good.

Brandon, oblivious as normal, nods. "Sure thing. Hannah? You want to come with me?"

Hannah shoots me a withering look before smiling at Brandon. "That's fine."

"See you at Vizzini's," Brandon calls, unlocking his car and opening the door for Hannah.

I climb into my Tahoe and toss my backpack onto the passenger seat.

Brandon drives out of the parking lot, and I follow for a few blocks before turning to get gas.

I shove the nozzle into the tank, fill the car, yank out the nozzle, climb back into my car, pull out my cell phone, and punch some numbers.

"Hello?" a sweet voice says.

"Hi, Hallie, it's Laurie Holbrook."

"Hi, Laurie!"

"We're still on for lunch today?"

"Yeah, I'm getting ready to head that way."

"Great! See you in a few minutes."

I can't keep the smile off my face, I tell you!

I drive directly to Merson's. Park out front. Pull out my cell again.

"Brandon?"

"You okay, Laurie?"

"Are you already there?"

"Yeah, we've already got a table."

I fake a groan. "I forgot I was supposed to meet Hallie for lunch today!"

"Who's Hallie?"

"I met her last night at Bible study. Red hair. Sitting in a sunbeam."

Brandon knows me too well. He doesn't comment on the sunbeam. "Oh. Well, don't worry about it."

"Tell Hannah I'm sorry."

"I will. Have a good time with Hallie."

I hang up, grinning.

Poor Hannah. She has no idea the extent of my genius.

My cell rings. I answer it without looking at the caller ID.

"Hannah, I'm sorry." My voice is a moan.

"It's Ryan, actually."

"Oh. Hey, Ryan." I grin.

"What'd you do to Hannah?"

I try to be evasive. "What are you talking about?"

"Uh-huh. Good try. What did you do?"

"She'll thank me for it one day."

"Oh man! It was that bad?"

"Will you relax? It is not bad."

"Is? Present tense? It's still going on?"

"Calm down, Ryan!"

"I have known you too long, Laurie Holbrook, to relax." He exhales. "What did you do?"

"I was supposed to meet her for lunch and wasn't able to. See? Not that bad."

He is quiet for a minute.

"Ryan?"

"You're not telling me something."

"Oops, my lunch date is here. Got to go. Bye!" I shrug. Let him worry for a while. I turn my cell off.

Hallie stands on the sidewalk in front of the door, holding a denim bag. "Hey, Laurie," she smiles, eyes slitting.

I grin at her and open the door. "Close your eyes and inhale, Hallie. And welcome to Dessert Heaven."

She walks in. "It smells *so good* in here."

I wave to Shawn. "Hey!"

He pulls the coffeepot out and pours coffee in an extra-large mug. "Laurie." He pushes the mug across the counter.

I point to my guest. "This is Hallie Forbes; she just moved here. Hallie, this is the desserts' creator, Shawn."

"Already a fan," Hallie says, distracted by the wall of sweets. "Wow."

Shawn watches her and smiles. "Take your pick. Coffee?"

"Yes, please."

"You're so polite," I tell her, but mostly to Shawn.

"Where are you sitting, Laurie?" Shawn asks.

"Want to sit at the bar?"

Hallie nods, eyes wide, still staring at the Sea of Sugar. I shove a stool underneath her.

"Looks like you found someone after your own heart," Shawn says, pouring another mug.

I sit and smile. Shawn looks at Hallie, pretty girl that she is, differently than he looks at, say, me. I am not offended in the least.

"Can I have that?" she asks him, pointing.

"What?"

"That fluffy chocolate thing." She squints at the sign. "Chocolate something."

Shawn pulls out a piece of chocolate mousse pie. "This?"

"Yes, yes, yes." She bounces in her seat.

A smile plays with Shawn's lips. He slides it to her. "Enjoy. Laurie? For you?"

"The German chocolate cake."

He hands it to me. "This is a new recipe, so let me know."

Hallie puts her fork in her mouth and closes her eyes. "Thi' i' swoo gwoo!" she says, mouth full. She forks off another bite.

Shawn watches her, shaking his head. "Look at her, Laurie. She just moved here, and you've already corrupted her."

I swallow my coffee and grin. "You know me."

"It's on the house, ladies."

Hallie blinks at him, swallows, and smiles. "Oh, thank you so much!"

Shawn returns her smile.

I stab my cake and hum, *"So this is love. . . ."*

———⊕———

I get back to the studio just in time for my two o'clock appointment, which doesn't leave much room to do anything but smile at Hannah and rush into the studio.

"Darn it, Laurie Holbrook!" she yells. Then in a nice secretary voice, "Hi, you must be the Franklins?"

The Franklins leave at three, dragging their six-year-old away from the stuffed *Blue's Clues* dog, kicking and screaming.

Ah, the joys of parenthood.

Hannah is on the phone, so I sneak down the hallway to Brandon's office, open the door, and slip inside.

Brandon looks up from his desk. "How was lunch?" he asks.

"Fine. How was yours?" I climb up on his desk and sit in front of him.

He nods. "Good. I had ravioli."

This is Brandon's idea of describing dates: Talking about the food.

"Really," I say. There's not a lot to discuss about ravioli.

"Yep. The one with the meat sauce, not just marinara. And I had them grate Parmesan cheese on top."

I am wrong.

"How was your conversation with Hannah?" I say, like I should have in the first place.

"Oh. Fine."

"What did you talk about?"

He looks up, squinting at me. "Why?"

"Just curious. What do you ever talk about with her?"

He leans back in his chair, fiddling with a pencil. "Stuff. You. Work."

"You're just the king of enthralling conversations, you know?"

He grins and points his pen at me. "Hannah's not so happy with you right now, so I'd steer clear of her if possible."

"I don't know why. I didn't do anything."

Brandon makes a noise in the back of his throat. "Uh-huh. Don't try that innocent act with me, Nutsy. We've been best friends since second grade."

"Which is why you defended my honor to Hannah, right?"

"Actually, I agreed with her. I know you're trying to get Hannah and me together."

I blink. "I am not! Why in the blue heavens would I ever want to set up my best friend? Then we couldn't be best friends anymore."

He frowns. "Why not?"

"Because, Brandon," I explain, rolling my eyes, "once you get married, you generally become best friends with your *bride*."

"Oh. Hey, how's your dad?"

"Fine. No change."

"Recovered from that fishing trip yet?"

My father decided to take a month-long fishing trip in March, and I accompanied him. We made it through the month, but just barely. Jumping into the lake with a millstone around my neck had been a viable option there toward the end.

And Dad? He ran out of instant hand sanitizer, and the one store within fifty miles of the cabin didn't carry it.

We both decided we hate fishing.

Fine by me.

But since then our house has been cleaner than ever because Dad has to find *something* to do with his time.

"Not exactly," I answer Brandon.

He laughs. "You have the weirdest family ever. Between Lexi and your dad, I can never guess what's coming next. Then there's Laney. . . ." His voice trails off, and he shakes his head. "Have you seen her lately?" he asks.

I nod. "She's big."

"She's *monstrous*! I'm not entirely sure it's just twins! I mean, she didn't get half that big with Jess and Jack."

My sister Laney is married to Brandon's brother, Adam, and has a five-year-old daughter and three-year-old twins.

Laney leads an interesting life.

"I told her she was giving birth to the Jackson Five," I say.

"I'm getting to the point where I believe you. She's only eight months along, and she hasn't been able to get behind the wheel of her car for the last two."

"Okay, that's a slight exaggeration."

"It is not!" Brandon defends. "Adam told me that either he or your dad has to drive her everywhere."

"I can believe that about Dad. He's been over there every day for the last three months. Laney's about to pull her hair out. And the kids are so clean they look starched."

Hannah knocks on the doorjamb. "Brandon, you've got a call on line one. From someone named either Deborah or Barbara. From First Bank. She chews her gum really loudly over the phone." Hannah makes a face. "Yuck."

I grin at Brandon. "I guess I should go."

"Are you done for the day?"

"Yep. I'm going home."

"Say hi to your dad for me."

I crawl off the desk and leave as Brandon picks up the phone.

Hannah waits for me in the hallway, arms crossed.

"Hi, Hannah. Sorry about lunch. I forgot all about Hallie."

"Mm-hmm. I bet."

I keep talking as I walk. "But we had a good time. And I introduced her to Shawn. And he gave us free dessert."

Now Hannah smiles. "Really? Shawn did? Gave you something for free?"

I point to her. "See? That was my reaction." I nod. "I think there's something serious going on here."

"Shawn and Hallie Merson," Hannah muses as we go back into the lobby.

You see, Hannah gets on me for my matchmaking tendencies, but she's just as bad as I am.

"Doesn't that sound good?" I grin.

"Not bad, not bad. What's next? Brownies?" she says, obviously recalling last night.

"No. Shawn makes better brownies than I do, so I don't think that will win him over. What could we do?" I twirl a strand of hair around my finger and lean against her desk.

"What are their common interests?"

"I don't know. I met Hallie just last night. And Shawn has only talked to me about what I'm doing."

Hannah taps her chin with her index finger. "Seems like the obvious choice would be a group dinner or something like we did for Nick and Ruby."

I pull out my backpack, thinking. "That could work. We could do it after church on Sunday, and then Shawn would have to come to church with us."

She nods. "I think we have a plan."

"I'll call Hallie today."

"What about Shawn?"

I give Hannah a look.

She nods and holds up her hands. "What am I saying? I'm sure you'll see him tonight or tomorrow morning."

I laugh. "See you tomorrow."

"Bye, Laurie."

———❖———

I open my Bible on my lap at eleven thirty. Dad's been in bed for the last hour and a half, and I've been watching some wedding reality show on TV.

Here's the problem with wedding shows on TV: I watch one show where the girl is dressed in a gorgeous, silky, bias cut, multiple-thousand-dollar Vera Wang gown, walking down the aisle to a guy who is looking at her like she's the only person on earth, and I go from being Single, Sassy, and Satisfied to sad, depressed, and lonely.

I stare at Psalm 45 without really seeing it until I read this: "All glorious is the princess within her chamber; her gown is interwoven with gold. In embroidered garments she is led to the king."

It reminds me of a verse I read once in Isaiah, and I flip to that book, hurriedly going through the pages until I find it in chapter 62. "For the Lord will take delight in you . . . as a bridegroom rejoices over his bride, so will your God rejoice over you."

Wow. Now *that* is cool! Definitely beats a Vera Wang gown!

Chapter Five

At seven Sunday morning my alarm clock goes off.

Here's something I hate: Alarm clocks.

Sickeningly perky classical music blares from my clock with the force of a crowd at one of those Running of the Bulls contests.

I sit straight up in bed, clutching my heart. I feel a pain in my chest. I know I do. I once read that heart disease is the number one killer in the United States, and since then I've been waiting for pains or aches near my heart. I will die of heart disease now.

Drat classical music!

I stumble out of bed and smash the snooze button.

Today is a big day. Not only has it been a week since Nick and Ruby's wedding, but it is also the day that Shawn and Hallie will officially fall in love.

Shawn wasn't hot about coming to church, but when the ultimatum included death to coffee makers and not seeing me every day, he decided to come.

Happily, of course.

I shower, dress, and take another twenty minutes just to dry my hair.

My hair is much too long. I will need to see about making a hair appointment.

Dad is already sitting at the breakfast table drinking his lemongrass tea when I get downstairs.

Ah, lemongrass tea. My first scent of each and every day.

Blegh.

I'm not sure how Dad stands to drink it. It's pale yellow and sludgy, and there're little flecks of lemon rind slodging around in there.

Slodge: (*v*) To drift, plod, or drudge along.

Perhaps this is the cause of my impending heart disease.

I think any drink you have to chew should be banned by the FDA.

"Morning, Laurie-girl. You look very pretty." Dad smiles, raising his cup to his mouth.

I pour a cup of coffee from our new coffeemaker. "Thanks, Dad."

"You're going out to lunch after church?"

"Yeah." I add sugar and milk and join Dad at the table.

"With who?"

"Hannah, Brandon, Hallie, Ryan, and Shawn," I say, ticking them off on my fingers.

Dad nods. "I think I'll go to lunch with Laney and the kids."

I swallow my coffee. "You're a brave man, Dad." I stand and refill my half-full cup.

"Aren't you going to eat something?"

"Probably not."

Dad frowns. "That's not healthy, Laurie-girl."

I freeze midway through spooning in the sugar. "Can skipping breakfast lead to heart disease?"

"I don't know."

"I mean, all those cereal boxes say they help keep the heart healthy."

Dad sips his sludge and shrugs. "It's possible then, wouldn't you say?"

I pour a huge bowl of some kind of wheat cereal.

Thirty minutes later I fall into one of the chairs in the singles' Sunday school room, next to Holly and Luke, who have been married for the last four months.

And, yes, they are still in the singles' class.

I can just see this turning into the young marrieds' and then the young families' class and all the parents asking me to watch their kids so they can go to the singles' Bible study on Wednesdays.

Possible heart disease puts me in a mood, I guess.

Ryan sits down beside me. "Hey," he says, poking me in the forehead. "You should blink more often; your eyes are glazed over. Still haven't gotten a new coffeemaker?"

"No, we did. But the caffeine hasn't reached my brain yet." I rub my face. "Have I said hi?"

"Nope."

"Hi."

He laughs at me, "Just try to concentrate on the fact that you'll be getting a Dr. Pepper during lunch after church."

"Mmm. Caffeine."

"The little addict." His forehead wrinkles. "Wasn't that the name of a movie? Like with Shirley Temple?"

"I think that was *The Little Princess*."

Stephen Weatherby, still filling in for Nick, clears his throat at the podium. "Hey, good to see all of you," he says, which is church-speak for "Please shut up and sit down."

Everyone follows the unspoken command. Ryan leans back beside me and shoves an elbow in my ribs.

"Ow." I rub my side.

He arches his head back, and I turn to see where he is motioning.

Brandon drops into a seat beside Hannah in the back row. She dimples at him, and he smiles.

I turn back to Ryan. "Score, home team."

"You've got it coming, Girl."

Stephen shuffles the papers around on his podium. "Everyone turn to 1 Peter."

I had an inkling that Nick would have us start this book. I teach the junior high girls during the school year, and we're going to study Peter's books starting in August.

~⊛~

After church everyone typically gathers in the small lobby area. I push through and stumble outside into the bright, bright, bright sunshiny day.

Ryan already stands outside, talking to Brandon.

"Hey, guys."

Brandon flicks my hair. "You need a haircut."

"Thank you. Good to see you too."

He smirks at me.

"Where's Hannah?" I ask. "And Hallie and Shawn?"

"I saw Shawn sitting in the back," Ryan offers.

"And since I don't know who Hallie is, I won't be much help there," Brandon says.

Hannah comes over and puts her arm around my shoulders. "Morning."

"Hi."

"Let's go to Vizzini's."

"Way ahead of you. Where's Shawn?"

She jerks her head back toward the church. "He's talking to Stephen."

This thrills me because:

1. Dr. Stephen is pretty cool. We almost went out. Long story.
2. He's black-and-white on the issue of salvation and will be quite upfront with Shawn about God's sovereignty and calling.
3. Shawn made a friend!

Hallie walks up, and I introduce her all around. Shawn finally breaks out of the lobby and waves at us.

"Sorry," he says. "I was talking to a guy who's going to be a doctor."

"Stephen," Hannah offers. "He taught Sunday school this morning. How are you, Shawn?"

"Good. I haven't seen you in a while."

"I'm trying to lose a few pounds."

I nearly swallow my gum. "You don't need to lose anything," I tell her.

She shrugs.

"Hi, Shawn," I say.

"Hey, Laurie. Gee, I haven't seen you in . . ." His voice trails off as he strokes his chin in an action that is entirely out-of-date. "Wow—like a day."

"Very funny."

Ryan grins at him. "So how are we driving?"

After much deliberation, Ryan and I end up driving, since everyone else except Brandon owns a little car. Brandon doesn't drive because no one in their right mind would ride with him.

Brandon and Hannah go with Ryan, and Shawn and Hallie climb into my Tahoe.

It's so perfect, it must have been arranged. Heh, heh.

I follow Ryan to Vizzini's, and fifteen minutes later we are all sitting around a huge table, staring at menus.

"What's good here?" Hallie asks.

"Everything," Brandon, Ryan, Hannah, and I say at the same time.

She giggles. "Okay. I'll get the spinach-filled ravioli."

"Except that," I say.

"That's *good*!" Hannah protests.

"Sure, if you like moldy cheese," I retort.

Ryan sets his menu down and frowns. "Isn't cheese by nature a mold? Is it redundant to say moldy cheese? Or is it just considered blue cheese?"

Hallie listens to him, her adorable little nose wrinkling. "Never mind, never mind. I'm getting spaghetti. At least I'll be able to tell that it's fresh."

Shawn looks at Ryan. "I think you're right. Cheese in and of itself isn't fresh. It's aged."

Brandon and I blink at each other across the table. "So," I say, "enough with cheeses. Hallie, how is the town treating you so far?"

"It's great." She grins. "I love it. I'm still looking for work, but it's a very friendly town."

"You're looking for work?" Shawn asks, staring intently at her.

I get a tingling sensation in my toes. I take it as a sign that the two of them are meant to be. Either that or my feet are falling asleep.

Hallie nods.

"Thought about waitressing?"

"I'm willing to consider just about anything now," she says. A mistake.

Brandon pounces on that one. "I might need someone to strip the discarded photos of color so we can reuse the film," he says seriously.

Hallie opens her mouth and then closes it.

Hannah smacks Brandon's arm. "Stop being mean. Don't listen to him, Hallie. There's no such thing."

"Want to hold Venus flytraps' mouths shut so I can work?" Ryan asks.

Totally disregarding the flytrap option, Hallie looks at Shawn. "Are you offering me a waitressing job? Because I'll take it."

Shawn chuckles. "You start tomorrow morning. Four fifty an hour plus tips sound good?"

"Sounds great."

"I'd negotiate for three fifty an hour, tips, and unlimited desserts and coffee," I whisper to her.

"See, Laurie, this is why I didn't want to hire you," Shawn says.

"As Ali Hakim says in *Oklahoma!*, 'I didn't want her either, but I got her,'" Brandon quotes.

"Hannah, hit him, please," I ask nicely. She smacks him upside the head.

"Ow!"

"I can't believe you'd even compare me to that girl," I spout. "She had the worst laugh on the face of God's green earth."

"It's your fault. You're the one who made me watch that movie." Brandon rubs his head.

"As I recall, it was that or *Clear and Present Danger*."

Hannah touches her throat. "Oh stop, please. Don't even say the name of that movie. That scene with the girl and the guy?"

"When he breaks her neck?" Ryan asks.

Hannah squeals and covers her head with her arms. "Don't say it!"

The waiter, a new guy I don't recognize with a name tag that reads "GUTHRIE," stops at our table.

"Good afternoon, everyone!" he yells, a huge smile on his face. "What can I get all you beautiful people today?"

This guy either loves his job way too much or is seriously angling for a big tip.

Everyone exchanges dumb glances that say, "Should I start?"

GUTHRIE helps us. "Let's start with this gorgeous girl," he says, pointing to Hannah.

He writes our orders down and slaps his pen into his apron pocket. "I'm glad you are here!"

He leaves.

Now everyone blinks at each other.

"Enthusiastic," Hallie mutters.

"He just wants a tip," Brandon says.

"I could give them some good tips about the way they make their coffee," Shawn says. "They need to grind the beans just before brewing and spread the grounds more evenly."

"Is that what's wrong?" I ponder. "Because I've noticed some cups are stronger than others."

"That's what's wrong. Don't order dessert, everyone. We can go back to my place. I made a batch of brownies yesterday that didn't get completely eaten. We can have those, and I'll make coffee."

I reach across Hallie and take one of Shawn's hands. "I love you, Shawn. Will you marry me?"

"Wow, the new *Fear Factor*," Brandon says. Hannah hits him again. "Ow!"

"And I didn't even have to ask, Hannah." I smile, letting go of Shawn.

"'We're such kindred spirits I can read her thoughts,'" she quotes.

Hallie gasps. "*Anne of Green Gables*! I love that movie! Marilla and Matthew are so sweet. I absolutely love them."

"I love Gilbert," I say.

Hannah puts her hand to her heart. "I'm with you, Girl."

"Who is Gilbert?" Shawn asks.

Ryan and Brandon both start waving their hands. "Don't get them started, please," Brandon begs. "I asked that same question one day and had to watch all *three* movies."

Ryan whistles. "Wow. And those are like three hours apiece."

"Trust me, I know," Brandon says.

"Nine hours of Gilbert?" Ryan shakes his head in awe. "My admiration for you just doubled."

Hannah turns to Shawn. "Gilbert is one of the best characters ever penned in the English language. He ranks up there with Mr. Darcy."

Hallie sucks her breath in again. "You guys like *Pride and Prejudice?*"

"Honey, this is basically *Pride and Prejudice* county," I say.

"Now, I *have* heard of Mr. Darcy," Shawn notes proudly.

"That's because Laurie frequents your shop often and mentions his name even more frequently," Hannah tells him.

"I'm marrying Mr. Darcy," I say to Hallie.

"I thought you just asked *me* to marry you," Shawn protests.

"I changed my mind," I say.

"Maybe we should have one of those discussion questions so we can get to know each other better," Hannah suggests. Everyone shrugs. "Okay, I'll come up with one. Um . . . I've got it. What's something you've always wanted to do but have never done?"

Shawn purses his lips. "I've always wanted to try a real truffle."

Hannah nods. "Good one. Good one, Shawn. Mine is that I want to go find Pemberley."

Hallie laughs. "And subsequently Mr. Darcy?"

"You got it. What's yours, Hallie?"

"I want to go to Paris."

Ryan smiles. "I want to design and build my own house one day."

Hannah looks at me. I clear my throat.

"I've always wanted to toss chocolate-covered raisins to the exotic leopards in an Australian zoo."

Everyone except Brandon stares at me like I have tassels hanging from my earlobes. Brandon laughs hysterically.

"Do I dare ask what yours is?" Hannah asks Brandon.

"I want to play the violin while skateboarding down Pikes Peak," he says.

While I laugh at Brandon, Hallie frowns at me. "You want to throw raisins to leopards?"

Ryan puts his arm around the back of my chair. "Welcome to the fast-changing and multifaceted world of Lauren Emma Holbrook."

———◈———

I get home a little after three. Dad isn't home, and the house feels big and quiet.

Not like it's a lot louder with Dad here. My father is a soft-spoken man. Odd how he ended up with me and my sister Lexi.

I turn on the computer and get on the Internet. Hannah told me that our local animal shelter has a website.

Here's what makes me throw caution to the wind: Puppies.

A picture of two little balls of fuzz pops up on the website. "ADOPT US!" it shouts.

"Okay," I say. I grab my keys and drive to the little brick building that houses the animal shelter. A young guy with really tacky black glasses sits at a desk inside, reading a book titled *Ten Secrets to Living with a Monkey*.

"Do you have one?" I ask, pointing to the book.

"Hi. Have what?"

"A monkey."

He turns the book around and stares at the cover. "Oh," he says finally. "Oh, no. It's illegal to own a monkey without a license, and monkeys are dirty pets. Nope. I just thought it might be interesting to know."

"In case you're on *Jeopardy!* or something?"

He stares at me like I'm the one reading the monkey book.

"Okay, then . . ." I move on. "I'm looking for a dog."

"Yours?"

"My what?"

"Dog," he says. "Did you lose it?"

"Oh. No. Does that happen often?"

"What?"

"Losing dogs."

He shrugs. "Fairly. Some dogs are prone to run off. Especially if there's not a fence involved."

"I'm looking for a dog to adopt."

He nods and stands. "Come on back."

He opens the door behind him, and yippy barks burst the silence. "This way." He goes through the door into a room where a bunch of cages line the walls, some occupied, some not.

"Got a certain age you're looking for?" he asks.

"Young as possible, I guess."

He nods and walks all the way past a herd of sad-looking cats and stops in front of a larger cage.

"Here we go."

I look to where he is pointing. "Hey, those are the puppies on the website," I say.

"Yep. Harry and Larry."

I give him a once-over. But then, I suppose a guy who wears glasses like that wouldn't have enough creativity to name a dog. "If I adopt one, would I have to keep the name?" I ask.

"Nope."

I bend down and stick two fingers through the chicken-wire cage. A little brown, black, tan, and red fuzzy puppy with a splotch of white fur drawing a line from his nose to his eyebrows bounds over and nips them. The other puppy yawns and goes back to sleep.

"Who's this?" I ask, tickling the little guy on the ear.

"That's Larry. He's a feisty little guy. Good puppy."

"Will he get big?"

"Fairly. He's only about seven weeks old right now and weighs five pounds. I'd say about forty pounds is where he's headed."

I grin as the puppy flops to the ground and yips at my fingers.

"How much?"

"Fifty dollars. Plus tax. And I'll need you to fill out a questionnaire."

"I have to take a test?" What do you know, I was right.

Guy With Bad Glasses laughs. "No, not a test. Just questions to make sure you have a yard and a job and stuff so little Larry here is taken care of."

I scratch the dog behind the ear, and he rolls over to his back, baring his tummy.

"I'll take him."

Bad Glasses jingles keys around his finger. "Thought you might. That dog likes you." He opens the cage door and Soon-To-Be-Renamed Larry bounds out and tackles my foot.

"Follow me back to the front."

I pay the man after marking the questionnaire that I do have a yard and a job. Then I take my complimentary collar, leash, and take-home box along with my new dog.

It doesn't hit me until I scoop up the little guy up in one hand and hustle the other stuff out to my car in the other hand: Dad is going to flip.

I set the box in the passenger seat and put the puppy inside. He puts two paws on the edge of the box and stands up, wagging his tail like, *Hey, look at me!*

"You're talented," I tell him.

He nods graciously.

I buckle the box in and go around to the driver's side, pulling my cell phone out of my pocket.

"Hi, Laurie."

"Ryan, you won't believe what I just did," I tell him, maneuvering the Tahoe out of the parking lot.

"Oh, I don't know. I've known you for a bit now. I don't think very much would surprise me."

The puppy yips loudly.

"What was that?" Ryan asks.

"Um . . ."

"You bought a dog?" Incredulous doesn't begin to describe his voice.

"You believe it, good."

"Lau-rie—"

I interrupt him. "Have you ever owned a dog?"

"Yeah, when I was ten."

"Could you meet me at that pet store on Maple? I need help."

He sighs. "Fine. I'll be there in ten minutes."

I drive to the store. The puppy has his front paws up on the box the whole drive, staring out the window like he is Dorothy and has been transported to Oz, his tail wagging confusedly.

He is cute!

I set him on my lap while I wait for Ryan to get there. The puppy puts his paws on the steering wheel and yips excitedly.

"Sorry, Pal. You can't get your license until you're sixteen."

He angles his fuzzy head back and barks at me.

I tap his adorable little forehead. "No exceptions."

He noses the steering wheel.

Ryan pulls up beside me and gets out. I open the door, and he immediately shakes his head.

"I can't believe you did this," Ryan says, staring at the puppy on my lap.

The puppy barks at him.

Ryan shakes his head again, but smiles, reaches out, and picks the little guy up. "He is kind of cute, though. Furry."

I climb out and rub the puppy's head. Ryan settles him in the crook of his arm.

"What's his name?" he asks.

"Fitzwilliam Darcy," I decide. "Darcy for short."

"I feel for you, Buddy," Ryan tells the dog. I swear the dog sighs. Ryan looks at me. "Promise me you didn't get this dog so you can look like Hannah."

"I promise. The website told me to adopt him, so I did."

"People like you should not have Internet connections."

I stick my tongue out at Ryan and rub Darcy's ears. "It turned out okay. Look at the little cutie, Ryan!"

He pushes me into the store. "What do you need?"

"Um. Everything."

Ryan and Darcy both sigh this time. "Better get started then."

⎯⎯⟡⎯⎯

Dad's car is in the garage when I get home with Darcy, along with three bags of supplies from the pet store.

"Dad?"

"In the living room, Honey."

I glance at Darcy. Dad sounds so calm. Darcy looks at me tiredly like, *What now?*

Dad doesn't have a problem watching other dogs while their owners are out of town, but a live-in, permanent dog might be different.

"Get cute, Buddy," I tell him.

Darcy snuggles deeper into my arms, his eyelids drooping. Poor little guy is sleepy.

I scuffle into the living room. Dad sits in his favorite chair reading a book, the lamp on behind him, a cup of steaming sludge in his hand.

"Before you get mad—" I start.

Dad looks up, and his mouth falls open at the sight of Darcy.

Darcy raises up in my arms and cocks his head at Dad.

"What is that?" Dad is in shock.

I think Darcy is asking the same question about Dad's tea.

"This is our new pet," I say, smiling much too brightly. "Hannah told me there's a bunch of mice near her place and her dog keeps them at bay." I lie not. This is a blatant truth.

Dad's mouth is still open. Darcy yips at him.

"He barks," Dad mutters.

"Well, he's a dog," I stutter. "Don't worry, Dad. If you hate him, I'll find somewhere else to keep him. I just thought, you know, we have a couple of acres here, and it's spring, and all those gross rats and mice are moving back to their homes, and Darcy will be a good companion for me."

Dad blinks. "Who's Darcy?"

"The dog."

Darcy yips again.

Dad stands and walks over to get a closer look at the intruder. I have had visions of this same scene happening when I announce my future husband.

He tentatively touches the dog's head. Darcy squirms closer to his hand.

"Dogs are just not clean," Dad says.

"I'll bathe him every week, I promise. More, if need be."

Darcy noses Dad's hand. A smile lurks around the edges of Dad's lips. "I used to have a dog," he says softly.

"You did?"

"Mm-hmm. He died when I was thirteen." Dad rubs Darcy's ears, and the puppy groans.

"I think this guy's been around too many cats," I say. "He just purred."

Dad chuckles. "Keep him here, Laurie-girl. I guess you can have a pet."

"Thanks, Dad."

I set Darcy on the floor, and he turns around in three circles, flops to the floor, and is asleep before I can blink.

Dad smiles. "So. Darcy."

"Darcy." I nod.

"What kind of dog is it?"

"A guy with bad glasses told me Darcy was part Australian shepherd, part border collie, and who knows what else."

"He certainly is . . . colorful. How big will he get?"

"Forty pounds?"

Dad nods. "Not too big then. Good. Just make sure he gets house-trained. And bathed."

"Yes, sir."

Dad sits back down in his chair and picks up his tea again. "You're going to be the death of me, Laurie-girl."

I slide into bed at eleven forty-five. Little Darcy is curled up on a fluffy pillow in a puppy kennel right beside my big, squishy chair. Apparently, shopping wears the dog out. He's been sleeping since I got home.

I pull my Bible over and yawn as I flip to Psalms. I'm having trouble keeping my eyes open tonight.

Psalm 46 says, "Be still, and know that I am God."

I smile sleepily and close the Bible. *You are God, Lord.* And then I fall asleep.

Chapter Six

I once heard that you can judge a good man by the way he treats his mother and his dog. I guess it reveals if he's respectful and could be a good parent.

Well, if this is the litmus test for future husbands, Brandon has failed miserably.

Here's what I have always wanted to do: Write a novel and have the opening line be, "It started with a scowl."

That's exactly how the day starts.

"What is that?" Brandon asks, his eyebrows jumping forward to stare at poor Darcy in an evil, crooked glower.

Darcy shudders under one of my arms, and I cuddle him closer. "It's my dog." I let the door to the studio close behind me and then set him down.

Hannah comes out of Studio Two. "Hey, La—" She halts, shrieks, and rushes forward. "Oh my gosh!" she squeals. "It's a puppy!" She kneels down in her skirt on the floor next to him. "Ooo, you such a cu-yewt wittle thing!"

Darcy sits and stares at her. So does Brandon, which is even funnier.

"Yes," Brandon says. "What is it doing here?"

"It's going to cheer my clients."

Brandon isn't convinced. "Uh-huh."

Hannah leans forward and cups Darcy's head. "Is you a wittle hawt-bweaker?" Darcy wags his tail, and I swear one of his brows is raised in confusion. "Yes, you is!"

"You're perplexing my dog," I tell her.

She looks up at me, her eyes sparkling, her long blonde hair shimmering down her back.

Hannah is beautiful; have I mentioned that?

"Oh, Laurie," she says in her normal voice. "He is too cute! Where did you get him? What's his name?"

"Why is he here?" Brandon asks again.

"I got him at the shelter, his name is Darcy, and for the second time, he's here to cheer my clients." I kick Brandon's foot.

He stands from the chair in front of Hannah's desk. "Is he house-trained?"

"Of course not. He's seven weeks old—which is why he's here, because this is not a house."

Brandon stares at me, eyebrows raised.

"Relax, Brandon, I'm kidding." I grin.

"You worry me."

I raise my hands. "Hey, I also provide a lot of entertainment, and I expect to be compensated accordingly."

He eyes my upturned palm, shakes his head, and joins Hannah on the floor. "You have a screwy mind."

"No raise, I guess."

"Nope." He wiggles his fingers at Darcy, and the puppy bounds forward and barks at them.

Hannah squeals again. "Look at his little behind! How *adorable*!"

Brandon shoots her a stare. "This is a work environment, Hannah."

"So?"

"So I think it's common courtesy to not gross out your employer."

"It's true!" she says with a pout. "Laurie, tell him it's true."

"It's true," I tell him. "It was one of the major selling points for this particular dog."

Darcy trots over and calmly begins attacking my flip-flops.

Brandon stands and goes to his office. "You two are disturbing." His door shuts with a bang. Then it opens again. "Laurie, if he goes on my floor, you're being held responsible . . . and there's carpet cleaner in the bathroom."

"I know, Brandon."

Bang! Opens again. He sticks his head out. "You named the dog *Darcy?*"

"Yes, it's a good name," I protest.

He shakes his head, mumbles something unintelligible, and slams the door again.

Darcy stares after him, head cocked.

"At least he recognizes a wacko when he sees one," I tell Hannah.

She grins at me. "I like the name."

"Me too."

"'I think it sounds refined.'"

"'But hopefully not unvarying.'"

"'Proud . . .'"

"'But not disagreeable, we hope.'" I kneel down beside Hannah, and Darcy hops on my lap. "Hannah, my dear, we have watched *Pride and Prejudice* too many times."

"We could give it up for Lent," she muses, reaching over and rubbing Darcy's ears as he noses my jeans.

"Isn't Lent in March?"

She shrugs and smiles. "Then we'd forget about it and not have to give it up. But our intentions would still be pure."

Ty walks in, blinks at Darcy, says nothing, and goes into Studio One.

I look back at Hannah. "I think I'm going to draft Darcy into the matchmaking business."

Hannah angles her head. "Oh, now you have a business?"

"'I just work for Vizzini to pay the bills. There's not a lot of money in revenge,'" I quote.

"*The Princess Bride*. Good choice."

"Besides, Darcy's so cute, people will fall over just to be near him." I cuddle my dog close to my chest.

"So you'll just make sure they land in the general vicinity of each other?" Hannah asks.

There are few people who can spar verbally with me. Hannah is one of them.

I laugh loudly. Darcy wriggles excitedly and yips.

See? Already we're a team.

Hannah fingers one of his ears. "So what are you going to do? Let Hallie borrow him?"

"Heck, no." I stop, set Darcy down, and he goes back to nibbling on Hannah's fingers. "Hey, wait a minute. . . ."

Hannah closes her eyes. "I know that look." She groans. "Laurie, I didn't say anything. Whatever you're thinking is a bad idea, I know, so just stop thinking now, please, before anyone gets hurt."

"What if Hallie came over to my house . . ."

"Laurie, please. For the sake of my mental health and Hallie's—"

"And I had Shawn come by, and Darcy would be there. And I'd have to run out and get something, and the two of them would be there alone with Darcy. . . ."

"Laurie? Laurie, listen—"

"They could fall in love over my dog!" I yell.

Hannah covers her face with her hands. "God, forgive me," she begs.

I pat her shoulder. "I'm sure He has." I pick up Darcy and stand. "And now, if you'll excuse us, we're going to go 'wait for the opportune moment.'"

"*Pirates of the Caribbean*," Hannah mutters, still on the floor. "If purgatory existed, I would have just landed another five million years."

At twelve thirty, after listening to "Oh my land, that dog is the cutest thing!" five times over, Darcy and I go home for lunch.

Poor guy. It must be tough to be so darn adorable. He curls up in the passenger seat, falls asleep, and only wakes up when I pick him up to take him inside. He trots right into his kennel and promptly conks out again.

"Laurie-girl?"

"Hi, Dad."

Dad comes out of the kitchen, drying his hands on a paper towel. "I didn't know you were coming home for lunch, Honey. I would have made another omelet."

I set my backpack down on top of Darcy's kennel and follow Dad into the kitchen. "Don't worry about it. I don't feel like eggs anyway."

Dad sits down to his steaming lunch. "How was your morning?"

"Fine. Darcy's a winner." I walk over. "What are you reading?"

Dad flips the brochure so I can see the glossy cover.

"Meet Your Match in Michigan," I read out loud. "What is that?"

"It's a retreat for older singles," Dad explains.

My jaw drops, and my knees start to buckle.

Dad, oblivious to my loss of muscle coordination, keeps talking. "Now, before you say anything, hear me out. Your mom has been gone a long time, and the house is too quiet when you're at work, and sooner or later you'll end up marrying someone yourself."

I sit down right on the floor.

"Honey, sit in a chair, please. I just waxed the floor."

I stand shakily, grab a chair, and fall into it.

"I know this is unconventional, but it's cheaper than buying lunch for half a dozen women before finding the right one, and it's not as dangerous as the Internet. Look, see?" He holds the pamphlet up, but I can't get my eyes to focus. "It's a Christian retreat."

"Christian . . . Christian singles' retreat," I mumble, my lips numb.

"Yes."

I blink repeatedly, open and shut my mouth a few times, and try the old shake-your-head-until-clarity-returns method.

It doesn't provide clarity, but it does give me a headache. I balance my elbows on the table, holding my head in my hands.

"Marriage?" I ask him, finally able to process a thought.

"I hope," Dad replies.

"Meet Your Match in Michigan?"

"Michigan." Dad nods.

What are the odds? I'm repulsed but strangely fascinated by alliteration. It's why I use it so frequently. Meet Your Match in Michigan is about as bad as Wealthy Women Wooing Wichita.

I am a matchmaker, am I not?

That saying about the shoemaker's wife going barefoot floats through my muddled gray matter.

Could I not find my father a wife if he truly needed one?

Of course I could!

I look at Dad, preparing to talk him out of Meeting Matched Michigan Matrons.

One look at his face stops me.

It suddenly occurs to me that my dad is lonely. That's a horrible word, *lonely*.

Mom died when I was eight. That's fifteen years he's had to deal with me alone.

Alone.

I manage a smile, reach over, and pat his hand. "Okay, Dad." I swallow. "I hope you find a nice lady in Michigan."

He colors and looks down at the brochure. "Well, I might not, you know. It's just to get me out of the house and back into the land of the living, Laurie-girl."

"You went fishing," I offer.

He rolls his eyes. "That was a mistake. I've never been so bored in my life. And that excuse for a cabin we stayed in was filthy. My hands are still chapped from all the hand sanitizer I used."

I inhale, get oxygen to my brain, and stand, fumbling, regaining enough mental strength from the change of topic to go make a sandwich.

"But I might meet someone," Dad continues.

I fall back on the chair with a *whump*!

Guess I'm going hungry.

Dad's eyes sparkle with excitement. "Wouldn't it be neat, Honey, if God arranged for me to meet your future stepmom in Michigan?"

I nod, unable to process the words. *Stepmom . . . stepmom . . . stepmom . . .*

My family would change. Again. I figured we had stood about as much change as possible a year and a half ago when Lexi got married.

Especially Dad.

Lord, this is weird.

I stand again, grab the back of the chair, and smile at Dad. "I need to go upstairs for a minute."

"Okay, Honey."

I stumble up the stairs into my room, grab my phone, go into the bathroom, and sit down on the edge of tub. Shock, however, throws my bearings off, and I end up *in* the tub.

I dial; it rings, stops ringing, and I hear chewing. Then a swallow.

"Hi, Laurie."

"Brandon?"

"Hi, Laurie," he says again. "Sorry, I'm at Bud's. What's up?"

I start and stop. Then start again. "Dad . . ."

"Is he okay?" Brandon yells. "I'm on my way, Laurie."

" . . . wants to get married," I stutter.

Brandon pauses. "What?"

"He wants to get married again."

"Mr. Holbrook? Your father?"

"Yeah." I rub my face and lean back against the end of the tub.

"Whoa." Brandon lets his breath out. "You're not taking it well, I gather."

"I'm in the tub, Brandon."

"I guess that means no."

"Maybe I'm overreacting."

"You? Overreact?" Brandon asks.

I rub my face on the shower curtain.

"Look, Laur, it'll be okay. All right? Maybe things will change, but think about how happy your dad will be."

This is what I like about Brandon: He has been my best friend for so long, he now knows exactly what I need to hear.

"Thanks," I croak.

"You're welcome. Now. You've got a two o'clock appointment, right? Want me to come give you a ride? Somehow the thought of you driving right now scares me."

"That would be good."

"Okay. Let me finish this hamburger, and I'll be there."

I pull myself up. "I love you, Brandon."

"I know. See you soon, Nutsy."

I hang up and stumble back down the stairs into one of the kitchen chairs. Dad looks up from his brochure.

"When is the retreat?" I ask.

"A little over two weeks. I already called and reserved my space. I fly out on a Thursday and come back on Tuesday. Think you can take some time off to drive me to the airport?"

I nod. "Um, sure."

"Good." Dad reaches over, pats my hand, and frowns at me. "You don't look so good, Laurie-girl. Are you feeling okay?"

"I'm okay."

He squeezes my hand. "Why don't you sit, and I'll make you a big cup of tea, okay?" He starts to get up.

I push him back down. "No, no, it's okay. I'm fine. I think I'll get some water, actually."

"Take some orange juice back to work with you. Lots of vitamins in orange juice."

Especially the kind we buy. Fortified with forty-seven vitamins and minerals. It's like trying to drink wet cement.

I stand and pour a thermos of the stuff.

The doorbell rings. Darcy barks. Dad looks up. "Who could that be?"

"It's Brandon, Dad. He's giving me a ride back to work."

"Something wrong with the Tahoe?"

I shake my head. "He just offered, so I figured free gas."

Dad smiles at me. "That's my Laurie. Always thinking ahead."

My dad's opinion of me is seriously skewed.

Darcy comes bounding out of the laundry room, where his water bowl is, whacks into the wall, falls, and spins in a circle on the wood floor. If it hadn't been so funny, I would have felt sorrier for the poor guy. He lifts his head and looks at the wall like it is the wall's fault.

I open the door in tears from laughing so hard.

Brandon steps in and shakes me. "It's not that big of a deal, Laurie!"

Darcy stands carefully, trots over, and attacks Brandon's shoes.

After drying my tears, I grab my orange juice and Darcy, and follow Brandon out to his car.

"Dog goes in the back."

I put him on the backseat, and he sits perkily, looking at Brandon in the driver's seat. It's a scary day when Brandon drives better than I do.

"Thanks for the ride."

He smiles at me as he turns the ignition. "You're welcome." He turns his Explorer around. "So when is this marriage taking place?"

I tell him about the retreat. "Want to know the name of it?"

"Sure."

"Meet Your Match in Michigan."

He grins. "That's good and corny. Michigan, huh? Long way from home for your dad. I figured the fishing trip had thwarted any desires he had to globe-trot."

"So did I."

"It could be good, you know. You might like having a stepmom."

"And I might not. Laney's been my surrogate mother since Mom died."

Brandon shrugs and smiles at me. "God's sovereign."

"I know."

He smacks my shoulder. "Then start acting like it." Darcy growls at him, and he takes his hand away. "That dog is going to spoil any chance you have of getting married."

I turn in my seat and grin at the little guy. He wags his tail excitedly and yips like, *Hey, I protected you, did you see?*

"Good boy, Darcy."

Brandon pulls into the studio parking lot and comes around to get my door.

"Thanks." I grab Darcy from the back and climb out.

I put my free arm around his neck and hug him. He wraps his arms around my waist, and I lean my head on his shoulder. "Thank you, Brandon."

"What are best friends for?" He lays his arm over my shoulders and walks with me into the studio.

Hannah stands when we come inside. "Here, let me relieve you of that burden," she says, snatching Darcy. "Do you want to help your Auntie Hannah with the paychecks?" she coos. Darcy licks her chin.

Brandon makes a face. "That's gross."

"Dog saliva has healing qualities," I say.

"I was talking about the Auntie Hannah part."

I laugh and go into Studio One to get it ready for my two o'clock.

Dad married.

Weirder things have happened, I guess.

Chapter Seven

Yawning, I pull my hair into a sloppy ponytail and trip down the stairs. Dad sits in one of the kitchen chairs. He's leaning over, talking to Darcy, who sits on the floor in front of him, head cocked.

"That's sit. See? Sit, Darcy. Good boy!"

Darcy sees me coming and hops up, flounces over, and jumps on my jeans. I pick him up and kiss his silky ears. "Hi, Baby."

"Is that what you're wearing tonight?" Dad asks, frowning and straightening.

Jeans and a white tank with a jacket. Casual? Yes. Comfortable? Yes. Thus, it meets my qualifications.

"I was planning on it," I answer Dad and set Darcy down.

He frowns again. "You don't want to get a little more dressed up? Maybe fix your hair?"

"My hair is fixed."

"Did you brush it today?"

I consider that question. A brush touched my hair today when I pulled it into the ponytail. But I did not technically brush it. Did that count? I settle for "Mmm"-ing my way out of it.

"You're never going to catch a husband if you look like that," Dad says.

"I'll keep that in mind." Really, is there an answer for this?

"Is Ryan picking you up?"

"Nope. I'm driving."

Dad pats Darcy's head. "You're picking him up?"

"No, we're both driving."

"I thought you were going to marry Ryan," Dad says.

My father must have marriage on the brain.

I bend down, kiss Darcy good-bye, stand, and kiss the top of Dad's head. "Well, I guess we'll see. Bye, Dad."

"Drive carefully."

"Will do."

I stop by Shawn's and catch him just as he is turning over the Closed sign.

He opens the door. "You're late." He hands me an extra-large coffee. "There's cream and sugar already in there."

"Wow, Shawn." I peer around him into the shop. "You wouldn't be trying to run me off quickly by having it ready, would you?"

He shoots a grin at me. "Now, why would I do that? Bye, Laurie."

"Hey! Don't you want to be paid?"

He pushes me back a few steps. "Don't worry about it. On the house. See you tomorrow."

The door shuts in my face, the Closed sign staring at me sympathetically.

Understand this: I rarely argue with free coffee.

But this is a dire situation. Hallie's car is still parked out front, and since this is her third day working and I *still* haven't seen her, I figure I should check up on her.

Shawn hasn't locked the door, so I open it.

He pauses, scrubbing the counter. "Not enough sugar?"

"The coffee's fine, Shawn. Where's Hallie?"

"Washing the last few dishes."

"So what's the hurry?"

He sets his sponge down. "Look, Hallie asked me not to tell you, okay? So go to Bible study, Laurie. Please?"

I frown at him. "You know I'll find out eventually."

"Yes, I do." He takes my arm and escorts me back outside. "See you later, Laurie."

The door shuts in my face again, and the Closed sign shrugs at me, proving that the theory of being a sign on a door or a fly on the wall does not necessarily mean that you'll hear every conversation.

I drive to Bible study, park behind Ryan's truck, trounce up the street toting my coffee, and open the front door to Nick and Ruby's house.

Ten people crowd in the tiny entryway, blocking anyone from entering.

I push through and find that the rest of the house isn't much better.

Nick is too good a teacher for his own well-being.

I ram into Stephen Weatherby, who is clutching his guitar like he is Kate Winslet and the guitar is Leo DiCaprio, drowning in a sea of people.

"Hi, Laurie," he says through gritted teeth.

"Ridiculous, isn't it?" I say.

He sighs. "I don't know whether to be happy that so many people want to come to a Bible study or kick them all out and meet on the street today."

"It's still light out."

He smiles and gives me a one-armed hug, his other hand still in a death grip on Leo Guitar.

"Good to see a familiar face, at least," he says.

I pat his shoulder and go to find Hannah, fighting my way through the crowd.

Nick's house is too small for this study.

Hannah grabs my ankle. "Don't step on me!" she shouts.

I sit down beside her, cradling my coffee, lest it die amid this pandemonium.

"Guess who just walked in?" she yells in my ear.

"Who?"

"Shawn and Hallie!"

"Together?"

"Forever and ever, amen." She grins, her incredible blue eyes sparkling.

I crane my neck but can't see anyone from the waist up. "Are you sure?"

"Positive," she affirms, giving me a hug. "Shawn will most definitely become a Christian now. You can't sit under Nick's teaching for very long before it happens. And I speak from experience."

— ❦ —

I find Shawn and Hallie afterward, crammed around the tiny kitchen table, talking with Dave and Natalie, a couple new to the study—and, yes, they're married.

People in this town just don't get the concept of a *singles'* Bible study.

"Hi, guys," I say. I throw my empty coffee cup in the trash can under the sink and pull a mug out of Nick's cabinet.

Natalie looks up. "Laurie, right? Good to see you. Do you know Hallie and Shawn?"

This mug was not washed before being put in the cabinet.

Eww.

I rub my hands on my jeans and step closer to the table. "Hi, I'm Laurie," I say to Shawn, holding my hand out.

He goes with it. "I'm Shawn. I've heard about you, actually. You once consumed sixty cups of coffee in one day, is that right?"

I shrug. "It was twenty cups under the lethal limit of caffeine, so I'm okay."

Hallie tips her head, red hair shining. "Eighty cups is the limit?"

"Yep. I read it in some newspaper. Caffeine overdose occurs after eighty cups of strong coffee. The thing that confused me was the fact that caffeine overdose is accompanied by severe trembling, headache, and nausea. How do you get that eightieth cup to your mouth if you're severely shaking?"

Shawn starts laughing. "Have you ever considered learning information that could be useful one day?"

"That's useful! One day someone might offer me my eightieth cup of coffee, and I'll have the knowledge to tell them no."

Natalie looks from Shawn to me and back to Shawn.

"We've met before," Shawn explains.

"Oh," Natalie says.

"Laurie comes to my shop every day."

Natalie's eyebrows raise. "Every day?"

I go back to the sink, squirt dishwashing soap in the mug, and turn the faucet all the way to the hot side. "That is a slight exaggeration."

I turn and stick my tongue out at him.

Hallie giggles.

"Coffee, anyone?" I ask.

Dave, Natalie's silent escort, shakes his head. Maybe he's a mime.

"None for me either, thanks," Natalie says.

Hallie and Shawn exchange glances. "Sure," they say together.

"What's in the pans?" Hallie asks, pointing to the counter.

I know because Hannah brought it. "It's a cobbler Hannah made." Unlike me, Hannah can cook beyond box brownies.

Nick's coffeemaker is one of those grind-and-percolate combos that requires a doctorate in mechanical engineering.

In case you're wondering, I do not have a doctorate in mechanical engineering. Truthfully? I flunked the mechanical section in the career placement tests I had to take in high school.

The odds of me making drinkable coffee tonight are not good.

I open the top of the machine and peer at the assortment of oddly shaped containers.

Here's what drives me crazy: Useless machines. Just buy already-ground coffee and a normal coffeemaker and save yourself the headache.

"Does anyone know where Nick keeps his owner's manuals?" I ask.

The four people at the table gape at me cluelessly. I go into the family room to find Stephen.

"Don't ask me," he says.

"But you're housesitting here," I say.

"Yeah. And I go to Starbucks every morning."

"Helpful, Stephen."

He smiles.

I go back into the kitchen. "Sorry, kids, no coffee." Natalie and Dave have gone, leaving just Shawn and Hallie at the table.

Shawn waves his hand. "No big deal. Let's just go to my place, Laurie."

"Okay," I say, putting the now-clean mug away.

"Want to see if Brandon, Hannah, and Ryan want to go?" he asks.

"I don't know. How much coffee are you making?"

Shawn rolls his eyes. "Enough, Laurie."

Hallie grins at me. "I'll ask them."

Hannah begs off, but Brandon and Ryan, like typical single guys, are not about to turn down free food. They follow us to the restaurant.

Shawn pours us all coffee a few minutes later and sits down at the table we are seated around.

"What are we talking about?" he asks, sipping from his cup.

"*The League of Extraordinary Gentlemen*," Ryan says.

"Ah. Good movie," Shawn says.

I shake my head. "Not a good movie."

"Is too," Brandon disagrees. "It's a great movie. Sean Connery is awesome in *LXG*."

Hallie and I exchange glances. I say, "The only reason I watched that movie was because of—"

Hallie joins me. "Shane West," we say together.

"Here we go again," Ryan says.

"He was cute in that movie." I nod.

"Just not cute enough to make me want to watch it again," Hallie adds.

"See? Exactly. That was my thought."

Brandon swallows his coffee. "Okay, so moving on. Hallie, how do you like your new job?"

"It's good."

"That's it?" I exclaim. "Just good? You *have* been giving her at least one free dessert a day, right, Shawn?"

Hallie laughs. "Okay, it's great. Better?"

"Much. So there *is* free dessert involved here." I put my hand to my forehead. "Oh, that I had discovered the job first!"

Ryan laughs. "Tragic."

"Want to hear something tragic? My dad is going to a Christian singles' retreat."

Ryan nearly spits out his coffee. "Your dad?" He is hacking.

Brandon wallops him on the back a few times. Ryan holds his hands up at him, coughing. "Stop," he croaks, standing. He inhales a few times and gets his voice back. "You would have to tell me this when my mouth was full, wouldn't you?" He sits again.

I smile broadly.

"A Christian singles' retreat?" he repeats.

"Yep," Brandon says. "Get the name: Marley's Michigan Marriage

Makers."

I cover my face.

Ryan's expression twists. "That's . . . interesting," he says slowly.

Hallie frowns. "If it's a Christian retreat, why is it called Marley's?"

"It's a denomination in Michigan," Brandon says. "Marlotist. I just call them Marley for fun."

I double over until my head hits the table.

"There is not a denomination called Marlotist," Hallie says.

"Is too. I visited one of their churches when I went to Michigan to ski one time," Brandon says.

My eyes blur with tears from laughing so hard and holding it all in. My shoulders start shaking.

Brandon levels a good kick to my shin.

"Ow!" I reach for my leg.

"What is the name of it, Laurie?" Ryan asks.

"Meet Your Match in Michigan."

Brandon scowls at me. "Spoilsport."

"When is he going?" Hallie asks.

"Two weeks."

"Hey, guess who's coming home on Saturday?" Ryan asks, changing the subject.

"Nick and Ruby," Brandon, Shawn, and I say together.

Ryan grins. "Yep."

"Nick teaches the Bible study . . ." Hallie begins.

"And Ruby is his new bride," I say.

Shawn points at me. "She got the two of them together," he tells Hallie.

"Oh. Got it."

"Guess what?" Ryan asks me.

"I know, I know. They're coming back on Saturday."

"Yep. Six in the morning."

"Ick."

"Guess what else?" Ryan prods again.

"What?"

"I have to work. With Mrs. Galen's Venus flytraps. Guess who's picking Nick and Ruby up?"

"Brandon."

Brandon huffs. "Ruby won't get in the car with me. You know that."

"Hannah?"

Ryan grins evilly.

"Oh no, I can't," I say.

"Why not?"

"I have a standing appointment with my pillowcase on Saturday mornings. He's trying to romance my comforter and asked for my help."

Ryan balances his elbows on the table. "I won't believe you until I hear names."

I blink at him. "Walter and Opal."

"Your comforter's name is Opal," he says.

"Yes."

"Thanks for picking them up, Laurie."

I moan.

Shawn reaches over and pats my hand. "Better start drinking the caffeine now, Honey."

Chapter Eight

Whistling screeches through the darkness.

I sit straight up in bed, knowing that World War III has started in our neighborhood.

Then I realize that the whistle is going to the tune of that annoying song in *The Parent Trap*.

I fall out of bed, stalk across the room, smash my alarm clock, and land on the floor.

Dad pokes his head in. "You up, Honey?"

"Mmfgh," I mutter, stretching prostrate on the carpet. *Heavenly Father, You made the sun stay out for Joshua. Could You please make the moon stay out for me?* Darcy shifts in his kennel and yips at me.

"Get off the floor, Laurie-girl. You'll be late picking Nick and Ruby up."

"They could take a taxi."

"Harold doesn't start until eight on Saturdays."

This fact should give you a basic knowledge of the size of our town. One taxi driver.

"Laurie-girl."

"I'm getting up." I sit on the floor, rub my hair, and look at Dad.

"What are you doing up?"

"This is my favorite time of day." Dad smiles in delight. "I get up at five every morning and watch the sun rise."

Weird.

I need to be on one of those talk shows where they find out if the kid really is the father's.

Then again, maybe not.

I pull myself to my feet with the help of my desk and stumble to the bathroom.

I dress in the dark because I don't want to permanently scar my pupils by turning on the light.

———— ❀ ————

Twenty minutes later I pull out of the driveway. Darcy sits on the passenger seat, staring at me like I'm a beaded necklace minus the string.

"Trust me, Kid, this was not my idea," I mumble.

I get to the airport at exactly six o'clock, and Nick and Ruby are patiently standing by the curb next to 513 pieces of luggage.

As I crawl out, Darcy jumps against the passenger window and barks at them.

"Laurie!" Ruby laughs, grabbing me in a huge hug. "I missed you."

Nick opens the back end of the Tahoe and starts the loading process. "Thanks for picking us up, Laur."

"Mmm."

"Who is that?" Ruby squeals, touching the window where Darcy peers out.

"Fitzwilliam Darcy. Darcy for short. He's my new dog."

"You bought a dog?" Nick asks, pausing in the packing. "Why?"

"Because of Hannah's abs."

He stares at me and shakes his head. "You're strange."

"I'm strange? You're the one flying in the middle of the night."

"We're on Caribbean time," Ruby says. "It's late morning there. Speaking of which, I'm starving. Can we stop by Merson's on the way back to our bungalow?"

I blink. "Your what?"

"Our house."

"You did not say 'house.'"

"What did I say?"

"You called it a bungalow."

"Oh. So?"

"So I've never heard anyone use that word," I note. "Especially this early in the morning."

"I'm sorry." Ruby gives a sheepish grin. "Now. Could we stop before we go home?"

"I've read it, but I've never heard it," I say.

"Merson's, Laurie. We have to stop at Merson's. I want a brownie."

"Nancy Drew used the word a lot, but I've never actually had someone tell me to drop them off at their bungalow."

"Look, will you get off the bungalow?"

"It even sounds weird. Bungalow, bungalow, bungalow—"

"Laurie!" Ruby yells.

Nick laughs. "I'll give you one thing, Laurie. Life with you is never boring."

"I'll take that as a compliment."

Nick closes the back end. "All set here. Sit in front, Babe."

"Do I get to hold the cute puppy?" Ruby asks.

"Sure," I say.

We climb in. I drive in the general direction of Merson's, but with the early hour, I can't be too sure.

"How's Orlando Bloom?" I ask.

Ruby sighs. "We didn't see him."

"Not even a glimpse?"

"Not even a glimpse. And trust me, I looked."

Nick leans forward. "Isn't that a nice picture, Laurie? Me on my honeymoon while my wife is looking for Orlando Bloom."

I shrug. "He's cute."

"Honey, he's more than cute," Ruby says, ruffling Darcy's ears.

"Excuse me. Nick, your husband, back here," he announces.

"Hi, Honey." She smiles at him. "I'm glad you're back there. So, no, I didn't see him. I once thought I saw him, but it wasn't him."

I have to laugh. "Sorry, Nick."

"This is all your fault, Laurie."

"It is not."

"You're the one who asked her to look for him."

"For me, not for her. She's married. I'm very available for Orlando."

Ruby holds Darcy up for Nick to see. "This dog is adorable! Can we get a dog?"

"Darcy has a brother."

"Really?" Ruby screeches.

Nick covers his face. "Laurie, when will you learn to keep your mouth shut?"

I grin at him. "Never."

I stop in front of Merson's.

"Oh, thank goodness he's open!" Ruby says. She hands Darcy to me and clambers out. "I've been wanting his coffee so bad."

"Coffee on the cruise wasn't good?"

"It was gross," Nick says.

"Yuck."

Ruby opens the door, and Shawn looks up from the counter. "Ruby Palmer," he exclaims and then stops. "I mean, Ruby Amery!" He comes around and gives her a hug. "You look fantastic!"

Nick shakes his hand. "How are you, Shawn?"

"I'm just fine. Laurie Holbrook, you may not bring that animal in this restaurant."

"Why?" I cuddle Darcy closer.

"It disturbs the customers."

I look pointedly around the empty room. "What customers?"

He frowns. "First customer and he's gone. Got it?" He turns to Nick and Ruby and puts on his nice voice. "What can I get the honeymooners? On the house."

"Wow, Shawn," I say. "What's with all this 'on the house' stuff?"

He ignores me. Fine by me. I know exactly what is with it. Love has a way of making stingy people generous.

"I want a brownie," Ruby tells him. "And the biggest cup of coffee you have."

Nick grins at his new wife with that "Wow, I can't believe she's really mine" look that most newlyweds have. "Coffee for me as well. Oh! And a piece of that chocolate cheesecake."

"The one I'm renaming 'The Laurie'?" Shawn asks.

"Very funny," I say. I set Darcy on the floor, and he trots around, sniffing the table legs.

Shawn sends the evil eye to my poor innocent puppy and hands Nick and Ruby their orders. I sit at a table and lay my head on it. "Want something, Laur?" Shawn asks.

"Coffee," I mumble.

"Decaf, I assume," Shawn says.

"Mmfgh."

Ruby sits down beside me and pats my head. "Poor little Laurie. Thanks for coming to pick us up, Honey." She fingers my hair. "Your hair is growing like crazy."

"It needs to be cut," I say, lifting my head a few inches and rubbing my eyes.

Nick sits opposite me. "Ruby could cut it."

"Really?" I ask, cheek against the table again.

"Laurie, your dog is behind the counter!" Shawn yells.

I clear my throat but don't move. "Darcy!" I croak. "Come here, Boy!"

"He's not obeying!"

"Just nudge him back, Shawn," I mutter.

Shawn comes over and sets a gargantuan cup of coffee in front of me that resembles a bowl with a handle on it. "Want a straw so you don't even have to sit up to drink it?" he asks, slinging Darcy onto my lap.

"That would be good."

"I was kidding." He sits between me and Nick.

Ruby bites into her brownie and basically purrs. "This is great, Shawn." She hits my shoulder. "This chocolate addiction is all your fault, Lauren Emma Holbrook. I was perfectly content with Slim Fast bars until I started hanging out with you."

I straighten a little and slurp my coffee. "Chocolate lovers live longer," I inform her. "And Slim Fast bars are gross."

"Laurie tell you about her dad?" Shawn grins at Nick and Ruby.

Nick swallows and shakes his head. "No. Is he okay?"

"He's meeting a match in Michigan," I tell them between sips.

Ruby frowns. "He's what?"

"He's going to a Christian singles' retreat in two weeks," Shawn says.

Ruby has the same reaction as her brother. "*Your* dad?"

Nick watches her and turns to me. "I don't know your dad all that well. Is this weird?"

"My dad is just not what you would typically call dating material," I explain.

Ruby pats my hand. "I'm sure it will be fine."

"Uh-huh."

"It will," she insists.

"Right," Nick agrees. "What's the worst that could happen?"

I blink at Nick. "The worst? He could meet a genetic scientist who wants to suck my lungs out so she can use them to create a cow or something."

The three of them stare at me.

"Like I said . . ." Nick sips his coffee. "Strange."

⚬❦⚬

I drop Nick and Ruby by the aforesaid bungalow, better known in the world of reality as Nick's house. They still haven't resolved the whole "Should we live at my house, your house, or buy a new house?" issue, so Ruby still has her duplex on the other side of town.

When we get home, Darcy trots right to his kennel and collapses. Dad sits at the kitchen table, drinking his tea and reading his favorite magazine, *Medical Mysteries and Common Occurrences*. This is the magazine that warns readers to tie plastic bags over their heads in order to avoid contracting the flu or polio or something infinitely more life threatening.

I have yet to follow the suggestion. For fairly obvious reasons.

"Nick and Ruby get in okay?" Dad asks.

"Yeah. We went to Merson's afterward. Ruby had a hankering for a brownie."

"There's coffee in the pot."

I pull out a mug, pour a cup, add cream and sugar, and sit down beside Dad. "Thanks, Dad."

"You're welcome. So I thought I'd go shopping today for my trip."

I nod, drinking. "Okay."

He watches me carefully. I smile at him, not getting the reason for his look.

"I thought maybe *we* could go shopping," he corrects.

"Ah. Got it. Sure, Dad."

"You have better taste in clothes than I do."

This comment is laughable. My sister Lexi always tells me I have no style at all. However, I must admit when compared to my father, I am a fashion diva.

"We should see if Lexi wants to go," I suggest.

Dad's eyes brighten. "That's a great idea!" he exults. "I'll call her right now."

He stands, leaving his magazine open to an article about a deadly virus straight from the rainforests of Mexico.

The prevention method?

I kid you not: Plastic bag over the head.

Dad comes back a few minutes later, holding the phone. "She can come. Ryan's over at her house right now."

I have to laugh. This past winter Ryan and Lexi's husband, Nate, built an entire porch plus four chairs, a table, and a chaise lounge for her. In the meantime, Ryan and Nate adopted each other, and Ryan has spent every Saturday since then with Nate.

"When is she coming?" I squint at the clock over the microwave. Eight o'clock. "Ryan was already over there?" I ask. The boy loves sleep about as much as I do.

"She said he and Nate were going to build a tiered garden in her backyard today, and they wanted to start before it got too hot. She'll be here as soon as she gets dressed."

That should tell you the level of comfort my sister has with Ryan. She's still in her pajamas when he's there.

The phone rings, and Dad answers it. "Sure, Ryan. She's right here." He hands me the phone and goes to his bedroom.

"Hi."

"Hey, Laur."

"Building a garden, huh?"

"Well, you know Lexi has high aspirations to become the next Martha Stewart."

"She doesn't realize those aspirations require perspiration."

He chuckles. "No, probably not."

"You and Nate are bored to tears, aren't you?" I grin. They've already built everything conceivable.

"Completely. We need you to come over. Things are never boring when you're around."

"That's the second time I've heard that today, and it's only eight o'clock."

"That's one reason I was calling. Nick and Ruby got picked up?"

"Oh no!"

"What?"

"I forgot! I forgot completely! Oh my gosh!"

"Oh, Laurie, you didn't!" he shouts.

"No, actually, I didn't. They're home and safe."

"Don't do that to me."

"Why not? Keeps your heart in shape."

"Hold on a sec." I hear him yell. "What, Lex? . . . I'll ask her!" He talks to me again. "This is going to sound really weird, but what are you wearing?"

I start laughing.

"Laurie," he says, and I can hear the grin in his voice.

"You said it wrong."

"Right. Sorry." He deepens his voice. "What are you wearing?" he asks sensually. I hear Lexi laughing in the background.

"Jeans and a sweatshirt."

He relays the message to Lexi.

"She said to change."

"I don't feel like changing."

"She said you have to or she's not coming."

"Tell her that if Dad can wear a kilt, then I can wear jeans."

Ryan tells her without laughing. I like that guy.

Here's the thing about my sister Lexi: She is the most gullible person on the planet.

"He's what?" she shrieks into the phone.

"Jeans and a sweatshirt don't sound so bad, do they?"

"He is not really wearing a kilt."

"Yes, he is. Red plaid."

"Laurie Holbrook, you are a pitiful little liar, and you're changing into something cute or I'm leaving you to the mercy of our dad in the mall," she threatens. It is the first time she's used my name in over a year.

Lexi doesn't like to use my name. Rather, I'm Honey or Baby or Doll-face or pretty much whatever suits her at the time.

I would have stuck my tongue out at her if we weren't on the phone. "Fine," I say.

"Here's Ryan again. Pink, Honey. Think pink."

"Hey, Laur," Ryan says again. "Sorry about the pink."

"This is all your fault."

"I'll make it up to you. Want to get dinner tonight?"

"I don't know. Is this like a date? Because I can never tell with you."

"Yep, this is like a date."

"Okay, I'll go."

"Good."

"Where?"

"Where what?"

"Where are we going?"

"Oh. I don't know. Pancakes sound really good right now."

"That's because It's eight in the morning. Speaking of which, why are you even there right now?"

"I had to work at Mrs. Galen's early this morning, remember? That's how you got saddled into picking up my sister and her husband."

"You're already done working?"

"I had to consult with her architect again. Took an hour at the most. He couldn't do it any other time but at six this morning."

"Very sad that people consider six to be part of the day."

"It is. I should go, Laur. Nate's trying to plan out the garden."

"That should be funny. You don't want to miss that."

He chuckles. "Have a good time at the mall."

I groan.

"See you tonight, Laur."

I hang up and climb the stairs. Pink. If I don't show up in something pink, Lexi will make me buy something pink.

I whip open my closet doors and stare. Nothing jumps out and grabs me by the throat, which proves the article in Dad's magazine about common closet critters to be false.

Thank goodness. A plastic bag will give me sack-head hair.

I find a pink rhinestone-studded sleeveless shirt with the tags still attached, which means that Lexi bought it for me for my birthday or Christmas and I have yet to wear it. I put on my khaki-colored jeans and spend a good thirty minutes on my hair.

I go back downstairs. Lexi stands in the kitchen, pouring a cup of coffee. "See? See, Baby? You can look so cute when you try."

"Good to know," I say.

She grins at me. Lexi is beautiful. My other sister, Laney, is cute, but Lexi is gorgeous.

She gives me a hug and finishes doctoring her coffee.

"Where's Dad?" she asks.

"I don't know. Changing out of the kilt, probably. You know why we're shopping, right?"

She shrugs. "He wants to get out of the house?"

"He's buying a new wardrobe for his trip."

She smiles at me quizzically and picks up her coffee. "What trip?"

"The Christian singles' retreat."

Lexi shakes her head, not believing me. "Uh-huh. Good one."

"I'm serious."

Dad comes into the kitchen and gives Lexi a hug. "I'm glad you're coming with us, Lex."

"Daddy, are we really shopping for clothes for a singles' retreat?"

He nods. "Good, Laurie told you. Isn't it exciting?"

Lexi's mouth falls open in shock. "Are you wanting to meet someone?" she stammers, setting her coffee down.

"Well, yes, Honey. That's why I'm going."

"Meet Your Match in Michigan," I tell her.

"In Michigan?" she gapes.

Dad nods, still giddy with excitement. "Yes."

"Michigan," she says again.

"It's a Christian retreat."

She shakes her head slightly and looks at me, her mouth still open. "Yeah, she told me."

"Are you ready to go, girls? It's already nine o'clock."

Dad drives, and we get to the mall shortly. Our mall is not big, but it's got a few good stores.

"I'm going to go look in here," Dad says, pointing to a men's clothing store.

"Okay," Lexi says. She grabs my arm before I can follow Dad. "I'm a little thirsty. We'll get something to drink and meet you in there."

Dad nods and disappears through racks of clothes.

Lexi blinks at me. "You don't think this is weird?" she asks.

Her mind is still on the singles' retreat, I guess.

"Sure, I do."

"I mean, you haven't been this calm the whole time, have you?"

"No. When he first told me, I fell into the tub."

She tilts her head at me but doesn't ask. "What if he meets some-one?" she frets.

"A genetic scientist, you mean?"

"Exactly," she points at me. "How do we know what kind of people go there?"

"Brandon told me to trust in God's sovereignty."

She lets her breath out. "Wow. That's all I can say to this whole thing. Wow." She looks at me. "Did you tell Laney?"

"No."

"Good. Don't tell her until after the babies come."

"She could deliver when Dad's gone, Lex."

"See? That's the other thing. Dad has been to Laney's house every day for the last three months to make sure she's okay. And now he'll be gone when she's hoping to deliver?"

"You know Dad. He can't take one of his kids bleeding."

Lexi thinks about this and nods. "Come to think of it, didn't he leave when Jess and Jack were born?"

I nod.

"Huh. Maybe you're right." Her eyes get big. "Hey, Baby, what if Dad's just going to this retreat because it's the same weekend Laney's due?"

I purse my lips and then shake my head. "No, he's too excited about it. That might be part of his decision, but I think he really wants to meet someone." I bite my lip. "Just as long as she's not a genetic scientist."

"What is it with you and the genetic scientist?"

"She'd bring rats."

Lexi laughs.

"I *hate* rodents. I'd have to move in with you, and Nate would prob-ably not appreciate that."

"Nate loves you to death, and you know it."

"Yeah. In the daytime. At night, though, he'd probably like to have privacy with his wife."

Lexi grins. "I don't know. I heard him asking Ryan if he wants to move in."

"He pretty much has."

"Yeah, well, Nate loves him too. Ryan has our vote for your future husband."

"I'll keep that in mind," I say.

Meet my sister, Mrs. Bennett.

Chapter Nine

The doorbell rings at six.

I open it and smile. "Hey, Ryan."

"Hi. New shirt?"

I raise my eyebrows and sigh. The pink top is not what you would call comfortable. "Your fault, you know."

He grins. "Want me to make it up to you?"

"I think dinner, dessert, and watching three movies that *I* get to pick out will take care of it."

"Oh man."

"Come on in. I need to find my backpack."

"Your ID wouldn't happen to be in there, would it?" Ryan asks, following me into the living room.

"Yeah. Why?"

He shakes his head and waves at Dad in the kitchen. "Evening, sir."

"How are you, Ryan? Did Lexi's garden turn out well?"

"The planning turned out fine, no thanks to Nate."

Dad chuckles.

"Dad, do you know where I left my backpack?"

"It's in your car, Honey. Remember? You left it in there when you got your sunglasses out."

I snap my fingers. "Right. Thanks, Dad."

"You're just begging for identity theft," Ryan says.

I start to shush him.

"Identity theft?" Dad asks, coming into the living room.

I close my eyes. "Ryan was joking, Dad."

"Were you?" Dad asks.

"Yes, sir. I think this is a safe neighborhood."

Dad nods. "It is. That's why Laurie's mother and I built here."

"Oh, I heard about your upcoming trip. Best of luck with that. I'll be praying for you," Ryan says sincerely.

Dad smiles at Ryan. "Thanks."

Darcy slinks past us, toward his kennel. Dad watches him. "Bet he got into the toilet paper again."

"I'll clean it up, Dad."

"No, no, you go. I can get it. Have a good time, kids."

I grab my backpack out of the Tahoe while Ryan opens the door to his truck for me. "So where are you taking me?" I ask.

He pushes the key into the ignition. "I guess we need to go somewhere to show off the pink."

"Funny. I was thinking the hot dog stand by the high school would be fine tonight."

"I've given up trying to figure out your thought processes."

"Then I could get mustard on it accidentally, and I'd have an excuse to never wear it again."

"You know, Laur, sometimes I wish you weren't so girly."

I laugh.

He drives to Vizzini's, and we wait ten minutes for a table.

"What are you getting?" he asks once we are seated with menus in front of our faces.

"Lasagna."

He squints at me. "Are tomato stains as hard to get out as mustard stains?"

I grin.

"They are, aren't they? You are something else, Laurie."

"You obviously have not spent enough time at Lexi's yet. You do not know my sister. Without a valid excuse, she'll make me wear this again."

"Forgive me for being male, but what is wrong with that shirt?"

"It's pink."

"So?"

"So I don't like pink."

"What do you like?"

"Red. Blue. Yellow."

"Primary colors?"

My mouth drops open in surprise. "Wow, Ryan!"

He shrugs apologetically. "I had to take an art class in high school."

"You had to?"

"It was that or drama class." He makes a face. "We were doing *The Sound of Music*, and I don't sing."

"Not even in the shower?"

"Not even."

"Singing in the shower constitutes a strong psyche," I say.

He raises an eyebrow and smiles. "Where'd you read that?"

GUTHRIE, the same guy from last Sunday, stops at our table. "Hi, I'm GUTHRIE, and I'll be your waiter," he says dully, staring at the table. "Know what you want?"

"GUTHRIE?" I ask.

He looks at me. "You look familiar," he says.

"You waited on us last Sunday."

He blinks. "Oh. Nice to see you again. Can I get you something to drink?"

I exchange a look with Ryan, who shrugs.

"Dr. Pepper," I order.

Ryan holds up two fingers. "Two, please."

GUTHRIE writes it down, sighs, and says flatly, "Need a few minutes for your meal?"

"I'm ready. Ry?"

"Go ahead, Laurie."

"Lasagna, please."

"Caesar or house salad?" GUTHRIE mutters.

"Is the Caesar really heavy on the anchovies?"

He shakes his head.

"Okay. I'll have that."

"And you?"

Ryan points to the menu. "I don't speak Italian, so instead of being laughed at by Laurie here, I'd like this one."

Even that doesn't produce a smile from our downtrodden waiter. He scribbles it down and exhales. "I'll have the drinks right out." He walks away, not in the bouncy clip he had on Sunday but in a sunken-shoulder plod that depresses me to see it.

Ryan waits until he's out of earshot. "What was that? Was that the same guy?"

"Looks like him."

"The same guy who was so loud your dad could hear him at your house?"

"I think so."

"The same person who called us all beautiful?"

I balance my chin on my hand as I think. "Should we ask him what happened between him and his girlfriend?"

Ryan blinks. "What?"

"I said, should we—"

He holds a hand up. "I heard you, Laur. I meant why in the blue sky do you think it's because of him and his girlfriend?"

"Did you see the way he walked?"

"Slowly?"

"Exactly. Sort of a snail-like, thudding walk. And he sighed a lot." I nod after him. "I think he probably said something wrong to his girl-friend, and she won't forgive him."

Ryan stares at me.

"What?" I ask.

"I can't decide whether I should be proud or worried that you can come up with this kind of stuff."

"It's a talent, but I try to stay humble."

GUTHRIE reappears with the two drinks.

"Here are your drinks," he says quietly.

"Hey, GUTHRIE?" I say. "What did you say to your girlfriend?"

He lifts sad eyes to my face and blinks. The next thing I know, he has taken a seat in the empty chair beside me and is pouring his heart out.

Poor guy.

"We were at that little coffee shop on High," he says.

"Merson's?" I butt in.

"Yeah." He looks at me. "How did you know?"

"She goes there every day," Ryan explains.

GUTHRIE exhales loudly. "I asked her if she wanted to go to the gym with me."

I shake my head, *tsking*. "Bad question."

"I know! I know that now. She got all uptight, threw down her fork, and said that if I thought she was overweight, I could have just come right out and said it."

Ryan raises his eyebrows. "Wow. Anger."

"A lot of it." GUTHRIE rubs his forehead.

"What was she eating when you asked her this?" I ask.

"Um. Cheesecake, I think."

I close my eyes. "That's really bad timing there, GUTHRIE."

"I don't think she's overweight! I think she's the perfect size."

"Have you told her that?" Ryan asks.

"I've tried."

"Since the Gym-iny Cheesecake Incident?" I ask. Ryan smiles at the name.

"Yeah."

"Not before?"

He pauses, thinking. "I don't remember."

I shake my head. "Not good, GUTHRIE. Not good."

"I don't know what to do!" He covers his face. "I love her. I thought we'd get married soon."

I clear my throat, push up my sleeves, and lean close to GUTHRIE. "Okay. Here's what you need to do. Go rent *The Prince & Me*, *A Walk to Remember*, and *French Kiss*. Watch them in that order. Ry, you have a pen and paper?"

He holds up empty hands. GUTHRIE hands me a Bic and his order notebook from his apron pocket. I write the movies down.

"But her favorite movie is *While You Were Sleeping*," GUTHRIE protests. "Shouldn't we watch that?"

"No, no, no," I say. "She has very good taste, but the reason she likes the movie is because the lead guy, Bill Pullman's character, is perfect. Okay? He's a total doll." I wave my hand. "That's not what you want her comparing you to right now. You two need to watch these movies together, and, subconsciously or not, she'll see that the guys in these movies, though they start out as jerks, turn out to be nice guys."

GUTHRIE blinks at me.

"Next, go to Merson's and buy four of the biggest chocolate-covered strawberries Shawn has, okay? Get two extra-large coffees and fix hers exactly how she likes it. Show up with all this stuff at her house tomorrow night, tell her you were a jerk and oblivious, give her the strawberries, tell her to sit down and relax, and put in *The Prince & Me*."

GUTHRIE nods. "I can do that."

"She'll be back in no time. Trust me. There's not a lot that can soothe a girl's heart better than romantic comedies and chocolate."

He smiles at me. "Thanks . . . I don't know your name."

"Doesn't matter. Hope everything turns out well."

"It will. I'll do exactly what you said." He thanks me again and leaves.

Ryan shakes his head.

"What?" I ask. "It's discernment, pure and simple."

"You know that quality is actually on my list for a future wife," Ryan says, reaching across the table and patting my hand. "I guess I just always pictured the display of it to be a bit more . . ." His voice trails off.

"Biblical?"

"Yes. Biblical in nature."

I grin. "I think it's important that qualities are well-rounded, don't you?"

"I think we should go to the gym afterward."

I laugh.

Chapter Ten

"Much as I like all of you, I have to say that I really dreaded coming home from our fabulous honeymoon with my gorgeous bride," Nick says the next morning in the singles' Sunday school room.

There are a few polite chuckles, and Ruby reddens.

"Anyway, we're back, and for those engaged couples here, I would highly recommend the Caribbean for a honeymoon. It was beautiful, quiet, and unlike going to a dude ranch, not naming any names or anything . . ." Nick coughs into his hand, ". . . Holly and Luke." He clears his throat, smiling. "It was private."

I grin.

Nick smiles at Holly and Luke. "Um, announcements . . . don't think we have any new ones . . . all right." He gets down to business. "Turn to 1 Peter."

Hannah elbows me hard between my sixth and seventh rib. I feel my lung puncture.

"What?"

"How was last night with Ryan?" she whispers, turning in her Bible to 1 Peter.

"Fine."

"What did you do?"

"We went looking for Rumpelstiltskin."

Hannah slaps her hand over her mouth, giggling.

Nick sends us a stare. "First Peter chapter one," he says loudly, mostly to the two of us. "You have been chosen according to the foreknowledge of God," he concludes an hour later. "Be obedient to Christ because of it. Stephen, can you take prayer requests?"

Young Dr. America pulls a pen from his Bible like a magician, uncaps it using his teeth, then spits it back into his palm.

"Okay," he says, "I'll start. I'm leaving at the end of next month for med school, so if you guys could pray that I'll get everything wrapped up before then."

Ruby raises her hand and Stephen nods at her. "Nick and I are still debating the house issue, so pray God's will in that," she says.

Stephen prays, and we leave. I came with Dad, so I relax in the passenger seat as he drives home.

We are two blocks from our house when I see the sign. "Stop, Dad!" I yell.

He pulls over. "What? What?" he shouts. "Are you okay?"

I point to the sign, jump out, and jog to the front of a cute ranch house with a big white sign in front of it: For Sale.

I pull a flyer out and get back in the car.

Dad has a hand on his heart and is mumbling to the ceiling of the car.

"Okay. We can go."

He closes his eyes. "Laurie . . ." he starts, pulling the car back on the road, "don't ever do that again."

"Yes, sir."

"Why do you want a flyer for that house anyway?"

I study the pictures and the price and smile. "Because this is Nick and Ruby's new house."

"They bought it? Shouldn't there be a Sold sign on there?"

"They haven't seen it yet. I just have this feeling . . ."

"Your feelings can get you into trouble."

I hum, *"Feeeeeelings . . ."*

Dad is not amused.

I call Ruby the moment I get inside the house, at the same time picking up Darcy, who is squirming in excitement.

"Hello?"

"Hey, Ruby!"

"Hi, Laur. What's going on?"

"I found a house for you!"

"Oh really?"

"More excitement would be appreciated, Ruby."

"Oh really!" she shouts.

"It's a little ranch house two blocks from here."

"A ranch house, huh?"

"Blue. It's open today from twelve to six."

"We're at the grocery store, and I left my watch on the bathroom counter. What time is it now?"

Okay, this is weird because:

1. Ruby is the Queen of Punctuality. If I'm ten seconds—I'm being literal here—ten *seconds* late for work, she pounces on me.

2. I always thought that Ruby's watch had been surgically implanted into her wrist.

3. The world will come to an end now, I'm sure. Earthquakes, tornadoes, etc.

"It's 12:20," I tell her, trying keep my balance as the floor shifts beneath my feet. It's started already.

"Okay. Here's what we'll do. Have you and your father eaten?"

"We had breakfast."

"Eaten lunch, Laurie," she says.

"No."

"Don't. I'll pick up some of this great soup here, we'll come to your house and eat, and then we'll go see the ranch house. Does that work?"

"It's June."

She pauses. "I left my watch at home, Laurie, not my calendar."

"No, I mean you're buying soup, and it's June."

"So?"

"I didn't know you were allowed to eat soup in June unless you had the flu."

She starts laughing. "We'll be there in thirty minutes."

I go into the kitchen and find Dad scrounging through the refrigerator. "Nick and Ruby are coming over and bringing *soup* for lunch," I tell him.

He smiles. "That sounds so good right now."

"Nick and Ruby?"

"Soup."

Apparently I am the only one who finds the idea of eating soup when it's ninety degrees outside to be marginally ludicrous.

Ludicrous.

I like that word.

Because my father is my father, our house does not need straightening, so I spend the next thirty minutes trying to teach Darcy that playing with the toilet paper is a privilege and not a right. He sits on the tiled bathroom floor and stares at me, his head in a puppy-cock.

The doorbell rings. Darcy hops, runs in a circle, dives out of the bathroom, and skids into the wall beside the front door.

I think my dog needs a lobotomy.

"Hi," Ruby says, coming inside. "Hi, little Darcy. Hi, Mr. Holbrook."

Nick shakes Dad's hand, and Ruby leads me into the kitchen, holding a paper grocery sack. "Could you start eight cups of water boiling?" she asks.

"Sure. What kind of soup is this?"

"Chicken enchilada soup." She pulls a container out of the bag.

"Sounds hot."

"Spicy anyway."

I squint out the window where the green, green, green grass shines white in the startling rays of the sun. A day like this demands icy cold watermelon slices and a swimming pool.

And I am going to eat spicy soup.

Yum.

I turn the stove on, set the saucepan over the flame, and turn to see Ruby pulling a bag of Oreos out of the sack.

"Yay!" I yell, springing for the chocolate.

She pulls it out of reach. "No, Laurie. Down, Girl."

My hands grasp for the bag. "Why?" I plead.

"It's for a dessert I make."

"You can make a dessert with Oreos?" I ask, my mouth open.

"Yes, Laurie."

I bow from the waist in respect.

Nick and Dad come in as Ruby laughs. "What are you doing, Laurie-girl?" Dad asks, *his* mouth open.

"I'm bowing with respect, Dad. They do it in Eastern countries."

"Well, this is America," Dad says.

I nod. "So it is."

Ruby takes a carton of ice cream, two jars of fudge sauce, and a huge tub of Cool Whip from the bag.

"You guys go relax," Ruby tells Dad and Nick. "Laur and I have this under control."

They leave, Nick mentioning that a baseball game is on.

"I'll help, but you have to agree that you have full knowledge of my inability to cook anything other than box brownies, and I am herewith absolved of any possible and quite probable mistakes," I say.

"Do I need to initial anything?" Ruby asks, one hand on her hip.

"In blood, please."

She chuckles. "There's nothing to this dessert except layering. And there's nothing to the soup but making sure it doesn't boil over."

"That's it?"

"You didn't think I was some kind of gourmet, did you?"

"You can make chocolate lava cake from a recipe."

"Honey, my uncle in Kansas has a monkey that can make that cake." Ruby digs in my pantry and comes out with a huge plastic bag.

"What are you doing?"

"No, you're doing it. Put the Oreos in this bag and crumble them up."

"You want me to destroy perfectly good Oreos?" I'll admit, I am aghast.

Thirty minutes later the soup is good and hot, and the Oreo dessert is in the freezer, awaiting its execution.

"Soup's ready!" Ruby calls.

Nick and Dad come back into the kitchen. "Smells good, Babe," Nick says, kissing Ruby lightly on the temple.

They are definitely newlyweds.

Nick says a blessing, and we eat. By the end of the meal, my tongue is crying for mercy.

"So dessert now?" I ask.

Ruby shakes her head. "Give it a few more minutes, Laur. Maybe we could go tour that house?"

I nod. I had given her the brochure for it, and they decided that it looked nice on paper and the price was good.

I know the person who answers the door is a Realtor because he is clicking a gold pen incessantly and his haircut is about twenty years out of date.

"Hi, come on in," he says. *Clickety-clickety-clickety.* "Just look around.

I'll be in the kitchen if you need anything."

He leaves, clicking.

The entry is small but nice. Wood floors throughout. High ceilings. One gigantic living room, three bedrooms, two bathrooms, a huge laundry room, and more kitchen than Ruby will ever need.

Needless to say, they both fall in love with it.

I like that it is two blocks from my home. They can dogsit; I can babysit. The arrangement is perfect.

I leave the two of them there to talk to the clicky Realtor and walk back to my house.

It is very hot outside. Very hot. I'm not exactly a nature girl, so two blocks seem more like two miles.

By the time I get home, I am sweaty, parched, and tired. I shuffle into the kitchen, backhanding my forehead, and find Dad sliding out the dessert.

"I heard you open the door. Where're Nick and Ruby?"

"Talking to the Realtor."

"They liked it?"

"A lot."

Dad smiles. "Good. It's not too far from here. You won't have to drive as far to go to Bible study now."

"Nope."

He puts the dessert back. "We'll wait for them."

Two hours pass before Nick and Ruby knock on the front door again. Darcy again runs from the kitchen, where I am petting his silky ears, skids into the entry, loses his balance, and cracks into the wall.

"Should I be worried about your dog, Laur?" Nick asks, staring at Darcy. Darcy stands wobbling, shakes his head, and trots over, off-balance.

"Probably. Why?"

"Every time we come in, he looks off-kilter."

I exchange a look with Darcy, who sits and stares at me innocently.

Ruby is glowing. Her brown eyes are lit up, a huge smile on her face. "Oh, Laur, it was perfect!" She lets out a wistful sigh. "The house, the backyard, the neighborhood . . ."

"The neighbors," I add, pointing to myself.

Darcy barks.

Nick nods. "Good going, Laurie. Finding the house, I mean."

"So it's a done deal then?"

"We're taking Ryan back tomorrow night and meeting the owners," Ruby says. "Ry wants to check the foundation or something."

This is what Ryan is like: Very protective of his big sister. It's a very endearing quality.

"I see that smile, Laurie, and I'll even be a good friend and not comment." Ruby's eyes twinkle at me. "Who's ready for dessert?"

Dad already has it out on the counter. "I heard you come in," he says to Nick and Ruby.

"Laurie, if we buy this house, you have to help me decorate."

"Me?"

"I saw what you and Lexi did to her house. It's so warm looking. I don't have that touch. Help me repaint? Right now there's this gross mustard color everywhere." She makes a face.

"Sure, I'll help."

"Where did you find the sofas in Lexi's place?"

"Furniture Mart."

"On Fifth?" Nick asks.

I nod and take the plate Dad gives me.

"Ryan could come with us and bring his truck," she says.

"Remember, the singles' group meets at your house, Ruby," I caution. "You probably won't want to get the same sofas." Lexi bought the cutest squishy white sofas three months ago. Amazingly, they're still white. My sister has all the coordination of a four-year-old.

Ruby sits at the table. "I was thinking we could have that protective spray put on it. That should help. But this living room is about three times the size of Nick's. I think if I keep some beanbag chairs in the guest room and bring them out for the study, I'll be all right."

My mouth is full of Oreo, ice cream, fudge, and Cool Whip, so I just nod.

This is heaven. I'm moving into one of their guest rooms.

"So, Laur, do you want to come with us tomorrow? You can help me plan out furniture while Nick and Ryan dig for grubs," she says, licking her fork.

"Can we keep the rest of this dessert?"

She grins. "Sure."

"Then I'll come."

She watches me put another bite in my mouth and close my eyes. "You're pitiful."

"No, just a chocoholic."

She shakes her head. "Same thing."

Chapter Eleven

I'm two seconds away from tiredly opening the door to The Brandon Knox Photography Studio. I have my coffee in one hand, my backpack slung over my shoulder, my other hand on the glass door when I see it.

Brandon is leaning against Hannah's desk, smiling shyly at the blonde beauty, and she's returning the smile!

My mouth drops open, and I drop my hand from the door like it suddenly turned into an R.O.U.S. I dart two feet to the side so I can still peer into the window, but I'm not in their line of sight.

OH MY GOSH!

I can't keep a grin off my face!

Ruby's curly head stops in front of me as she walks up the sidewalk. "Hey, Laur. Why are you standing outside?"

She makes a move toward the door, and I grab her shoulders and yank her back. "Don't!" I screech.

She jerks away. "Why not?"

"Brandon and Hannah are in there."

She levels a gaze at me. "So?"

"So they're in there together."

She shakes her head. "They work together, Laurie. I thought you realized that by now."

"Very funny. No, I mean they're in there *together*."

She stares first at me and then at the door. "You mean like together-together?"

"Yep."

"Together-together-together?"

I grab her again and point in the window. "Look!"

She blows her breath out. "Wow."

"I know!"

"Brandon and Hannah?"

"Isn't it cool?" I'm bouncing, I'm so excited.

"Who would've guessed?"

I keep my mouth shut, which turns out to be a bad idea. All those self-help books that tell you to shut up and listen? Worthless.

She pins me with a look. "Laurie Holbrook . . ."

"Yes, Ruby?"

She sets her briefcase and purse down and grabs me by my shoulders this time. "I'm going to ask you a question, and I want you to be completely, 100 percent honest with me. Got it?" she says sternly.

"Um . . ."

"Did you or did you not set those two up?"

"Which two?" I fidget.

"Lauren Emma Holbrook . . ."

Oy. The full-name treatment.

"Brandon and Hannah. Did you?"

I wince. "What exactly do you mean by set up?"

She lets go of me and starts pacing. "Oh man. Oh man. This is bad. This is very bad."

"What?"

"You are trying to get the two of them together."

I roll my eyes and rub a hand through my hair. "There's a huge difference between encouraging and forcing, you know."

"Oh my gosh." She moans, covering her face with her hands.

"Hey, I did it to you."

She freezes. Drops her hands from her face. "What?"

"You and Nick."

"You what?" she bursts.

"I put the two of you together. You didn't even notice. See? I am beyond amateur; I get to skip directly to professional!" I grin, rubbing my hands together excitedly.

Her mouth hangs open in shock.

"Ruby?"

"What did you do?"

"To Brandon and Hannah? Nothing. I just reminded Brandon how he thought she was pretty, and Hannah has always had a small crush on him."

She is shaking her head. "No, no, no. To Nick and me." She looks at my hands. "And stop doing that; you look like Scrooge."

I hold my hands up. "Sorry. Oh. Well. Uh, when you guys first met? I kind of did that."

"We first met in the seventh grade, Laurie. You were barely even born."

"Okay, not your first meeting. But the first time you actually *talked.*"

"At Bible study."

"Yes. At Bible study. I made brownies."

"You made brownies," she echoes dubiously. "What does that have to do with this?"

"Ruby, I knew that God had destined the two of you for each other, and everyone knows that chocolate and falling in love go together," I explain.

She blinks. "So you think Brandon and Hannah are meant for each other?"

"I think so. Why wouldn't they be? They're both funny. She's organized; he's a slob. She's teachable; he's a good teacher. She's gorgeous, and he's pretty cute, which guarantees that their future children will be good-looking." I stop, cross my arms over my chest. "Of course, she's blonde, and he's got brown hair, so there is the whole Natural-Blond Theory to think about." I frown. "By the way, if a guy has brown hair, is he called a brunette or a bruno or just brown-haired?" I throw my hands up. "I never know."

Ruby's mouth is open again. "The Natural-Blond Theory?"

"Yeah. You know. That in fifty years there won't be any more natural blonds, so if you are a natural blond, it is your civic duty to marry another natural blond to prevent extinction."

She stares at me, slack-jawed and round-of-eye.

Brandon pushes open the door. "What are you two doing? You don't get on the time card until you are inside the building."

"I thought it was on the premises. And so did Ruby, right?" I point to Ruby, who still has that Dorothy-with-the-Munchkins look. "Never mind."

Ruby follows me inside, and I smile at Hannah and Brandon. "Morning, you guys." I'm humming Dean Martin.

"Hey, Laur. Stop humming. I hate that song." Brandon gives me a once-over. "You need a haircut. I'm in my office if anyone needs me."

He leaves.

I watch him go. Come to think of it, Brandon was born with blond hair. I don't think his hair darkened until puberty.

I wonder if there's a clause in the Natural-Blond Theory. A trip to the library is in order, I guess.

Ruby gives Hannah a pitying look. "My heart goes out to you, Honey."

It's Monday night. I'm standing in one of the bedrooms in the ranch house with Ruby. "We could put my desk here." Ruby points to one wall.

"Could." I pop a Tootsie Roll in my mouth and look around, chewing. "You were right. These people liked yellow."

"It's not even a cheery yellow, though. It's a yuck yellow."

"Might want to keep your voice down. I think I just heard them come inside."

Nick and the present owners, Bill and Erma, have been outside watching Ryan check the foundation.

Ruby puts her hands on her hips and looks around. "It's perfect, isn't it?"

"Yep. Great house for kids."

"Let's not go there yet."

I grin.

Ryan comes into the room, grabs me by my shoulders, and aims his boot-encased foot at my shin.

I yelp, even though his foot hasn't touched me. "What are you doing?"

"Checking your foundation."

"By kicking it?"

"It's a standard test, Laurie." He grins, his eyes crinkling in that cute little-kid smile he has.

Ruby looks at him. "You kicked the house? That's it? That's why you wanted to come tonight?"

Ryan slings one arm around my shoulders. "Well, that and to see if the house was infested with termites or something worse."

"Like what?" I ask, handing him a Milky Way from my pocket.

"Like squirrels."

"Mice would be worse, Ry," Ruby says. "That and this paint," she mutters under her breath.

"It is kind of gross, isn't it?" Ryan remarks, not lowering his voice at all.

I elbow him in the ribs, and he almost spits up his half-chewed Milky Way. "Be quiet," I whisper.

"So does it have your approval?" Ruby asks.

"What?" he says, swallowing.

"The house, Ryan."

"Oh. Sure, Sis. I think it's a great house. It'll make Bible study a lot easier. That living room is huge. You sure you can afford it, though?"

She nods. "I've been working full-time for the last twelve years, and so has Nick. And when we sell both of our houses, I think it will come out fine." She touches the walls. "I just want to repaint before we actually move our stuff in."

"Laur's good at that," Ryan says, squeezing my shoulder.

"She's already helping."

"Good. Want me to help?"

I shake my head. "No, thank you. I've seen you around paint."

"*You're* the one who got it all over you."

"You have to be relaxed around paint. You're not. And Lexi is the one who painted my backside, for the thirtieth time."

"You can help pick up the new furniture when I find it," Ruby tells him.

"Okay. Hey, Nate could help too."

I have to smile. Those two are tighter than the proverbial peanut butter and jelly.

Ryan sees my grin. "What?" he asks, nudging me.

"You guys are just cute, that's all."

"Thank you for noticing."

Nick, Bill, Erma, and Clicky the Realtor come into the guest room then. "Well, Ryan gave his okay, Babe," Nick says.

Ruby smiles at her brother, who still hasn't taken his arm off my shoulders. "He told me."

"You ready to sign then?" Clicky asks. "Bill and Erma need to close fast so they can settle their house in Dallas."

Nick and Ruby look at each other. "It feels right," they say at the same time.

Ryan chuckles. "So sign it. Laurie and I are going back to her house, though."

I say good-bye and let Ryan push me out the door. "Thank you," I say. "I really didn't want to walk home."

"We could walk and leave the truck here."

"Let's not and say we did."

He squints at the full moon. "It's a nice night, though."

"Yes, it is. Good night for hanging out inside with a cup of coffee."

He chuckles and opens the passenger door. "You're funny."

"Want some coffee?" I ask when he climbs in.

"Sure."

"We still have some of Ruby's Oreo dessert thing she made. Want that too?"

"With the ice cream in it? Did you have to ask?"

"I was waiting for the lecture about how much chocolate I eat. And since this would be dinner . . ."

He shrugs. "Like you said, chocolate's healthy. And the Oreo dessert is the best-tasting thing since . . . um . . ." His voice trails off as he thinks.

"Worcestershire sauce on shrimp?"

He makes a face. "How can you compare shrimp with Oreos?"

"My dad used to put Worcestershire sauce and lemon pepper on shrimp and then barbecue it."

"It sounds good, Laur. I'm not arguing with that. How you can compare seafood with chocolate is what I'm questioning."

He stops in front of my house, gets my door, and I go up the walk and open the front door.

Darcy skids into sight and rams smack into my legs.

"Whoa!" I yell. "Easy, boy." I reach down, scoop him up, and hand him to Ryan.

"Hey there, Darcy," he says, holding the dog at eye level. "Looks like you've been growing."

"By leaps and bounds."

He settles my puppy in the crook of his arm and follows me into the kitchen. "Where's your dad?"

"I don't know." I go into Dad's bedroom. No Dad.

"Dad?" I yell.

"Hey, Laur, there's a note on the kitchen table."

"Where is he?" I ask, going back to where Ryan stands.

"Laney called and asked if he wanted to go to dinner." He looks up. "Okay, where's the Oreo dessert?"

— ❖ —

Dad gets home about nine thirty, says something about Laney's kids tiring him out, and goes straight to bed.

Ryan leaves about eleven. "I should go. Have a good day tomorrow, Laur," he says, standing up from the couch and stretching. I flick off the TV. We were watching—of all things—a *Full House* marathon.

I follow him to the front door. "Yeah, have a good day working," I say.

"I will." He gives me a hug.

I close the door after him, carry a sleeping Darcy upstairs, and read Psalm 47. It was a good day. I turn off the light. *Thanks, Lord.*

Chapter Twelve

It is the Wednesday night before Dad will leave, and I cannot move my arms. Or for that matter, my toes. I've spent the previous week helping Nick and Ruby paint their new house, and my arms are sore from using the paint roller. My toes are sore from gripping the ladder.

I hate ladders.

Clicky the Realtor hadn't been kidding when he'd said that Bill and Erma wanted to close quickly. Nick and Ruby signed the papers last Monday night and closed Tuesday afternoon. Clicky was pretty much hyperventilating to keep up.

Then again, so was I. Once Ruby had her hands on a new house to decorate, she morphed into a drill sergeant.

And since my dad, bless my poor heart, picked the earliest flight he could possibly find, I am once again driving to the airport before it's even light outside. I sincerely hope there's not a limit to how many before-light hours one person can take in a month, because I am probably coming very close to it.

Thus the reason I'm skipping Bible study tonight. I am a heathen.

Dad holds up a beige-colored sweater that I hate and Mom hated even more, which tells you how old it is.

"Should I bring this?"

"No, Dad."

He frowns and fingers the sweater. "Why not? It's very warm."

"It's June."

"Yes. But in Michigan, it could be colder."

"Or warmer. It's humid in Michigan. You could take a sweater, but I wouldn't take that one. Take the blue one."

"Why the blue one?"

"It matches your complexion better."

Dad hangs the beige sweater back up, making a face. "I am almost fifty years old; you'd think I would have learned to dress myself by now."

"I guess that's why God gave you daughters."

He pulls the blue sweater out, folds it, and lays it in his suitcase. I crunch back on the pillows, waiting.

"Blue suit or gray suit?"

"Both."

"Two pairs of khakis?"

"Mmm . . . I'd be safe and go with three."

"Tennis shoes?"

"Yuck. With khakis, Dad? Gross."

"So I have to wear my loafers the whole time?"

"Take a pair of jeans, then."

Dad sighs in unison with me.

He smiles at me ruefully.

"Lexi's better at this than I am, Dad," I say.

"You're doing fine, Laurie-girl. Thanks for staying home with me tonight."

"Sure thing." I pluck a stray thread from a pillowcase Laney sewed for him when she was in high school. "This is the first time I can remember you taking a trip without taking one of us along."

"I think it is." He looks up from his suitcase, alarmed. "You will be fine here by yourself, right, Laurie-girl? Because if you won't, I can stay home."

I hold up my hands. "I'll be fine. I am twenty-three years old, am I not? Surely I can stay here by myself for a weekend."

He relaxes. "I love you, Laurie-girl."

———— ❖ ————

Whitney Houston wakes me up in the middle of the night. "Iiiiiii-eeee-iiiiiii-eeee-iiiiii will allllllllll . . ."

I jerk straight up in bed, stumble across the room, and smash down my alarm like I am on *Deadliest Catch* and it's a king crab from Alaska.

Dad knocks on my door as I throw open my closet.

"You up, Honey?"

"Mm-hmm."

"Can I come in?"

"Mmm."

He opens the door, grinning at me, his eyes flickering in unconcealed excitement. "Oh, Honey, I'm so nervous about this trip."

I have to smile. I *don't* have to open my eyes, though. "Don't be nervous, Dad. You'll have a great time."

"What if I meet someone? Wouldn't that be wonderful, Honey?"

A bowling ball whacks me in the stomach. *Squuuwish.*

Maybe I am not as prepared for this trip as I thought.

"That'd be great, Dad," I manage to say, grabbing the nearest pair of jeans and something at least resembling a shirt. "Let me get dressed, and I'll be ready."

"Okay, Honey. I'll go make your coffee."

I close the bathroom door and lean against the counter, staring at myself in the mirror.

"It's okay," I tell the wide-eyed, sleep-deprived, ghostly looking woman. "Nice people live in Michigan. The odds of him marrying a genetic scientist, a rose gardener, or a paint sniffer are highly unlikely."

I nod, inhale, and dress.

Why the rose gardener, you ask?

When I was fifteen, a friend of a friend of a woman who worked with Dad thought I was the next Mother Teresa and asked me to babysit her two kids. Since I hate letting people down, I said yes.

The kids were quite odd, the woman was odder, and the father grew roses in horticulturally sound, temperature-, humidity-, and soil-regulated cages in the backyard and forbade his children to play out there. Instead, the kids got to play inside, where it was dark, somewhat moist, and smelled like a mixture of cloves and fish oil.

I babysat them once. That is all.

And ever since then, I have a strong aversion to rose gardeners.

Dad hands me a thermos filled with coffee when I get downstairs, smiles so wide his cheek muscles pop, picks up his suitcase, and pats my shoulder.

"Let's go," he says.

I drive to the airport and stop in front of the drop-off area.

He turns to me, leans over, and kisses my cheek. "Thanks, Laurie-girl. Hold down the fort?"

"Sure, Dad. Be careful. Don't eat anything that looks suspicious, stay away from Kool-Aid, and, Dad?"

He opens the door and smiles at me.

I sigh. "Just be careful."

"You take good care of me, Laurie-girl."

"And have fun," I call as he climbs out, hoisting his suitcase with him.

"I will. You be careful too, Laurie. Stay away from sick people and check on Laney every day."

"I love you, Dad."

Unexpectedly, Dad's eyes tear up. He sets his suitcase down and leans back into the car, pulling me into a huge hug. "Bye, Baby Girl."

He closes the door, grabs his suitcase, and walks through the swishy automatic doors without looking back.

I watch him disappear. Then I drive away.

The clock tells me it is 6:17.

Shawn will be open.

I drive to his place, tumble out, and open his door, yawning.

He turns from where he is putting salt and pepper shakers on the far table in the corner.

"Laurie Holbrook?"

"Hi, Shawn."

"Is it really you?"

"Be quiet, Shawn."

"It's six thirty in the morning." He grins at me. "The Laurie I know would never be here this early in the morning—especially *twice* in one month."

I collapse onto a bar stool and lay my head on my arms.

"So what are you doing up so early, Laur?"

"I took my dad to the airport," I say through a yawn.

"Oh yeah. For that Matchmaking Michigan Maids Making . . . Matches . . . and I don't remember the rest of the alliteration. I hate alliteration."

"Me too." I lift my head a few inches. "And it's Meet Your Match in Michigan."

He smiles and goes around the counter. "You missed last night."

"Honey, I had to get up at 5:20 today." Then I blink. "You went to Bible study again?"

"Yep. Want coffee?"

Now I sit all the way up. "Wow, Shawn, I'm so glad you did."

He passes me an extra-large mug filled to the brim. "Here. Have a doughnut." He hands me a chocolate-iced, ring-shaped piece of the Pearly Gates and leans on the counter.

Hallie comes through the door and smiles curiously at me. "Hey, Laurie."

I smile over the rim of my coffee cup at her.

"Hey, Hallie." Shawn grins.

"Hi, Shawn." Hallie walks over and sets her purse on the counter. She touches my sleeve. "What are you doing here?"

"She dropped her dad off at the airport," Shawn says, handing Hallie a cup of coffee.

"Ohhh," Hallie nods. "For his Michigan matching thing. Wow. That is so cool, Laurie."

"As long as he doesn't meet a rose gardener."

Shawn frowns at me. "I thought it was a genetic scientist you were worried about."

"I'm worried about both."

"What are you going to do this weekend, Laur?" Hallie asks.

I shrug. "I don't know. A whole empty house to myself and not one person to limit how much coffee I drink or chocolate I eat."

Hallie laughs. "Wow, look at that smile, Shawn!"

Shawn closes his eyes.

"What are you doing?" I ask.

"Praying for your future husband."

I could be mad, but instead I'm thrilled. "Praying, huh?"

He opens his eyes and hooks a thumb to the door. "Go home, Laurie. Get some sleep. And thank you for not bringing your dog this time."

"You're welcome." I find my backpack and hop off the bar stool. "Bye, Hallie."

"Good-bye, Laurie. Have a good day."

Darcy is whining in his kennel when I get home, so I let him out into the backyard and sink down on the sofa. I know I won't go back to sleep because once I brush my teeth and have some caffeine, I can't return to sleep until the afternoon hours. I have the whole day off from work. Plenty of time for sleeping later.

Dad doesn't make a lot of noise, but the house feels really quiet without him.

I hate quiet.

This could be a long weekend.

The phone rings. I look at the clock before reaching over for the extension. No one other than my oldest sister would be calling at seven.

"Hi, Laney."

"Hey. Dad get off okay?"

"Yep. Should be sitting in the terminal waiting right now."

"Oh good. Say, could you do me a big favor?"

"Sure."

"Adam's already at work, and the kids are still in bed, and I'm looking through my refrigerator, and I don't have any milk. And I knew you were up because you took Dad, and I can't fit behind the steering wheel . . . "

I stand. "Say no more, Laney. I'll be there in an hour."

"Thanks, Laur. Hey, get some Oreos and green beans too, okay?"

"Oreos and green beans." I repeat this while holding my rolling stomach. *Blegh.*

"The two together taste awful, but that's what I've been craving this last week."

I make a face to Darcy through the window.

"And I heard that."

"I didn't say anything."

"You stuck your tongue out."

Rats. My oldest sister is too smart for motherhood. Her kids are going to wind up being psychotic wackos who spend their days looking backward and fidgeting.

Sort of like their aunt, I guess.

"Okay, sure. Anything else?"

"Not that I can think of," she says. "Take your cell. I'll call if I do think of something."

"See you later."

I hang up, open the back door, and pick up an excited little puppy. "Want to come to the store and Auntie Laney's house?"

Darcy barks.

Laney opens her door for me exactly an hour later. "Hi." She squints at me. "What's with the Peter Pan shirt?"

"First thing I saw this morning."

"Well, it obviously wasn't a comb." She grins.

"Hey, am I or am I not the wonderful sister who went to the grocery store at the earliest hour known to man for you?"

"You are."

"Thank you."

She lets me in, smiles at Darcy, and gives me one of those pregnant woman hugs—you know the kind: one arm—and stubs her toe against mine.

I grin at her. "Hi, Laney."

Laney has brown-blonde hair, is well-kept, and has one of the driest senses of humor I know of. She's also normally thin.

Today, though, she resembles more of a sideways Alp.

I pat the Alp. "Gee, are Junior and Junior still growing?"

She rolls her eyes. "I'm really missing being able to see my feet, Laur. Not to mention my kids. Yesterday they were playing hide-and-seek, and Jess hid under my stomach."

I laugh and follow her into the kitchen and put the groceries on the counter.

"That's the other thing I'm missing." She watches me make a pot of coffee.

Laney is one of those women who keeps a full pot of coffee on all day long. Pregnancy has been hard, to say the least.

"Where are the kids?" I ask as I pour myself a cup.

"Still in bed."

I sip the coffee. "You're kidding."

"Nope. Adam had them up until eleven thirty last night teaching them how to play poker."

"Laney Holbrook Knox . . ."

"What? I couldn't do anything about it. I can't even get off the sofa without help anymore."

I laugh.

"I'm just glad today is Dorie's day off from preschool."

She sits slowly at the kitchen table, and I join her. "Teaching a five-year-old and two three-year-olds to play poker," I mutter.

She shrugs and rubs her stomach like pregnant women do.

"So Dad got off okay?" she asks again.

"Mm-hmm."

"He excited?"

"Unbelievably."

Laney smiles. "I'm glad. Dad deserves some happiness."

"Yeah."

"You don't sound very convinced."

"I just don't want him to end up meeting a rose gardener or a genetic scientist or something like that."

Laney laughs. "You are still dealing with the Hodges!"

"Give me a break, Laney. They were weird!"

She shakes her head. "Not every rose gardener is like that."

"You don't know that. How many other rose gardeners do you know?"

She opens her mouth, stops, and blinks. "None."

"See?"

"I'm sure that the odds of Dad meeting a rose gardener are few. Rest easy."

"Right. Sure." *Rest easy.*

Not in this lifetime.

Chapter Thirteen

The doorbell rings at six fifteen, and I stop and turn away from the kitchen.

Ryan Palmer stands on the front porch, looking constructiony. "Hey, Laur."

"Hi, Ryan. Was I expecting you?"

He shakes his head. "I was helping Nick and Ruby move some bookcases. I remembered your dad was gone, and I thought I'd see if you wanted to get something to eat." He grins his cute grin.

I smile at him. He wears worn jeans and a big flannel shirt with the arms rolled to his elbows. A backwards baseball cap smashes his hair down.

"I don't know, Ry. You're so dressed up. It will take me awhile to get ready."

He rolls his eyes. "Funny, Laur. Come on, get your shoes and whatever else you need."

He comes inside, and I search for my tennis shoes.

"Did your dad get there okay?"

"He called about two hours ago and was at the conference center."

"Good."

I find my shoes in the living room.

"Where's Darcy?"

"Sacked out on my bed."

He grins. "What'd you do to that poor dog?"

"We went to Laney's today."

He starts laughing. "Oh, I see. Twins and a five-year-old. Poor dog."

I sit down on the couch and start tying my shoes. "So I guess Dad's retreat thing starts with a dinner tonight before all-day activities for the next few days."

Ryan sits beside me. "You're worried sick."

"I am not!" I protest.

"You are too, and you know it." He freezes me with a stare. I blink innocently.

"I am *concerned.*"

"Liar."

I finish tying and lean back. "I'm apprehensive."

He grins. "You're in denial."

"I'm uneasy."

He shakes his head, stands, and pulls me to my feet. "You should have knocked photography and went for a career as a thesaurus."

"I'll take that as a compliment."

He puts an arm around my shoulders and escorts me out the door. "Your dad will be fine, your future stepmom, if she exists, will be normal, you will be okay, and I'll still be perfect. See? Life is good."

I roll my eyes.

"I have to tell you I heard a rumor that your dad left because Laney's thinking she'll deliver this weekend." He looks at me, eyebrows raised. "Tell me that isn't true."

I laugh.

"It's true." He opens the passenger door of his truck and helps me climb in. "Your family is unbelievable, Laur."

I wait until he climbs in. "Why?"

"Laney's pregnant with the cast of *Full House*, Lexi's just plain odd, your dad takes a trip to Michigan to meet women, and you . . ." He looks over at me and grins. "You . . ."

"Me what?"

He shifts gears. "You, Laurie Holbrook, are beyond words."

I can live with that.

"Where are you taking me?" I ask.

"Merson's."

I can live with that too.

"I was there this morning, actually."

He shrugs. "So what else is new?"

"Very funny."

Ryan smiles.

"Hallie and Shawn went to Bible study last night."

"I know. I was there. You, however, were not there."

"I wasn't?"

He rolls his eyes.

"I drove Dad to the airport, remember? I stopped for coffee afterward."

He smiles at me and then turns right. "So that's where you heard that Shawn was at Bible study."

"Isn't it great?" I am ecstatic.

"And Brandon sat next to Hannah again."

I did not know this little bit of information. "Really?"

Ryan grimaces at the innuendo in my tone. "Oh no."

"Hey!" I protest, smacking his arm. "When Hannah is Mrs. Brandon Knox, everyone will thank me."

"Has anyone you've set up thanked you?"

I wave my hand airily. "That was a rhetorical statement."

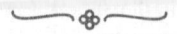

Shawn looks up from handing a lady a piece of cheesecake when we come in and grins. "Hey, Laur. It's been awhile. Hi, Ryan." He finishes with the lady. "What do you want?"

"Food, preferably," I say.

Shawn gives me a look and then turns to Ryan. "How you stand it, I don't know."

"Well, she's not boring."

"Hello, gentlemen? I'm standing right here. Save that stuff for later."

"Yes, Laurie. What would you like to eat?"

"A dinner salad with ranch dressing and a slice of the German chocolate cake, please."

Ryan smiles and holds up two fingers. "Works."

Hallie comes around from the back, holding a tray with sandwiches. "Laurie, Ryan, how are you?"

"Fine, thanks," Ryan says.

"Staying for dinner, I hope?"

I nod. She smiles so wide her eyes turn into slits.

Man, she's cute. I sneak a look at Shawn and catch a glimmer, not a glint.

A glimmer is much better than a glint. Glints are harder. A glimmer is soft and affectionate-like.

Ryan calmly elbows me in the ribs. I jump, and the glimmer in Shawn's eyes dissolves.

"I should get this to the tables," Hallie says and leaves.

Shawn pushes numbers in the cash register. "And coffee to drink," he mutters.

I hold up my hands. "Whoa, whoa, whoa," I say. "I do not remember ordering coffee. Ryan, do you remember ordering coffee?"

He thinks about it and shakes his head. "Afraid I don't, Laur."

Shawn huffs. "Fine. What do you want to drink?"

I stare at the drink menu, suspended above the coffeemaker. "Umm . . ."

Shawn taps his foot, annoyed.

"I think I'd like . . . coffee, please," I say.

Ryan nods at me, his eyes twinkling. "Sounds good, Honey. Make it two, please."

Shawn stares at both of us, mouth pursed. He mumbles as he totals our order.

"What was that?" I ask.

"I don't chew my cabbage twice."

"Glad to hear it," I tell him. "Chewing cabbage even once is disgusting. I once heard that red cabbage promotes bone mass and liver functions, so I don't eat it."

Ryan frowns. "Why not? Those are good things."

"Yeah, but those two things are completely unrelated to each other. How do I know that the cabbage won't get confused when it gets into my system?" I shrug. "What if I end up with a liver mass and malfunctioning bones?"

Shawn covers his eyes. "Laurie, Laurie, Laurie." His voice is a moan.

"I told you she'd make you start praying," Ryan says.

"Cash or credit?" Shawn says weakly.

Ryan hands him a ten and tells him to keep it. I take our tray to a corner table.

Hallie comes by as we set out our meal. "I'll take that," she says, pointing to the tray. She looks back at the counter and frowns. "Hey, what's Shawn doing?"

"Praying," Ryan says.

She blinks. "Really?"

I nod. "Really."

"Wow!" She grins at us. "That is fantastic! I am so happy!" She goes to the counter immediately and gives Shawn a big hug, pulls away, and goes into the back.

Apparently she did this without explaining the reason for the hug because he stares after her like a blank sheet of paper.

You know. Blankly.

Ryan turns and grins at me. "You're pitiful."

"I did not tell her to hug him. In fact, you're the one who told her he was praying." I look at him over my coffee.

"I guess it was inevitable, hanging around you. You've sucked me into your web of . . . of—"

I cut him off. "How long have we known each other?"

He blinks at the change in subject. "Uh. Like five months."

"Five months? And you're only now stricken speechless?"

He laughs.

———— ❖ ————

Ryan drops me off at my house two hours later, and I trudge up the front walk, open the door, and wave as he drives away.

I close the door and look at Darcy, who sits in the middle of the living room floor staring at me, cock-headed.

Creepy. I am twenty-three years old, and yet I have never stayed a night alone in this house.

I take a deep breath, smile reassuringly at Darcy, and clear my throat. "I can do this. It's not like it's any different with Dad home. He'd be in bed by now."

Darcy nods at me.

"And I have a trusty guard dog."

Darcy nods again.

The ice machine in the freezer kicks on, and I grab Darcy. "Okay, we're going to Lexi's."

Darcy licks my chin, nods once more, hops to the floor, and trots to his kennel like, *Okay, I'm ready.*

⟜❖⟝

Lexi opens her front door, takes one look at me, my backpack, Darcy, and the kennel, and sighs. "Why, hello, Kid Sister."

"Want to have a sleepover?"

She smiles gently. "Weird at the house?"

I step inside and drop the empty kennel to the floor. "Worse than weird. Dad makes a lot of noise in his silence."

"Who's at the door, Honey?" Nate yells from the kitchen.

"Laurie!" Lexi yells back.

"Hi, Laurie!" Nate yells.

Nate and Lexi yell *constantly.* Even when they are two feet apart, they yell. Not in anger; they're just loud. I worry about their future children. Scratch that. I worry about my cardrums and their future children.

"Can we stay here?" I ask. Darcy lays his head on my arm and blinks at Lexi pitifully.

Lexi can't help it. "Awww, of course," she coos, rubbing Darcy's ears and kissing my cheek.

"Honey!" she screams.

"Yeah?"

"Baby and Darcy are staying tonight, okay?"

"Sure thing!" He comes out of the kitchen, wiping his hands on a towel. "Hi, Laur. Hey, Darce, how's my man?" He comes up behind Lexi, wraps his arms around her waist, and kisses her ear. "Guest room, Babe?"

I watch them, smiling. These two kicked off my matchmaking tendencies.

Lexi nods. "Yep."

"Want me to go make sure the sheets are clean?" Nate asks.

"Sure." She smiles at him, and he squeezes her waist and leaves.

Darcy struggles in my hands, so I set him down.

"He is carpet-trained, right?" Lexi says warily, watching the puppy nose her new furniture.

"Yep. Sees carpet and goes."

Lexi does not find that humorous.

"Yes, Lexi, he's carpet-trained. You think any dog in the presence of our father would not be carpet-trained within forty-eight hours?"

"Speaking of our father," she says, relaxing, "did he get to the camp safely?"

"Yeah." I check the clock on Lexi's living room wall. "He should be done with dinner and *socializing* now."

She gives me a look. "Good grief, Baby, it's a Christian camp. And he's almost fifty years old. He can take care of himself. Lighten up."

"But, Lex, it's *Dad*. He's so . . ." I wave my hands, not finding the words.

Nate comes back into the entry and picks up my backpack and the kennel. "Naive?" he suggests.

"That's it. Naive. Trusting. In fact, it was Mom who taught us— including Dad—not to take candy from strangers."

Lexi rolls her eyes. "Okay, now you're exaggerating. And it wasn't Mom who taught us that. It was Laney."

"And who insisted on locking the front door at night?"

"Laney."

"See?"

"Like I said before . . . Baby, it's a Christian camp. Relax. Breathe. Pray. Okay? Last time I checked, God was still sovereign in Michigan."

"I heard that too." Nate smiles.

"Do me a favor and read Psalm 16, all right?" Lexi says, hands on hips.

"Okay."

Darcy looks up, sees his home in the hands of Nate, and freaks out. He runs over, yipping like crazy.

"I'll just set this down in the guest room," Nate says.

Darcy follows him down the hall.

"What time do you need to be at work tomorrow, Hon?" Lexi asks.

"Well, Ruby's back, so nine o'clock."

"What does Ruby being back have to do with anything?"

"She's the human stopwatch, remember? Marriage doesn't change everything."

Lexi snickers and goes back into the kitchen. "Spoken like a true single. Okay, I'll set the coffeepot so it's ready for you in the morning. Still drinking ten cups a day?"

The early, early, early morning is beginning to catch up with me. "Eleven."

She grins. "Go to bed, Sweetheart. See you in the morning."

"Night, Lex." I pass Nate in the hall and tell him goodnight too.

He gives me a hug. "Glad you came to our house, Laur."

My brother-in-law is not like a typical brother-in-law. *Of course.*

I close the door to the guest room behind me. Darcy, also woken up at the crack of dawn, is fast asleep in his kennel.

I change into my pajamas, climb into bed, and grab my little pocket-sized Bible. I open to the psalm Lexi suggested, and verses 8 and 9 catch my eye. "I have set the Lord always before me. Because he is at my right hand, I will not be shaken. Therefore my heart is glad and my tongue rejoices; my body also will rest secure."

Closing my eyes, I drift to sleep.

Chapter Fourteen

The day is beautiful as I drive to the airport. The sun is shining and a slight breeze ruffles my hair through the open windows. It's a beautiful day for suntanning.

Darcy sits perkily in the passenger seat, barking excitedly as we approach the pickup area for Dad's airline. Dad stands on the corner, his ever-present sweater over one arm, his other arm around . . .

A tall, imposing woman with a beautiful mane of long, shimmering brown hair and eyes covered with designer sunglasses stands next to him.

I stop at the curb, gawking.

"Laurie! I have something exciting to tell you!" Dad exclaims, pulling the woman close to the car.

"Hi . . . D-Dad," I say weakly. The woman pulls her shades off, revealing eyeliner reaching far up to her forehead, Egyptian-style.

Creepy.

Darcy shrinks under her condescending gaze, whimpers, and darts under my seat.

"This is Dr. Elizabeth Melora, my fiancée and your future mother!" Dad says, his eyes brimming with excitement and love as he looks at his future bride.

*The woman extends a hand through the open window to me. "Hello,"
she says, her voice unnaturally guttural. "I am Dr. Melora. You may call me
Dr. Mother."*

*I swallow and blink a few times, but the woman's hand and face do not
disappear.*

*I reach out and shake her hand, chilled by its iciness. "Hi," I squeak.
"Um . . . what kind . . . that is to say, what type of . . . what is your doctorate in, uh . . . Dr. Mother?"*

*"Do not stutter!" she suddenly shouts, her already hard features crystal-
lizing in diamond-like sharpness. "I abhor stuttering!"*

"I'm . . . I'm sorry, Dr. Mother," I plead. Darcy whimpers.

*Dad's arm tightens around the woman. "Dr. Elizabeth is in biochemi-
cal studies and evolutionary concepts in organic science."*

I blink.

*Dr. Mother sees my confusion and rolls her eyes. "I am a genetic
scientist."*

*My eyes widen. It suddenly occurs to me that this woman's hair doesn't
have a single strand out of place, like the whole mass could be lifted up and
taken away and not move in the process.*

"A . . ." I gulp. "A genetic scientist?"

*"Isn't it wonderful, Darling?" Dad says. "She's invented a vaccine to
fix cell breakdowns that lead to the common cold. I've already been injected
with it."*

*Music begins playing from the car stereo. Odd. I have not turned the
radio on. Sad violins grind out hauntingly beautiful notes that wind through
the Tahoe.*

*"A genetic scientist," Dr. Mother says. Her eyes narrow evilly, like the
stepmother on* Cinderella. *"Breathe for me."*

"No, Dad, don't marry her!" I screech. The violins get louder.

"Breathe for me!"

"Daddy, please!" I yell.

Dr. Mother rips open the passenger door, her breath hot in my face.
"BREATHE FOR ME!"

I scream and jump to a sitting position, my hair falling over my face in an odd reenactment of that scene from *The Princess Bride*.

Darcy yelps.

I blink, my breathing harsh, my heartbeat off the charts, not having a clue where I am or how I got here.

Blue.

Lexi's guest room.

I sigh and fall back on the bed, breathing deeply.

Dreams don't have meanings these days, do they?

Violins softly invade my brain and I turn. The alarm clock radio is going off on the table beside the bed. It's Friday morning.

Darcy shakes his kennel, yipping again.

I hit the off button and sit up again, much slower this time. Darcy, now being able to see me, calms somewhat, staring at me wide-eyed.

"Freaked me out too, Kid," I mutter.

I open his kennel door and lead him down the hall and out the back door so he can go in the backyard. Then I stumble to the guest bathroom.

I come out thirty minutes later, tired and still shell-shocked, but dressed with my hair fixed.

Lexi smiles at me as I go into the kitchen. "Hey, Baby, sleep well?"

I blink at her, get a huge mug of coffee, and fall into a chair at the kitchen table.

"Apparently not." She grins. "Strange bed? Strange noises? What was it?"

"I dreamed that Dad was engaged to a genetic scientist." I set the coffee down.

Lexi looks at me and shakes her head. "Okay, seriously, Honey, you're getting way too worked up about this." She pulls a box of doughnuts from the pantry and sits beside me at the table.

"But she wanted me to breathe for her!" I say, reaching for a chocolate-iced with sprinkles.

Lexi just looks at me. "Did you read Psalm 16?"

"Yeah."

"And?"

"And God is in control."

"Of what?"

I swallow a piece of sugary goodness. "Of everything."

She keeps prodding. "Including?"

"Dad."

"Thank you." She sips her coffee smugly.

⎯⏑⎯ ❖ ⎯⏑⎯

I go to work, open the front door of The Brandon Knox Photography Studio, and come face-to-face with a very mad woman.

It isn't Dr. Mother, however. *Thank goodness.*

Hannah doesn't look much nicer though.

"Lauren Emma Holbrook!" she shouts.

I frown. "Yeah, that's me."

She doesn't smile. "This is all your fault!"

I push her gently into one of the chairs in front of her desk. "What happened?" I ask soothingly.

"Thanks to you, the *entire* Bible study thinks Brandon and I are *engaged*!" she yells.

I sit down opposite her. "What?" Apparently Ryan left a few details out regarding Hannah and Brandon sitting together.

"Yeah! They think we're engaged! This is *not* okay!"

I wince. "Look, stop yelling and tell me what happened."

She huffs and slumps back in the chair, crossing her arms over her chest. Her hair is yanked back in a sloppy bun, and she's wearing only mascara and lip gloss.

"He sat down next to me," she starts, her voice icing over.

"Okay," I say. "So?"

"So he sat there and then was talking to me afterward, and Dr. Stephen came up, and he and Brandon started joking about when the wedding was." She leans forward and covers her eyes.

I'm not seeing what the big deal is. "So?" I say again.

"So everyone heard! *Everyone!*"

"Uh-huh."

"Oh, Laurie, it was terrible." She is moaning. "Everyone was staring, I turned red, Brandon was laughing, and you weren't there to patch things up."

"I'm sorry, Hannah. I wanted to go, but I couldn't. I had to drive Dad to the airport by six the next morning."

She lifts her big, sad, gorgeous blue eyes to mine. "I mean, what if my future husband was there and he's not going to talk to me now because he thinks Brandon and I are engaged?"

I rub her shoulder. "First of all, you're being ridiculous." She gapes at me and I continue. I didn't win the Most Likely to Speak Her Mind award in high school for no reason. "Half the guys there are already married anyway, and don't forget about God." I wave my finger in her face.

"I know." She rubs her eyes. "It's just that then everyone started talking, and all the girls wanted to know when the wedding was and where my ring was and how he proposed. . . ."

I'm really trying hard not to laugh. "What did you say?" I ask, covering my mouth.

"I said, 'We're not engaged!'" She shakes her head forlornly. "I don't think anyone heard me."

I grin. "Well, look at the bright side, Hannah."

"What bright side?"

"I'll throw you a shower and you can score some awesome gifts." I start laughing as she sends a look the temperature of a snow cone in my direction.

"Laurie."

"I'm kidding, I'm kidding." I whack her on the shoulder. "Perk up, Kid, and smell the silver lining."

"So many mixed metaphors," she mumbles, then exhales loud and long. "I guess it wasn't too bad the other night."

I look at her. "After all that drama?"

"Well, you know Tina and Kyle?"

I roll my eyes and point to the life-sized portrait of them hanging on the lobby wall. Flawless Tina and her now-husband, Perfect Kyle.

She giggles and immediately turns from downtrodden Hannah to bright-eyed Hannah. "Right. They're pregnant. That drew most of the attention the other night. You know, them being the first couple in the singles' Bible study to get pregnant."

My mouth drops open and my chin hits the floor like weights have been inserted between my bottom teeth. "What?" I yell.

"They're pregnant," Hannah repeats. "Two months along, apparently."

"With a baby?" My eyes are wide.

Hannah recovers her old self. "No, Laurie, with a fish tank. Yes, with a baby!"

"They're having a baby?"

"We've been through this." She holds my face in her hands. "Yes. Tina and Kyle are having a child. Soon it will be born. Then it will grow. One day it might have its own child."

I stare at her. "I mentored her through seventh-grade English!"

"We know, Laurie. We heard this whole spiel when she got engaged.

And again when she got married."

Ruby comes through the door, frowns at the clock, and smiles at us. "Hi, girls." Nick and I sold our houses yesterday.

"Tina is pregnant!" I yell.

"Hey, congratulations!" Hannah says to Ruby.

Ruby sets her purse in her cubbyhole and nods at me. "That's right, you weren't there on Wednesday. She is. Exciting, isn't it? And yes, Laurie, I know you mentored her through English."

"She is nineteen years old," I assert.

"No!" Hannah says sarcastically.

This is unbelievable. In the last year, Tina has managed to find a guy, get married, and start a family. And me? Nothing. I suddenly feel very, very old and worn out.

Since when did growing up get to be so . . . complicated?

My mom and dad's courtship wasn't complicated at all. He saw her; she saw him; they dated for several years and got married. A year later, they had Laney.

Granted, my parents met when they were in the fifth grade.

But still!

I take a deep, calming breath.

God is still sovereign, yes?

Yes.

I am still Laurie Holbrook, right?

Right.

So this little emotional firecracker did not need to happen. Correct?

Correct.

I exhale and smile at Hannah, who shakes her head.

"You go from piping mad to serene in less time than it takes to change a tire," she states. "I don't know whether to worry or not."

Ruby smoothes my hair. "I think that's a good quality. How's your dad, Laurie?"

"I haven't heard from him since he first got there."

"But he did get there?"

"Yeah."

She nods. "Good. I'm sure he'll have a good time."

"How many genetic scientists do you think are in Michigan?"

Brandon comes through the door, humming. "Morning, guys."

"Hi, Brandon," Hannah says.

Brandon's eyebrows go up. "Hey, she speaks!"

Hannah smiles at him, and his eyebrows go up further. He looks from her to me and back to her.

"You're talking to me again?" he asks her.

She shrugs. "Well, Laurie and I talked. I guess we can talk too."

He doesn't look away from Hannah, but speaks to me. "Laurie, I love you, you know that?"

I smile. "Yeah, I know that."

Ruby starts to chuckle, but I put a finger to my mouth to hush her.

Brandon's brown eyes are soft and warm as he smiles at Hannah, who in turn smiles at him, a faint blush stealing up her cheeks charmingly.

"I'm sorry about the other night," he says gently.

"Me too. It's okay. It will be all right," she murmurs.

"Yeah. It'll all work out." He pauses, still looking at her eyes. "What are you doing for lunch today?"

She shrugs.

"Want to go get something with me?"

She nods, the blush deepening. "Okay."

He grins. "Okay."

I feel Ruby looking at me and turn, flinching, ready for the verbal lashing about matchmaking I have coming.

Her arms are crossed over her chest, and she shakes her head slowly side to side.

I smile hopefully.

Brandon touches Hannah's shoulder gently. "I guess I should get some work done before then."

She grins, the old Hannah back, blush receding. "Work? You work?"

"Till lunch, Hannah," he says. He smiles at me on his way down the hall to his office. "How's your dad?"

"I had a dream."

"Oh boy."

"I'll tell you later."

He clutches his chest. "Be still my heart." He laughs and disappears through his office door.

Hannah clears her throat, steps around her desk, and turns on her computer.

Ruby is still looking at me.

I hold my hands up and back toward Studio One. "I didn't do a thing, Ruby."

Hannah looks at her and then at me. "You didn't do a thing with what?"

Ruby turns to Hannah and pulls out the messages in her box. "Just start praying now, Hannah." She closes the door to Studio Two behind her.

Hannah blinks at me. "Praying about what?"

"Um . . . could you send the Myers in here when they come?"

I close the door on Hannah's totally confused expression and fall onto the sofa.

My cell phone rings in my pocket, and I answer it, not recognizing the number. "Hello?"

"Hi, Honey, it's Dad."

"Hi, Dad. How's the retreat?" I hold the phone tighter. "Meet anyone with a doctorate?"

"What? No, no doctorates . . . yet, I guess. It's going well. Dinner was good last night. Chicken. Cooked all the way through, so don't worry about food poisoning."

"Um . . . all right. Have you met anyone yet?"

He pauses. "I've met lots of people, Laurie-girl. It's a big retreat."

"I meant women, Dad."

"Oh. Not really." He pauses again. "Well . . ."

My fingers are beginning to spasm around the phone. I switch hands. "Well?"

"Well, I did meet one woman last night who was interesting."

"Interesting?" Interesting women can be good or bad.

"Her name is Joan Abbot."

"Joan Abbot," I repeat.

"She's a widow, her husband died ten years ago, and she has two kids."

Kids.

There is an angle I haven't thought to worry about yet. "Kids?"

"Older kids. One's twenty-five, and the other is twenty-six. They're both married."

My palms are sweating. "Wow, Dad, you sure know a lot about her after just one evening."

"Well, like I said, she's interesting. She's very nice. She's a seamstress but works from her home."

"Where is her home?"

"New Mexico, actually. But her son, the twenty-six-year-old, lives about fifty miles from us."

Fifty miles.

My heart is palpitating. If I didn't already have heart disease, I'm contracting it now.

"We're planning on having lunch together today, so I'll let you know more later."

"Okay . . ."

"I need to go, Sweetie. Tell Laney and Lexi hello for me."

"All right . . ."

"Bye, Honey."

He hangs up.

I pull the phone away from my ear and stare at it like it is a squid with a bad case of the measles.

Then I dial. Wait. Just about give up when he answers.

"Ryan? Dad met someone. And she has kids who live near us, and she's a seamstress," I say in a rush.

I hear him laughing. "So no genetic scientist? No brain-wave machines or suctioning devices?"

I smile sheepishly and feel my heart rate returning to normal.

"She sounds normal, Laur. What's her name?"

"Joan Abbot. I wonder what it means?"

"What *what* means?"

"Her name. Names have meaning, you know."

"So look up what Joan Abbot's name means. But it's a good, normal, nice-sounding name, Laurie. Calm down."

"She has two kids, Ryan. I never even thought about the other person having kids."

"Is that bad?"

"I don't know."

"I don't think it is."

"What if they're psychos?"

"Then they'll fit right in."

"Funny, Ryan." I rub my head. "I hope she's nice."

"I'm sure she is. Your dad has good taste in friends, remember. "

"Yeah, I guess he does."

"See? There's nothing to worry about. Your dad has been married before, he knows what marriage looks like. He'll go slowly with this relationship or any others."

"I guess you're right."

I can hear his grin. "Hey," he says slowly.

"What?"

"You came to me."

"What are you talking about?"

"You came to me with your problem. Not to Brandon."

I blink.

"That's quite a compliment, Laurie; I thank you."

"Thanks for calming me down."

"You're welcome. Anytime. But I really need to go now, Laur. Mrs. Galen's plant is about to eat my left elbow."

"Yeah, you need to go. I happen to be very fond of your left elbow."

He laughs. "Bye, Laur. Don't worry about your dad."

I hang up and stare at the camera equipment in front of me.

Dad . . . married again?

Me with a stepmom?

I shake my head, stand, and go back into the lobby. Hannah looks up from the computer.

"Hey, your nine fifteen, the Myers? They just called; they're canceling."

I sit on the edge of her desk and lean over her shoulder. "Could you get on the Internet and look up name sites?"

"Name sites?"

"Yeah, you know. Meanings of names sites."

She raises an eyebrow but does as I ask. "Type in Joan and Abbot," I tell her.

"J-O-A-N?"

"I guess so."

The screen flickers and I lean closer. "'Joan,'" I read out loud. "'God is Gracious.' What does Abbot mean?" She types. "'Spiritual leader,'" I read, sitting back.

Hannah closes the window and turns to me, her hands folded principal style. "Why did we just look up those names?"

"Well, Dad—"

Brandon comes out of his office, waving a paper at us. "Hannah, we made a copy of this paper, and I can't find the original."

"What paper?"

"This paper." He gives it to her and smiles at me. "Hey, Nutsy. Shouldn't you be snapping pictures of someone?"

"Should, but I got cancelled."

"The Great Laurie? They cancelled on you?" Brandon asks, eyes open in shock.

I put a hand to my chest. "It's a devastating blow to my ego, let me tell you."

He rubs my arms in sympathy. "I feel for you."

"Can I have a raise?"

"I don't feel that much." He pinches the back of my arm and I shout.

"Why did we look up Joan Abbot?" Hannah asks, reading the paper Brandon gave her.

"We didn't. There is nothing on that paper that says we looked up Joan Abbot. Who is Joan Abbot?" Brandon asks confusedly.

"Why did we look up Joan Abbot, *Laurie*?"

"Dad met someone named Joan Abbot," I mumble.

Hannah looks over the paper at me. Brandon's face settles into a grin.

"Is this a good Joan Abbot?" Brandon asks.

"I think so."

"Is this a serious Joan Abbot?" Hannah asks.

"I guess so."

"Your dad said he liked Joan Abbot?" Brandon rocks back on his heels. He blows out his breath and draws out his words. "Hooooooolyyyy cow."

"You said it."

"Wow. Imagine. Mr. Holbrook, married. Another Mrs. Holbrook. Weird," Brandon says.

"It could be good, Laur. I mean, you could have an older woman, you know, like in Titus where Paul talks about that stuff," Hannah fumbles.

"I thought that was in one of the Timothys," Brandon says.

"I don't remember. Laur?"

I rub my eyes. "Yeah?"

"You okay?"

"I'm getting heart disease."

Brandon sends Hannah a look that says, *Yeah, right, she's a hypochondriac just like her father.*

"I am not," I say.

"You are too," Brandon says.

"What?" Hannah exclaims.

Brandon knuckles my head and starts back to his office. "Thought reading, Hannah. Hey, let me know when you find the original for that copy, okay?"

His office door slams.

Hannah watches him leave and then turns back to me. "I wouldn't worry, Laur. It's not like there's a preacher on the premises out there. They can't come back married. So if you get a stepmother, at least you'll have good warning."

She goes back to typing.

I stare off into the distance and have yet another thing to worry about: A preacher is one of the speakers at the retreat.

Chapter Fifteen

On Saturday Hallie hands me a turkey sandwich on wheat and surprises me by sitting down opposite me at the corner table, tucking her tray in her lap, and sneaking a look toward the counter.

"Laurie, I have to talk to someone, and you're the first person who came to my mind," she says, her green eyes wide with worry, apprehension, and something fluffy and pink like cotton candy. Hallie is smitten with someone, I think.

I set my coffee down and smile. "Hallie, you can always come to me," I say psychotherapist style, patting her hand.

"It's about . . ." She clears her throat and lowers her voice. "Shawn."

I lean closer. "Go on."

"Hallie! Order's up!" Shawn calls from the counter.

She immediately sits up straight. "Listen, meet later?"

"Sure, you can come to my house. Dad's still gone. It'll just be us and Darcy, and he's good at keeping secrets."

She smiles, her eyes slitting. "Thanks, Laurie. I'll call you." She stands and goes, leaving me alone with my turkey sandwich.

I'm in the middle of debating whether a song about a loner who finds a best friend in a turkey and then eats him for Thanksgiving will be a radio hit when Ryan comes through the door, sees me, and sits down at my table.

"Hey."

"Hi," I say, swallowing. "What do you think about this for a song title: 'Thanks to You, Clucky, I'm Clucking This Thanksgiving'?"

Ryan stares at me, steals one of my potato chips, chews it, and then answers. "I think you should stick to photography."

"Rats."

"Who's Clucky?"

"The guy's best friend."

He nods. "I figured. Sounds cannibalistic."

"It's poetry, Ryan. Didn't you ever study Emily Dickinson? It's not supposed to make sense." I gesture with a chip. "It's like *Mission: Impossible.*"

"Not catching the connection, Laur."

"*Mission: Impossible* didn't make sense."

He laughs.

"Hey, Ryan, thought I saw you come in. Want something to eat?" Shawn asks, holding a notepad.

"Hey, I had to go to the counter to order," I protest. "Why didn't you make *him*?"

He rolls his eyes. "Well, Honey, the answer to that should be obvious."

"You like Ryan better?" I flutter my eyelashes pitifully.

He ignores me. "So, Ryan?"

"Um, that sandwich actually looks good."

"Another Clucky through the slicer," I say, chomping a chip.

"On wheat?" Shawn asks.

"Sure." Ryan shrugs. "And a Coke, please. Unlike Miss Folgers' here, my system can only take so much coffee before it crashes."

"Tragic," I commiserate.

"Eh, I've moved on."

Shawn bites back a smile. "Be up in a second." He leaves.

"Hey, so how's Joan?" Ryan asks.

I sigh. It's the third day of the retreat, and when Dad called me just before I headed to Shawn's for lunch, he was still favoring Joan of Abbot.

"Still there."

"Still in high standings?"

I nod. "Pretty much the only standing."

Ryan grins.

"I told Dad he needed to socialize more, but apparently this woman is perfect to him."

"Don't you mean *for* him?" Ryan steals another chip.

I shake my head. "No, because only a third party can determine that. Dad thinks she's perfect, thus, she's perfect *to* him."

He leans his arms on the table and smiles at me. "Guess that makes sense."

"See? I was right. I told you I had sense."

"I didn't say you *had* sense. I said what you said *made* sense."

I frown. "Wouldn't that imply that I *had* sense as well?"

He exhales. "No comment. How is she perfect?"

I tick the points off on my fingers. "She knows what hand sanitizer is and carries her own pocket-sized version. She hates buffalo wings, she has blue eyes, and she's allergic to polyester."

Ryan's eyebrows go up. "That makes her perfect?"

"Dad's always had a soft spot in his heart for people with allergies."

He starts laughing. I keep going. "And the clincher: She is a fellow subscriber to *Medical Mysteries and Common Occurrences.*"

He stops laughing, and his jaw goes slack. "You're kidding." He blows his breath out. "Wow, Laurie, what are the odds?"

"I know. My life as I know it is over." I pick up a potato chip and kiss it. "Good-bye, dear friend."

"I'm not even going to ask," Shawn says, handing Ryan his sandwich and Coke.

"You don't have to ask. I could just tell you," I say.

"Don't want to *know*, either."

"But isn't that part of your job description as a small-restaurant owner? Listening to the woes of your loyal customers?" I point to myself.

"Nope," Shawn says cheerfully. "Try the bar on Birch for that. Anything else, kids?"

"Can I have a piece of cheesecake?" I ask, pushing my empty plate to the middle of the table.

"You just ate an entire turkey sandwich," Shawn says.

I purse my lips. "And I also had chips minus the two Ryan ate. And coffee. And a Tic-Tac before I came. Now that we've completed the rundown on my afternoon's consumption, can I have a piece of cheesecake?"

Ryan grins at me.

"Your heart attack," Shawn mutters and goes to open Dessert Heaven.

"What kind, Laurie?" he yells across the restaurant.

"The turtle one!" I shout back.

He pulls the slice out, brings it over, and sets it in front of me. "Here you go."

"No whipped cream?"

"Nope."

"Are you out?" I protest.

"Yep. Just. I'm about to send Hallie to the store."

"You're lying through your palate," I accuse.

"It's through your teeth, Laurie. And you don't need whipped cream." He leaves.

"I guess it's over for cheesecake too when Joan comes, right?" Ryan asks, crunching a chip.

"Only in my closet will I be able to enjoy such calories." I stick my fork in the cheesecake and smile. "I like the consistency, Shawn!" I yell, and I hear his sigh all the way across the restaurant. "My goodness, he's grouchy," I tell Ryan.

Ryan grins again and wipes his mouth on a napkin. "I think you should go easy on him," he says.

"Why?"

"You're going to give him a conniption fit one day."

My mouth drops open. "I beg to differ," I say, tossing my head. "My father says that God puts different personality types around you in your single years to show you what kinds of personalities your future children will have."

"Your dad's college friends must have been really something."

"Very funny."

"Hey, isn't today when Laney's hoping to have the babies?" he asks.

"Yep. Last Saturday in June."

"How is she?"

I lick my fork. "Big."

"Still no . . . water breakage or whatever is supposed to happen?"

I grin. "No, their plumber guaranteed the kitchen sink for another three years, so I think they're set."

He narrows his eyes at me. A rarity among men, Ryan is. Most guys cannot do anything remotely talented with their eyes. It's my personal philosophy of why Solomon warns the reader about women seducing with their eyes, not men. Men are not gifted like that.

"I meant with Laney." He waves his hands as he tries to explain. "Something connected with water is supposed to break or bend or leak . . ." He stops when he sees me doubled over laughing. "Never mind."

"You're funny, Ryan."

"Just let me know when the kids come, okay?"

I salute. "Yes, sir!"

"And I should go."

"But it's Saturday. You don't work."

He stands and pulls out his wallet. "Nate and I are trying to build that tiered garden today."

"Still?"

"Sure. Last time we just decided *how* we would build it." He pulls out a twenty and tosses it on the table.

"You two need a hobby or something," I say, finishing the last of the cheesecake. "Don't you get tired of building all the time? Maybe something new?"

"I'll take that to heart. What are you doing now?"

"Going to Laney's."

He smiles sarcastically and sings to the tune of that State Farm commercial: "Like a good sister, Laurie is there."

I grin. "Yep. I figure Laney spent a good amount of her junior high and high school years raising me after Mom died. I should probably be there for the birth of her fourth and fifth children."

I find my backpack at my feet and dig around for my billfold.

"Don't worry about it, Laur. That covers yours too." He points to the twenty.

"That's very nice, Ryan. Thank you very much."

"And you're lying about feeling a responsibility toward Laney," he says, holding the door for me and waving at Shawn.

I gape at him. "No I'm not!"

"You are too. You just want one of those kids named after you." He laughs at my expression.

I put a hand on his shoulder. "Ryan, *Dear*, this family can only handle one Laurie."

His eyes twinkle at me. "Guess you're right."

I suddenly realize how close we are standing and that my hand is on his shoulder. That weird squirmy feeling like a hundred ducks are attempting the Flying V in my stomach starts, and I quickly yank my hand away and smile naturally. "I'll probably see you later today," I say, clearing my throat. Cheesecake crust crumbs are stuck in there, most likely.

Ryan must have a potato chip or something in his throat as well. He coughs and smiles at me, a weird expression on his face. "Yeah, probably. Say hi to Laney for me."

"I will. Bye." I climb in the Tahoe, start the engine, and sit there, staring at the front windows of Merson's.

He buys my lunch, he asks about my dad and sister, he's concerned about my daily life, I get queasy around him. . . .

These should all add up to something, but for the life of me, all I can figure is that he likes my family and I must be allergic to his deodorant or fabric softener or something.

I put the car in reverse and am getting ready to back out when Hallie comes running out the front door, waving to me.

I stop and roll down my window. "Hey."

"Hey," she says breathlessly. "You left your keys." She holds up a key ring.

I stare at her. "Hallie, my car's running."

"I know," she says. Then she frowns. "Wait a second . . ." She covers her face. "I'm sorry. My brain is not working lately."

Ryan strides up. "I think I left my keys in . . . Hallie . . ." He grins, seeing her holding the keys.

"These are yours?" she asks, giving them to him.

"If not, they probably belong to a nicer truck, so I'd take them," I tell him.

He acts hurt. "You don't like my truck?"

"Honey, it's older than you are."

Hallie watches us, a half smile, half frown on her face.

I smile gently. "Hey, don't you have a break coming up?"

She nods.

"Come with me then," I say, my tone not giving her room to argue.

She seems to appreciate it. "Okay. Let me put my apron back and tell Shawn that I'm leaving." She goes back inside.

Ryan looks at me and frowns. "Leave it alone, Lauren Emma Holbrook."

"What?" I protest loudly.

"You know exactly what."

"Now I can't even invite a friend to hang out with me? Suddenly all my activities are tainted?" I rant.

He pats the hood of the Tahoe and starts humming the extremely annoying song from *Fiddler on the Roof.*

"Matchmaker, matchmaker, make me a match . . ."

"Good-bye, Ryan," I say, batting my eyes at him. "I hope you plant poison ivy by accident!"

"Don't mention ivy. Mrs. Galen's entire living room wall is covered in ivy. I'm convinced it's poisonous."

I laugh, then smile genuinely at him as Hallie comes back outside apronless and carrying a flowered purse.

"See ya." I grin, roll up the window, and turn to Hallie. "I'd like to introduce you to someone," I say.

———⊕———

Five minutes later I ring the doorbell at Laney's and then try the handle. It's unlocked, so I walk in, Hallie behind me.

"Hey, it's me!" I yell.

"Kitchen!" Laney shouts.

Three little kids start screeching from the direction of the bedrooms. "Auntie Lauren! Auntie Lauren! Auntie Lauren!"

Jess and Jack come running, attack my legs, and then hop up and down excitedly. "Guess what?" Jack shrieks, his blue eyes wide. "Mom's having babies!"

I laugh and tousle his hair. "You're just now figuring that out, huh, Jacky-boy?"

Dorie comes into the living room, then grins at me and smiles shyly at Hallie. "Hi, Auntie Lauren. I made you a painting."

She shows me a crudely drawn house with blobs scattered around it. "That's me," she says, pointing to one of the blobs. "That's you, and those two are our new babies," she announces.

"Very pretty," I say, bending to give her a hug.

Hallie nods. "Beautiful."

"Are the babies girls or boys?" I ask Dorie sweetly.

"I heard that!" Laney shouts from the kitchen.

"Will you please just tell me?" I plead, walking through the doorway to see Laney sitting at the kitchen table, drinking coffee.

"No," she says.

"That had better be decaf." I point to the coffee.

Laney smiles placatingly at me and then turns to Hallie, smiling brightly. "Hi, I'm Laney, and normally I weigh a hundred and fifteen pounds."

Hallie bursts into laughter, her eyes slitting cutely. "I'm Hallie."

"What do you weigh normally?" I smirk, pulling a mug from Laney's cupboard. Laney rolls her eyes. "Coffee, Hallie?" I ask.

"Please."

I pour the coffee, hand one of the mugs to Hallie, and we join Laney at the table. "So, Laney, as Ryan said, any sign of water breakage?"

She hacks on her coffee and wipes her face. "You couldn't wait to ask me until I had set the cup down, could you?"

I grin at her over the rim of the mug. "Today's Laney's hoped-for due date," I say to Hallie after I swallow. "She always takes the official due date and subtracts three weeks from it. Good coffee, Sis."

"Thanks," she says to me. "I've been early delivering with both of my other births," she tells Hallie. "My hoped-for due date has become obsolete."

"I don't see why you don't just take the date the doctor tells you, subtract only two weeks, and then call it your due date," I say. "Then we'd avoid this, 'Oh no, I've passed my due date' depression."

"Is that the scientific name for it?" Hallie smiles.

Laney sets her cup down. "I like her," she tells me. "She can talk back to you."

I shake my finger at my sister. "Keep it up, and I'll start telling pregnancy jokes," I threaten.

She dismisses my threat and continues. "You're the kind of person who needs to be surrounded by people who ridicule you on a constant basis."

Hallie giggles.

"Hallie, you know how some women call their unborn child a bulge?" I say, smiling angelically.

"Lauren Holbrook," Laney rebukes me harshly, shifting positions, one hand on the Alp.

I grin innocently.

"I'm sorry you have to deal with her, Hallie," Laney says.

I sip my coffee. "You wanted to talk to me, Hallie?" I ask.

Hallie nods. "Laney, can you keep a secret?" she asks, only half-serious.

Laney grins and holds up crossed fingers.

"Okay, Laurie . . . Laney," Hallie says, pushing her coffee to arm's length. "Laurie, you might have . . . noticed this because I heard from Shawn that you're, like, real big on coupling. . . ."

Laney smiles.

Hallie keeps going. "But um . . ." She lets her breath out slowly. "I need to talk about . . . Shawn."

"What about him?" I say lightly.

"He's uh . . ." Her voice trails off and she fidgets in her chair.

"Annoying?" I suggest.

"No . . ."

"Hard to get along with?" Laney asks. Laney knows who Shawn Merson is.

Hallie shakes her head again. "No . . ."

"Uncanny?" I continue.

Both of them stare at me.

"What?" I protest. "Is he?"

Hallie blinks. "I don't think so."

"Well, what is he then?" I ask.

She fidgets again and lowers her head until her face is hidden by shimmering red hair. "He's *wumsdbl.*"

I exchange a glance with Laney and, based on her brief head shake, neither of us caught the last mumbled word.

"What?" Laney says.

"He's wonderful!" She starts banging her forehead on Laney's table.

"Whoa, whoa, whoa!" I shout. Laney stares first at her and then at me like, *Why did you bring this nutcase into my house?*

Hallie stops giving herself a concussion and sighs, her forehead resting on the table.

I try very hard—well, moderately hard anyway—to keep a sympathetic look on my face and not bust out into song and dance. You know, like those old cheesy musicals. Guy and girl start to exhibit the universal signs for attraction, and before any shy "Hey, want to go out with me?" can be established, they burst into song and spill their guts right in front of each other. What I don't get is that after this great lovey-dovey "Gee, I like you, let's get married" refrain, the music stops, and suddenly it's like the song didn't happen and the two lovers are still totally oblivious to each other's feelings.

I don't understand musicals.

Here's what I like: Confessions of love.

Sounds like the title of a Mariah Carey CD, huh?

Hallie lifts her head, and I pat her hand, my eyes compassionate.

Laney keeps staring and then in her typical tactless, to-the-point way she has says, "Well, what's wrong with that?"

I close my eyes.

This is not the way to encourage a romance.

Hallie blinks several times and then mutters, "Uh, well, see, he's um . . . not a, that is to say, he's my boss, and he's not . . . he's not a believer."

"In romance?" Laney asks.

I swear Hallie shudders. Her eyes open wide. "Romance? No, no, no. Not romance. In God. Not romance. Actually, I'd rather not talk about it anymore."

Laney shrugs. "Okay. Hey, Lauren, when was the last time you went to Old Navy, and did you happen to get their latest ad?"

By this point, I have to shove my hands under the table they are shaking so badly with the bloodthirsty urge to wring Laney's neck. If she weren't pregnant . . .

—⚛—

Fifteen minutes later I step outside her house, the tendons in my knuckles crusting over with arthritis. Hallie looks haggard the whole drive back and doesn't say a word until I drop her off at Merson's, even though I attempt to calm her nerves.

"Thanks for the break, Laurie. See you tomorrow."

Then she closes the passenger door, trudges up the sidewalk, and disappears into the fishbowl of desserts.

I watch her go, knowing my life will one day be one of those made-for-TV documentaries on the Lifetime channel titled, *Her Family Made Her Psychotic: The Lauren Holbrook Story.*

I'm driving out of the parking lot trying to untwist my seat belt when my cell rings.

"Hello?" I say, managing a precarious balancing act with my phone, the steering wheel, and my seat belt. Safety first, my dad always says.

Odd how little we have in common.

"Yes, Laurie?" a female voice I do not recognize asks.

"Yeah?"

"Hi. We haven't met. My name's Joan Abbot."

Chapter Sixteen

I pull the Tahoe over, coming to a stop in front of the pickup gate at the airport. There stands my father, dressed in khakis, tennis shoes, and that terrible beige sweater—a living, breathing testament to the fact that any fashion sense I have comes from my departed mother.

My father's arm rests lightly around the shoulders of a short, bookish woman wearing a faded blue polka-dot dress and bright red sandals. Over her shoulder a huge beach bag hangs, a long string of yarn looping out of it, her hands working double-time to knit or crochet or needlepoint something also blue and polka-dot.

"Honey, this is Joan Abbot," Dad says, grinning proudly at the woman.

"Hi," she says and smiles.

"And there's more!" Dad says, his eyes sparkling.

"To her name?" I ask.

Dad shakes his head, the smile not leaving his face. "We're married! Surprise!"

Joan Abbot holds up the blue-yarned concoction. "This is your new comforter!"

"But my room's not blue!" I protest.

Joan Abbot waves her hand dismissively. "Not to worry, Darling. It will be." She hums knowingly, the needles clicking. "It will be."

I blink and nearly run into the curb.

"Laurie?" Joan Abbot says over the phone.

I clear my throat. "Yes," I squeak, clearing my throat once more. "Yes," I say again.

"I'm sorry, Dear, are you busy?"

"No! No," I say, gentler. "Not at all."

She gives a slight giggle. "You sound so shocked your socks are probably being electrocuted."

"It's okay. My shoes are rubber," I mutter. *Joan Abbot is on the phone!* I shake my head and try to pinch the back side of my arm like they do in the movies for reality checks.

Joan Abbot laughs. "Oh, your father told me you have quite the sense of humor!" She changes the subject. "You're probably wondering why I'm calling you."

How do you answer that? "Yes," and then she'll feel uncomfortable for calling me; "No," and she'll think I'm insanely odd.

I decide silence is golden and keeping my eyes on the road is even better. I stay quiet.

"Right," Joan Abbot says after a moment. For some reason, I can't separate her two names. She keeps going. "I'm calling because I need to propose something to you."

Ack!

"And if you feel in any way uncomfortable with this, please tell me."

I pull into the parking lot of Mickey's Laundromat, stop the car, and close my eyes.

"Laurie, your father and I have decided to elope, stay here in Michigan, and open an infirmary for underprivileged donkeys. We'd like you to move here as well, but the option is yours. If you stay, however, could you please

pick up the mail at my son's house? I forgot I was supposed to housesit this weekend."

"What is it?" I ask weakly, leaning my head against the steering wheel.

"I'd like to meet you . . . in person," she stutters. "I've been looking at my calendar, and this weekend—the first weekend in July—is free and clear. I was wondering . . . well, your dad and I were wondering . . . what you would think if I came out there for a few days."

I stare at my toes, my brain waves stalling. I suddenly start noticing things I've never noticed before. Like the pattern in the mat on the floor of the car is a 3-D logo for Chevrolet, and at some point in the two years I've been driving this car, I must have eaten a Fruit by the Foot in here because an eighth of an inch of the fruit is stuck there.

Cherry flavored, I think.

Then I start thinking about those little disclaimers on the packaging of Fruit by the Foot saying they'll replace the product if it is unsatisfactory, and I wonder if being an eighth of an inch short of a foot is reason enough for them to send me a free roll.

"Laurie?"

I bite back a sigh. "Sure, Joan . . . Abbot. That . . . sounds . . . fine," I say haltingly, like Elizabeth Bennett standing there staring at a drenched Mr. Darcy after he inquires about her family.

"Aye . . . yes . . . they're all in excellent health. . . ."

"You can just call me Joan," she says. "And you're sure?"

"Mm-hmm!" I hum brightly.

I hear her exhale. "Wonderful! I'm so excited. It will be so great to meet you, Laurie. I've heard so much about you."

"Looking forward to it too," I falter.

"Good-bye, Dear."

She hangs up.

I still haven't lifted my head from the steering wheel. I can feel the stitching pressing into my flesh.

Swell. Now I'll look like a psychotic lobotomy patient.

Someone taps on the window and I jump.

Mickey from the laundromat stands there frowning at me. "Something wrong, Laurie? Did Jeff try to sell you that glunk of his?" he spouts.

"No, Mickey. I just had a headache, that's all."

He keeps frowning at me. "You don't need laundry done?"

I smile at him. "On my way out."

I drive home, and Darcy meets me at the door, watching me curiously as I dump my backpack on the floor and slouch onto the sofa.

He yips and hops in my lap.

"Hey there, Kid," I say, rubbing his ears. "What do you think about Joan Abbot?"

I swear the dog purses his lips in thought.

The phone rings and I hold up a finger to him. "Hold that notion, Darce. Hello?" I answer.

"I just got a really weird phone call."

"Lexi?"

"Yeah. From Joan Abbot."

"She called you too?" I say, perking up. Finally. Now someone will see things my way for once.

"I think she sounds nice," Lexi says.

Hopes crumpled, I smile sadly at Darcy, stroking his silky ears. "Mm-hmm."

"You don't?"

"She sounds . . . maternal."

"Honey, she's a mother. That's natural. When did you last talk to

Laney? She even sounds maternal."

"Not maternal as in motherly, maternal as in . . . matronly."

I can almost hear Lexi thinking. "What?" she says after a pause.

"You know. Like, older maternal."

"Dad is an older *pa*ternal. I'm not seeing the problem here, Baby."

I let my breath out. "She tell you she's coming?"

"That was the weird part. First weekend in July?"

"What's weird about that?"

"Think Laney, Doll-face."

I squeal. Darcy jumps. "Laney's babies!"

"Yup."

Laney has without fail had each of her kids exactly one week before her due date. I guess Dad was thinking positively with this trip.

"She wants to be here for the birth!" I scream. Darcy hops off my lap and leaves, shaking his head back and forth.

"That's what I can figure."

My mouth hangs open slapely, and I blink repeatedly.

Slapely: (*adv*) Loosely, without muscular assistance.

Is Joan Abbot trying to weasel her way into my family?

"Sweetheart?"

"Can I call you back?" I choke and hang up on Lexi's protest.

I stand, fumble to the kitchen, pull out the coffee carafe, and start washing. Joan Abbot. She will be here a week from today.

I dump the soapy water into the sink, dry the pitcher, shove it back in the coffeemaker, and open the bag of grounds sitting on the counter next to it.

Eight . . . nine . . . ten. Ten cups of coffee might help. *Mmm.* I wrinkle my brow. *Nah. Eleven . . . twelve.*

For the life of me, I can't figure out why I'm the only one in my family who is worried about Dad possibly getting remarried. Laney thinks it's great, Lexi thinks it's about time, and I think . . .

I push the power button, and the coffeemaker starts gurgling.

What *do* I think?

On the one hand, I'm glad Dad will be happy. On the other, I live in this house, which means I get to live with her too. It'll be like one of those twenty-four-hour breakfast joints: *"All day, every day . . ."*

The phone rings again just as the coffee is done. The caller ID says it's Lexi.

"Sorry, Lexi," I answer.

"Hey, Lex, she apologized!" Ryan yells, not into the phone. "Hey, Laur."

"Ryan." I tuck the phone between my shoulder and my ear and pour a huge mug of coffee.

"So Joan Abbot called you?"

"Nosy."

"Actually I prefer 'In Search of Knowledge.' Sounds more intellectual."

I nod, even though I'm on the phone. "She called my cell phone."

"When you were at Laney's?" he asks.

"No, when I was driving home."

"Not safe to drive and talk on the phone, Laurie."

"I parked at Mickey's."

"Uh-huh. Hey, you didn't buy that sticky stuff that Jeff's trying to sell, did you?"

I frown, tipping up the sugar bowl and pouring a good three table-spoons into my coffee. "No."

"Good. It doesn't work. So anyway, what do you think?"

"I don't know. Did Lexi put you up to this?"

"No. She told me you hung up on her. I got worried."

"That what?"

He pauses. "That *what* what?"

"Why did you worry?"

"I don't know. You all alone in that house . . . you never know what you might be doing."

I pour a small amount of milk in the coffee, stir it, and set it on the living room coffee table. "I'm drinking coffee and getting ready to watch *Speed*."

"Oh." He stops. "Wait a minute. Did you just say *Speed*?"

"Yeah."

"You do realize that's an action flick, right? It's not a romantic comedy. You know that, right?"

"Yes, Ryan."

"There're bombs and suspense, and people die."

"I've seen it before, Ryan."

"You must really be in a mood. No wonder you hung up on Lexi."

"Hey!"

"What?"

"Just because I'm not watching *Emma* means that suddenly I'm out of my mind?" I protest seriously.

"No, no, no," Ryan soothes.

"Then what?"

"Never mind."

"No, there's no never mind now, Ryan Palmer. What did you mean?"

"I don't even know why we're arguing about this!"

I blow my breath out.

"Can I come watch it with you?" he asks in a small voice.

"I don't care."

"Okay. I'll be there soon."

I hang up.

Darcy is in front of the sofa when I come out of the movie closet holding *Speed*. He watches me quietly, waits until I return to the sofa, and hops back onto my lap.

I rub his ears. At the moment, his sympathetic silence is wonderful.

The movie starts, and I watch the interminably long ride down the elevator shaft, aimlessly reading the opening credits. For a movie titled *Speed*, you'd think the travel through the shaft would be a little faster.

I hear a knock and then the front door opens. "Laur?" Ryan calls out.

"Living room," I answer.

He comes in holding a jumbo-sized Milky Way. I smile sweetly at him.

He chuckles at my look, hands me the candy bar, and settles down next to me on the couch. "Lex had it in her pantry," he says in answer to my unasked question of how he got here so fast if he stopped by the store first.

Lexi gave up candy bars a good year and a half ago because of the calories, so there's no telling how old this Milky Way is. But it's chocolate, and I figure chocolate is similar to diamonds in at least two ways:

1. It makes women happy.

2. It's often used for anniversaries, birthdays, etc.

So why not a third way—longevity?

Darcy leans across my lap and noses Ryan's hand.

"Hey there, Big Guy," Ryan greets him. "You've been busy growing."

"And gaining weight," I say, ripping open the Milky Way. "He's getting heavy."

The music in the movie intensifies as people start climbing on the Forbidden Elevator, and Ryan and I direct our attention to the movie. About halfway through, he nonchalantly slides his arm around my shoulders.

Two hours later the credits start rolling, and Ryan stretches. "Good movie, good movie," he mumbles, rubbing his eyes. "I haven't seen *Speed* in about five years."

"I like Sandra Bullock's hair," I say.

Ryan grins. "Oh boy, here we go."

"Here we go with what?"

"Your rundown of the movie. Go ahead."

I narrow my eyes at him. "And I like Keanu Reeves' hair short like that because I think it makes his eyes look bigger, and since he has small eyes to begin with, they need all the help they can get."

Ryan nods. "Very good."

I bow as best I can sitting on the couch with Darcy snoozing in my lap. "Thank you."

He grins at me and brushes a finger along Darcy's ears.

"Hey, Ryan?"

He looks at me again.

I smile. "I'm glad you came."

"I know."

I roll my eyes and stand, pushing Darcy onto the sofa. He blinks and goes right back to sleep. "Smart aleck."

Ryan groans. "I can't win!"

"At least you recognize it."

I go into the kitchen and pour my third cup of coffee, spooning in the sugar and milk.

Ryan follows me. "So is this depression related in any way to Joan Abbot?" he asks, leaning against the counter, watching me search the pantry for a bag of M&Ms.

I stop, holding a container of powdered lemonade mix in one hand. "What depression?"

"Laurie."

I put the mix back on the shelf and push a few cans of chicken noodle soup out of the way, ignoring him.

"You're drinking gallons of coffee, you're watching an R-rated—for violence and language, I'll add—movie, and now you're digging through your house looking for chocolate."

I stand up, my hair flopping in my face. "How did you know?"

"What?"

"That I'm looking for chocolate?"

He rolls his eyes. "The half-crazed look might have something to do with it. Reminds me of the first time we met."

I frown. "I had a half-crazed look the first time we met?"

"You were hiding Oreos under your coat, Laurie." He gives me a long look and continues, "So Joan Abbot?"

I sigh loudly, yank out a kitchen chair, and sit, glowering at him. He is undeterred.

Here's what drives me crazy about Ryan: The boy has more determination than the pyramid-building Egyptians.

It's a bad quality. The list of spiritual gifts Paul has? Notice determination isn't on there.

Ryan pulls out the chair next to me and sits calmly. "Going to talk?"

"No. I need M&Ms."

He flicks my arm. "Answer my question, and I'll take you to Merson's."

"Bribery," I say, but I can feel the muscles in my cheeks relaxing into a smile. Merson's. Good place, good place. Good coffee. Good cheesecake. Good brownies.

Ryan stares at me, shaking his head. "Unbelievable," he mutters.

I blink innocently at him. "What?"

"You are such an addict!"

"But a nice addict." I smile.

"Answer the question."

I sigh again, just for his sake. He doesn't budge. "All right," I mutter. "Yes."

He frowns. "Yes what?"

"Yes, it's about Joan Abbot."

His frown deepens. "What is?"

"My depression, Ryan! Gee, for asking the question in the first place . . ."

"I asked it like five minutes ago!"

"You can't remember what you said five minutes ago?"

He covers his face.

I pat his shoulder.

He lets his head fall back and stares at the ceiling. "What have I done?"

Funny. It's the same question my dad always asks the ceiling.

I decide not to point that out to Ryan—delicate mental state he's in right now and all.

"Can we go to Merson's now?" I ask, still patting his shoulder.

He turns and gives me this wide-eyed "You must have cheese twisties in your brain" look.

"Can we?" I ask again.

"Fine. But we're talking at Merson's."

"Sure. It would be boring if we just sat there staring at each other."

I run upstairs, slip on a pair of flip-flops, come back downstairs, pick up a sleeping Darcy, and put him in his kennel. "Ready," I announce as Ryan flips his keys around and around his finger.

"You do realize that we were just there about four hours ago," he says.

I open the front door. "Yep."

"And you already had cheesecake today."

I push him out, close the door, and lock it. "Mm-hmm."

"And that as the proprietor, Shawn has the right to refuse you service."

I stop dead in the middle of the sidewalk. "What?"

Ryan nods. "It's true."

This Is Bad.

"Shawn didn't even give me whipped cream on my cheesecake today," I say.

"I know."

"He probably won't give me a dessert!"

Ryan puts a hand on my arm. "Calm down, Laur. We'll just go to Vizzini's."

"But they don't have good brownies!" Any relaxation I previously experienced vanishes like a long-haired Chihuahua after a haircut.

"Laurie, calm down. It's not a big deal. We'll go get coffee and then go get M&Ms. All right? Okay? Come on, Honey, get in the truck."

He opens the door and helps me in, then climbs in the driver's side. "Good grief, Laur. I can just see this happening when we've got three kids and a dog clambering for attention. What are you going to do then?" he mutters.

I blink. He just used *we* to describe *our* future children.

I turn to look at him as he backs out of the driveway.

"Whose kids?" I ask.

He opens his mouth, pauses, then grins impishly. "Never mind."

He drives to Merson's, and we both climb out. Shawn looks up from handing a teenage guy a ham sandwich.

"Didn't I just see you here?" he asks, wiping his hands on his ever-present dishtowel.

"I've had a rough day." I approach the counter, my eyes downcast. "Can I please have a large coffee and a . . ." I clear my throat, "brownie?"

I sneak a look. Shawn stands there staring at Ryan, who lifts his shoulders like, *Don't look at me; it wasn't my fault.*

Shawn taps the counter. "Look at me, Laurie Holbrook."

I look up sadly.

"If in the very likely chance you develop any disease, malformation, or social problems based on all these desserts you consume constantly, I want you to promise that you will not sue me. Got it?" His eyebrows bunch sternly.

I nod. "Promise. Can I have the chocolate mousse pie instead, please?"

A smile lurks around his lips as he pulls the pie out from Dessert Heaven. "How do you stay so skinny?" he asks me. I assume he doesn't want an answer because he keeps talking. "Ryan? Anything for you?"

"Ummm . . ." He squints at the glass-covered display case and then at the menu. "Do you have just a bowl of carrots or something?"

Shawn's eyebrows rise. "Carrots?"

I freak out. "Carrots?" I shriek.

"I think at least one of us should be healthy." He points to the pie. "That is not healthy. So it falls to me."

Shawn rubs his mouth, and I know he is trying not to smile. "Sure, Ryan," he says gruffly. "One bowl of . . ." he coughs, "carrots coming right up. Two large coffees?"

"Extra-large, please," I say.

He scowls at me. "You said large earlier."

I puff my bottom lip out pitifully. "I had a really rough day."

"You don't know the meaning of rough," he retorts, but grabs two extra-large mugs.

Ryan takes my arm and leads me to a corner table. "You're going to push that man to his grave," he says, his eyes twinkling.

"Not before he falls in love with Hallie," I say.

"Speaking of her, what did you talk about earlier?"

I frown. In the wake of Joan Abbot's call, I forgot about the incident with Laney.

Shawn sets my coffee in front of me. "What's the sad look for?" he asks.

"My sister doesn't think," I tell him.

"Oh. Here you go, Ryan."

"Hey!" I yell as Shawn turns to leave. "You don't want to know what she doesn't think about?"

He shrugs. "Not really."

I gape at him. "How rude."

"Sorry about that. But I did give you pie."

I smile brightly at him again. He shakes his head and leaves.

Ryan bites off the end of his carrot. "Okay, so I know you didn't take Hallie to see Lexi because I was at her house, so even though Lexi fits the bill for not thinking, it's not her. You took Hallie to see Laney?" he asks.

"Yeah."

"But Laney's the thoughtful one," he points out.

"Not when she's pregnant. When she was pregnant with Jack and Jess, I was trying to pick out a dress for prom and—"

"Whoa, hold it!" Ryan swallows, holding up his hands. "You went to prom?"

I blink at him. "Yes. Should I not have?"

"Well, who did you go with?" His forehead creases in a frown.

Small confession: I kind of, sort of, might have liked seeing that proprietary look on his face. I once heard on a commercial that it is nice to feel needed. What do you know? The cheeky-smile lady was right.

I look down at my mousse pie. "Derek Maxwell."

"Derek Maxwell?" Ryan repeats slowly. "Who's he?"

"He was captain of the football team. I was a cheerleader." I nod. "It was meant to be."

He pushes a carrot around in the bowl, not looking at me. "So what happened?" he says dully.

I rub my cheek. "Oh, you know. He got a scholarship to play for

UCLA, but Lexi and Laney had both moved out, and I felt like I should stay with Dad. So we broke up." I shove a bite of pie in my mouth.

Ryan makes a noise deep in the back of his throat and presses his lips together. "Oh."

I chew my pie, and the table is quiet for a full three minutes before Ryan frowns deeper and his head jerks up. "*You* were a *cheerleader*?" he says.

I lick my fork carefully before looking up to meet his eyes.

I grin evilly. "Gotcha!"

"Laurie Holbrook!" He covers his eyes.

I point my fork at him. "Hey, you're the one who believed me."

He pulls his hands away from his face, shaking his head. "Why do you do this to me? What have I ever done to you?"

"Gee, Ryan, I didn't know you cared so much." I bat my eyelashes.

He stares at me for half a second, a weird expression on his face. Then he shakes his head slightly, and the expression melts away. "Who did you go to the prom with?" he asks again.

"Brandon."

He gives me a once-over. "You went to the prom with Brandon."

"Yep."

"Why?"

"Why not?"

"You two are basically siblings."

"'We are really not so much brother and sister as to make it at all improper,'" I quote, forking off another bite.

Ryan holds up a hand. "Let me guess. *Pride and Prejudice*?"

"Nope."

"English accent, formal verbiage," he mutters.

"Wow, Ryan. Verbiage. That is not a word I hear every day." I raise an eyebrow at him. "Especially from construction workers."

"We try our hardest to disguise the fact that we do have intellect, but occasionally it slips." He shrugs, grinning.

"Ah, I see. If your heads got too big from being complimented on your language skills, the hard hats might not fit."

"Exactly. Is it *Emma*?"

"Good job," I congratulate him.

"So who spoke that line you just gave me?"

"Emma."

"To who?"

"Mr. Knightley."

He leans his elbows on the table, his eyes twinkling. "Where?"

I match his pose. "Outside the ball at the Crown."

"Why?"

"Because Mr. Weston told everyone to start dancing again."

Ryan leans back and picks up his coffee, shaking his head. "I don't know whether to be impressed by this or not." He sips his coffee and squints at me. "When was *Emma* published?"

I grin at him. "1816."

"How old was Jane Austen when she died?"

"Forty-one."

"How many books did she write?"

"Six, but the last two were published after her death."

He gestures to me with his coffee mug. "Who played in last year's World Series?"

"The uh . . . and um . . ." My voice trails off as I rack my brain. No idea. I shake my head and lift my shoulders in defeat. "I don't know."

"What country is above Sudan?"

"Umm . . ."

He starts laughing. "I saw this underlined in your Bible. What is Romans 8:28?"

"'And we know that in all things God works for the good of those who love him, who have been called according to his purpose.'" I cross my arms over my chest. "What is the point of this, Ryan?"

He holds up a hand. "One last question. Without turning around, tell me where the coffee is located on Shawn's menu."

I glare at him. "Far left, bottom corner, underneath the muffin varieties."

He looks at the menu suspended above the counter and grins. "I guess it's all about the important things in life."

Chapter Seventeen

July starts with a day so hot, I know the sun moved a few inches in our direction. I drive to church and stare at the corner right before the turn-in to Grace Church. I could have sworn there was a fire hydrant on that corner, but now there is just a mustard yellow stain on the sidewalk.

The hydrant must've melted in the heat.

I park, run through the front doors, waving a hurried hello to Greg and Nina, this week's volunteer greeters, race through the hallways, and drop into a chair beside Brandon just as Nick takes his place at the front of the classroom.

Brandon elbows me in the ribcage. "You're late," he whispers. "Gee, could your dad still be out of town?"

"Shh."

Hannah leans across from the other side of Brandon. "Hi," she whispers.

I smile at her.

Brandon turns from me to Hannah, since her blonde head is right in front of his face. Her eyes, still twinkling from smiling at me, sparkle at Brandon, and I see The Look cross his expression.

Remember in *The Princess Bride* when Buttercup asks Westley to fill

erynn mangum

the buckets with water? He gives her The Look and then says, "As you wish."

Once, at the beginning of my role as matchmaker when I was working on Lexi and Nate, I tried to find a definition of The Look. It doesn't exist. To be very profound, it is defined by its lack of definition.

I need to remember this profound thought so I can impress Ryan.

Brandon's eyes darken into a deeper, chocolaty color, and his mouth softens. I *know* if we weren't in a Sunday school class and Nick hadn't chosen that exact moment to clear his throat to start teaching, Brandon would've kissed her.

Hannah jumps fully back into her seat as Nick rakes a hand through his short hair and looks around the packed classroom. Brandon loses The Look and replaces it with the studious, serious expression he gets when he's taking notes during Bible studies.

"Morning, everyone," Nick croaks, then clears his throat again. "Sorry about the voice, guys. I didn't get my full cup of coffee before class today. Which is why I sent my new brother-in-law to get one for me."

Ryan comes in and walks up to the front, handing Nick a steaming Styrofoam cup. He smiles at me, then sits in the front row.

Nick takes a long drink. "Thanks, Ry," he says, voice almost frog-free. "Brother-in-laws . . . nice to have around. Get one if you can. Uh, announcements . . ." He looks at his notes and then at his wife.

Ruby grins at him from the first row next to Ryan. "Sundaes," she tells him.

"Oh yeah! Hey, plan to come to Bible study Wednesday. It'll be the first Wednesday night in our new house, and we'll be throwing a housewarming party complete with ice cream sundaes, music, and lots of other food. We'll be taking a temporary break from studying the life of Christ to just have good fellowship." He angles a look at Ruby. "That's a good church word, Hon, don't you think? Fellowship."

Ruby turns in her chair to face the group. "I have maps for those who need directions."

I slouch down in my chair and feel myself smiling. Those two? A match made on the golden streets of Paradise. I'm glad I saw it. Those hours I forewent beauty sleep and made brownies? Totally worth it.

"Hey, everyone, turn to 1 Peter 1:13, please." Nick flips his Bible open as does everyone in the room. Nick clears his throat. "'Therefore, prepare your minds for action; be self-controlled; set your hope fully on the grace to be given you when Jesus Christ is revealed.'"

"Hope in the grace God has given you," Nick finishes an hour later. "People, circumstances, and things will let you down. Grace from God never will. Let's pray."

I shut my eyes, lean my head against my knees, and do as Nick says.

Once class is over I swap seats to the other side of Hannah. "Hey," I greet her.

She gives me a hug. "Hi."

I touch her hair shimmering down her back. "Your hair looks pretty."

"Thanks. I changed shampoos. During the summer I use something that has a chlorine protectant in it since I spend a lot of time swimming in the apartment complex pool."

I nod, peeking to make sure Brandon is watching as I fiddle with her hair.

She *hmms* and leans forward more. "I love when people play with my hair," she says in a low voice. "Relaxes me."

"You must love going to get your hair done then."

Brandon clears his throat and looks away from Hannah's hair. "You obviously don't, Laur," he says to the back of the seat in front of him.

I frown. "Why?"

Again, he doesn't look across Hannah to me. "When was the last time you saw a hair stylist?"

I pick up the ends of my hair and stare at them. Now that I look, I do see some split ends. "Three months? Four?"

Hannah grins.

"Your hair has grown a lot lately," she says, fingering my hair.

"I know," I say. "I have to admit having long hair is nice."

"Isn't it?" She nods. "Bad hair day? Easy to do a ponytail and forget about it."

"And guys typically like longer hair." I grin.

"I'm a guy. And I think you should cut it," Brandon says.

Ryan straddles the chair in front of Brandon. "Who should cut what?" he asks Brandon. He smiles at Hannah. "Hey, Hannah. How are you?"

"Good. Thanks for asking."

"Laurie needs to cut her hair," Brandon tells him.

Ryan looks at me, reaches over, and rubs the ends of it. "I don't know, Brandon. I like it long."

"Ha!" I gloat to Brandon. I smile at Ryan. "Thank you, Dear."

He raises his eyebrows, smirking. "You're welcome, Sweetheart."

Hannah sends Brandon a look that says, *I told you so*, and then says, "Hey, Laur, when is your dad coming home?"

"Tuesday. Conference ends Tuesday morning."

Ryan hooks his thumb back at Nick. "Are you going Wednesday?"

I shrug. "Probably."

"You should bring business cards with you," he says. "People are going to want to know who helped Ruby with the house."

"Ryan, all I did was paint and go with her to Furniture Mart. That's it."

He nods. "Yeah. And their house looks great. When Ruby was growing up, her room had plain white walls and an old ratty red comforter on the bed, and she told my mom it was decorated because there was a dried flower arrangement on her desk." He smiles. "Mom worried quite a bit about her future house."

Hannah grins. "Well, I saw it, and I think it looks pretty." She leans back in her chair. "Are you supposed to bring gifts to a housewarming party?"

We all stare at each other cluelessly.

"I don't know," Brandon says finally. He looks at me. "Did we take one to Lexi's?"

"Umm . . . yes. We got them a CD, I think."

"So you are supposed to bring something," Ryan says.

"Know what I'm going to bring?" Hannah grins. "A baby-name book."

Ryan's eyes widen. "Okay, this is my sister we're talking about. And they have only been married for a month."

"Ryan, look at Tina," Hannah whispers. "Ruby is in her thirties. Tina is pregnant and *nineteen*."

"I am really curious to see what that child will look like," I confess.

Three pairs of eyes stare at me. "Why?" Brandon asks finally.

"Well, okay, case in point. Prince Charles and Princess Di. Not exactly the most beautiful people on the planet, right? But Prince William . . ."

Hannah nods. "Quite good-looking," she agrees.

"Exactly. See? Not-so-pretty people end up with gorgeous kids. So. Both Tina and Kyle are very good-looking. It just makes me wonder if there's a reverse property going on."

Hannah purses her lips. "You know, I never thought of that. Huh. Now *I'm* curious to see what their kid will look like."

Ryan and Brandon exchange glances and shake their heads.

"Hey, we should all go get lunch after the service," I suggest.

Hannah smiles at me. "House quiet?"

"Very."

"I'd love to," she says. I see Brandon watching her carefully. "But I can't," she continues. "I'm completely out of groceries."

Brandon declines then too, like I knew he would. "Shouldn't, Laur.

I need to get some stuff done around the apartment today."

I look at Ryan pleadingly, and he grins, reaches over, and ruffles my hair like I watched him do to three-year-old Danielle last week after Sunday school.

"Sure, I'll go with you," he says.

No wonder I never know where I stand with Ryan. One minute he's giving me looks that send Jell-O cubes dumping into my stomach, and the next he's treating me like I'm his favorite sister.

"So then he gave her The Look," I tell him later at Vizzini's, after the waiter left us with the menus and a vague promise to return.

Ryan puts his arms on the table, not looking at the menu. "The Look?" he questions.

"Yeah. You know." I glance up and give it to him. Ryan blinks and then laughs.

"Very nicely done," he compliments.

"Thank you. That's how I know Brandon will suddenly realize he's out of milk and have to accidentally run into her at the grocery store."

"You know, I think I've used that excuse before," he says, staring off into the distance, thinking.

I lean back, fiddling with my napkin. I must be hungry. My stomach starts cramping.

"With who?" I ask, tracing the design on the napkin.

"Oh, this girl from where I grew up. You don't know her. I think she still lives there," he mutters. "Maybe not. Anyway, her name was Mallory Clayton."

"Mallory Clayton?" All of a sudden I have this picture of a Tina-like girl. Model looks and a pliable personality. Girls named Mallory are usually like that, right?

"Yeah, Mallory." The way he says her name rankles me. "She had to go to the grocery store, and I followed her. Except I think my excuse was Eggo waffles, not milk."

"How did you . . . meet Mallory?" I ask, trying to keep my voice smooth as I stare blankly at the menu.

"Oh, I was captain of the football team, and she was a cheerleader."

My head whips up and he starts laughing.

"Gotcha!" he exclaims, the cute little-kid grin on his face.

I smile despite myself and toss my napkin at him. "That was mean!"

He throws it back. "Hey, you did it to me."

"Completely different."

"Yeah?" He leans forward over the table. "How?"

I am speechless. His eyes twinkle with victory. "See?" he demands.

"Did you really know someone named Mallory Clayton?"

He nods. "Well, by sight. She was a cheerleader." He quirks his head at me. "And Derek?"

"Was really the captain of the football team."

He grins, reaches over, and picks up my hand. "So do you concede we were both cruel?" he asks.

"Yes. 'I think I have finally learned the importance of being earnest.'"

He narrows his eyes at the look on my face. "Another Jane Austen line?"

"Oscar Wilde. But he was another nineteenth-century writer, and it's also a good present-day movie." I squeeze his hand. "You're learning."

"With you, it's always best to be as learned as possible."

"So I'm a challenge?" I smile.

The waiter comes then, silencing Ryan's retort, but his eyes sparkle dangerously.

"You know what you want?" the waiter asks.

I look up at him. "Ravioli and a Dr. Pepper, please."

Ryan hands him his unused menu. "Lasagna for me. And a Coke."

He writes down our order and leaves.

Ryan leans back in his chair but fiddles with my fingers. "Are you liking the 1 Peter study?"

"I am. It's interesting learning about the early church. And Peter has always been my favorite disciple. It's adding a new dimension to two of my favorite books."

Ryan nods. "I can believe that. You remind me of Peter sometimes."

I frown. "How?"

"You're both loud and obnoxious."

"Hey!"

He leans forward again and keeps a firm hold on my hand. "But still used of God," he soothes.

I look at him, a warm feeling spreading through my chest. "You think I'm used by God?"

He smiles. "Yeah, Laur. I mean, I give you a lot of grief about this matchmaking thing, but if you hadn't done something, Nick and Ruby would still be just acquaintances. I would never have seen the possibilities for them. That's more than talent, Laurie. I think it's a gift from God."

"It's not on any of Paul's lists," I say dubiously.

He shrugs. "Neither is construction, and that's what God's gifted me for. How is the memorizing going with the 'delight' verses?"

"I'm up to ten." I look at him. "You?"

"Fifteen."

I shake my head. "That's a gift from God, Ry."

He tips his head. "What is?"

"The ability to memorize."

"You think?"

"Yep." I smile, meet his eyes, and watch, startled, as they start to soften.

"Ry? Laurie?"

I blink and look up to see Nick and Ruby standing there, grinning. A waitress carrying their menus stops a few feet past our table when she realizes they aren't following anymore.

"Hey," Ryan says, grinning nonchalantly at them, dropping my hand, and leaning his chair back on two legs. "Had the same idea as us, huh?"

"I really had a hankering for spaghetti, and I didn't feel like cooking," Ruby says.

"Want to join us?" I ask.

They look at Ryan, and he shrugs his okay. The waitress stares at them. "Staying here?"

"Yes." Ruby smiles at me, sliding into the close chair. Nick walks around and sits in the chair opposite her.

The menus are set on the table, and the waitress disappears. Ruby watches her go, a slight frown on her face. "The help they've had here recently hasn't been that great. Whatever happened to your friend JACK, Laurie? He was a nice guy."

I shrug. "Doesn't work here anymore, I guess."

"Pity. He was nice-looking too."

"You're married now, Ruby," I remind her.

She grins across the table at Nick. "I am, aren't I?"

Nick shakes his head and leans over to Ryan. "When you two get married, take this piece of advice: Never let her out of your sight."

Ryan and Ruby laugh. I sit here feeling like ten thousand oysters have crawled across the restaurant floor and clamped electric pincers onto my flesh.

Shell-shocked.

Nick just assumes that Ryan and I will get married someday.

What is this?

I am a matchmaker, right? If I'm going to marry Ryan, you'd think I'd know innately.

Ruby squeezes my shoulder. "You okay?"

I look up and smile. "Yeah, yeah. Just thinking. Don't worry about me."

Ruby shrugs, and she and Nick start discussing the plan for the party on Wednesday night. Ryan looks across at me, and I see the concern in his expression.

I smile at him and sip my Dr. Pepper.

Maybe I'm just missing whatever signs everyone else seems to see that tell them Ryan and I are supposed to be together. I have been pretty busy with Hannah and Brandon and Shawn and Hallie. And freaking out about my dad and Joan Abbot. *And* trying to teach Darcy that toilet paper is not a toy.

Life hasn't been boring.

I watch Ryan smile at something Nick says, and I smile too.

If people want to assume that Ryan and I are more serious than we are, it's not that big of a deal.

Right?

Chapter Eighteen

Tuesday at three o'clock I drive to the airport, feeling overwhelmed by déjà vu. How many times have I driven this in my nightmares? How do I know this isn't just another one?

My arm is starting to bruise as I pull to the curbside at the airport. I pinch myself again and look at Darcy, who has two paws on the window, his tail wagging excitedly.

I wait anxiously. How do I know he won't show up with his arm around a blue-yarn-crocheting, rose-gardening genetic scientist?

The automatic doors swish open and a stream of people come out carrying luggage.

There is Dad.

Alone!

I jump out of the car and race around, laughing. He drops his suitcase and opens his arms, a huge smile on his face. Wrapping my arms around his neck, I kiss his cheek. "Dad, you look great!" I yell.

"I missed you, Laurie-girl." Dad grins, keeping his arms tight around me. He pushes me back a few steps. "Let me look at you." I grin at him. "You look perfectly the same."

Dad's face has a healthy tan as a result of a few days outside. "Was it nice?" I ask him, hefting his bag into the back of the Tahoe.

"It was wonderful."

I toss Dad the keys, and he climbs into the driver's seat while I scoop up a squirming Darcy and slide into the passenger side.

"Gracious, Darcy is getting big." Dad gawks.

"He's not having any trouble eating, if that's what you mean."

"He hasn't cleared any coffee tables yet, has he?" Dad asks, worried.

"No, not yet."

I can almost see him mentally calculating how much furniture polish he will need.

I can't help the grin. "Dad," I say, laying a hand on his arm, "it's good to have you back again." *Alone*, I silently add.

"Laney didn't have the twins," he says dejectedly. I detect the disappointment in his voice.

I keep grinning. "Nope. It's now become the Blame Game."

"The Blame Game?"

"Yeah. First it was my fault she's late delivering because I sat on her abdomen too many times growing up. Then it was Adam's fault because he's her husband. And it was Lexi's fault because . . ." I rack my brain. "I can't remember. Either because Lexi never taught Laney how to do the splits or because Lexi never figured out the art of French braiding."

Dad sends me a look.

"The reasons get more elaborate every day," I tell him.

"Apparently," he says. "I think we'll go home before going to Laney's."

"I think that's a good idea."

"So you can bail out?" Dad smiles. He pulls to a stop at a red light and digs out his instant hand sanitizer. I push my hand over without being asked.

My hands scream, *No! Don't subject us to this!*

But my brain calmly tells them, *It could be worse to refuse.*

My hands capitulate and grudgingly open.

Dad squirts a big puddle of the gel into my palm and a larger one into his. Snapping the lid shut, he rubs his hands together vigorously.

"So, Dad, what do you want to do on your first day back?"

Dad looks out the window dreamily. "I want to sit in front of our fireplace and drink a big cup of tea."

I really must be adopted.

The phone is ringing as we walk through the door, and I lunge for it. "Hello?"

"Lauren? Good, you're home. Is Dad home too?" Laney asks in a harried voice.

"Yep. Just got back from the airport." I stop talking for a second. "Um, Laney, are you panting?"

Dad looks up at me sharply. I grin. She is, I can hear her.

"Adam's at work, and I can't reach him." She's breathing hard.

"Where are the kids?"

"Coloring." I hear her inhale harshly through her teeth. "Oh, Lauren, my water just broke!"

I can't stop smiling. "All right, Laney, hospital, here we come!" I say, giddy. "I'll be right over!"

I hang up laughing and turn to Dad. "She's in labor!" I announce. "I have to drive her to the hospital."

Dad's face pales. "She's in labor? Now?"

"Yeah! Water just broke! Are you coming with me?"

He licks his lips. "You know, Laurie-girl, you get her to the hospital, and I'll come along later. Okay?"

"Okay. Hey, call Lex. See if she can stay with Dorie, Jack, and Jess." I fish my keys back out of my backpack and run down the front steps to the Tahoe.

I drive frantically and get to Laney's five minutes later. She stands by the door. Lexi, having the shorter distance to drive, has one arm around her, coaching her breathing.

"Let's get her to the car, Baby," Lexi says to me, her eyes sparkling madly, a huge grin across her face.

Laney's mouth makes an O, and she breathes in and out slowly and regulated. Dorie, Jack, and Jess stand just inside the front door, mouths gaping at their mom being loaded into my Tahoe.

I wink at Dorie. "Don't worry, Hon! She'll be fine!"

I close the passenger door after helping Laney with her seat belt and turn to a beaming Lexi. "I'll keep trying Adam!" she yells. "Better drive quick, Doll-face; she said her contractions started two hours ago."

"What?" I shout.

Lexi hugs me quickly and pushes me to the driver's side. "Bye, Cakey, I love you!" she shouts to Laney.

Laney manages a terse smile, obviously in the middle of a contraction.

I jump in the car and speed out of the driveway. Laney grips the door handle so tight her fingers turn neon purple.

"Okay, Laney? Are you okay? Just don't have them here! Laney? DON'T HAVE THEM IN THE CAR! Please!"

She doesn't answer me until I'm on the highway. "Trust me, Kid," she huffs. "I wouldn't have you delivering my kids if my life depended on it."

I grin, breathing hard, my leg starting to ache from the way I'm pushing the pedal down. "Good." I exhale. "Good. Remember that. I'll be a bad obstetrician. Very bad. Keep that in mind."

She looks over and smiles tightly through her teeth, then gasps and starts panting, short *eeks* coming when she inhales.

"Hold on!" I yell, my heart rate matching hers.

The hospital, thank God, is only ten minutes from Laney's house. I zoom into the entrance, stop in front of the sidewalk, and jump out, running around to Laney's side.

"Lauren . . . don't . . . no . . . parking . . . zone . . ." she wheezes, unfastening her seat belt, keeping one hand on the Jackson Five.

"Don't worry about it!" I shout in her face.

"Calm . . . down . . . not . . . deaf . . ." she says between breaths, scowling at me.

I grin.

An orderly must see us coming because he comes running out, pushing a wheelchair.

He helps Laney into it calmly. "Laney Knox?" he questions.

"That's her," I yell, wrapping a hand tightly around the wheelchair.

The guy smiles nicely at me. "Your sister said you were coming. I've got her, miss," he says, wrenching my hand off the chair.

I grab Laney's hand instead and run with him as he pushes her through the automatic doors and around a corner to the obstetrics, questioning her about how long her contractions have been going on and when her water broke.

"What's your name?" he asks me.

"Laurie. I'm Laney's other sister."

"Laurie, don't worry about Laney. She's in good hands." He sees Laney's wedding ring. "Your husband is coming?"

Laney, in the midst of a contraction, groans.

"We hope so!" I say.

He smiles again at me. "Laurie. It's okay. Laney, would you like Laurie to stay with you? You prearranged a birthing room, I hear."

Laney nods, her hand compressing mine until it feels shriveled.

The orderly pushes us through yet another set of doors and down a hallway.

"If you could wait here for a moment, Laurie, we'll get your sister set up in the room," he says.

I look at Laney. Her face is white and sweaty, her gray eyes huge. Brown-blonde wisps fall from her ponytail. She looks about thirteen.

"Go, Lauren, I'll be fine." She's hissing through clenched teeth. "It's not the first time I've done this."

I lean down and kiss her hair. "I'll be there soon, Laney, I promise."

She nods, the orderly smiles again, and he pushes her down the hall. I watch until they turn a corner and disappear.

It is then that I notice I'm standing in front of a desk. Behind it is a short, black-haired person with the same fake, annoying smile the orderly had. "Just go ahead and take a seat, Miss Knox."

"It's Miss Holbrook, actually."

Smile. "Miss Holbrook."

"I'll be right back," I say, running. I move the car and run back to the waiting room. I sit on a lumpy red waiting room chair, sigh, flip through the magazines stacked beside me, sigh, shift on the chair, sigh, go through the magazines again . . .

I have never understood why they stock hospital waiting rooms with magazines like *Physician's Weekly* and *Your Child's Health*. If you can figure out your child's health with a magazine subscription, why do you need to come here?

Sigh.

My phone rings then, shattering the quiet flipping-through-magazines silence. I smile apologetically at the three pregnant women sitting in the room and catch the annoyed look of the desk lady.

"Sorry," I whisper. I answer it. "Hello?"

"LAURIEISSHEOKAYAREYOUATTHEHOSPITAL!"

I squeal, pull the phone away from my ear, whisper another sorry, and step back into the first hallway.

"Adam. Calm down. Yes. We are at the hospital."

"HOW LONG HAS SHE BEEN IN LABOR?"

I rub my ear, grimacing. "Listen! You need to be quieter. She's been in labor for about two hours, she thinks."

"TWO HOURS?"

"Adam!"

"Two hours?" he says quietly. "I'm on my way. Stay with her, Laurie.

Hey, did she bring her overnight bag?"

I think about it. "Um, no."

He groans.

"You're not going to get it, are you?"

"Lauren Holbrook, my wife is in *labor*!" he exclaims. "No! She can stay in a hospital gown! Listen, I'm on the freeway. I'll be there in ten!"

He hangs up.

Laney hates hospital gowns.

I peek through the window of the waiting room, see no change, and dial another number.

"Hey, Laur."

"RyanLaney'sinlaborandIneedyoutogetherhospitalbagokay?" Yikes! I am starting to sound like Adam.

Anytime you start sounding like one of the Knoxes, it's a bad thing.

"Wait, okay, Laney's in labor?" he yells. "Where are you?"

"I'm at the hospital. I brought her, but we forgot her bag, and Adam's on his way. Can you get it? Lexi's at Laney's house with the kids."

"Yeah, sure, sure, anything. Do *you* need anything? A book or a magazine not medical-field related?"

"You've obviously been to this waiting room."

"All hospital waiting rooms are like that."

I rub my forehead, pacing the hallway. "No, I'm okay. She'll just want her bag." I look through the window and see a white-coated man standing in the room, looking around. The desk lady points to the door I'm behind.

"I have to go," I tell Ryan.

"I'll be there soon."

I hang up and walk back in just as the doctor steps my way. "Are you Lauren?" he asks me kindly.

"Yes, yes. Is Laney okay? Is she hurting? Does she need something? I forgot her bag," I say in a rush.

The doctor stares at me for a second. "She'd just like your company. Are you okay?"

"Fine. I'm fine. Where is she?"

"Right this way, miss."

I follow him around the hallway and suddenly realize that though I clutch my phone, I am missing another critical item.

"I forgot my backpack." I hold up a finger. "One second." Run back to the waiting room. Find the backpack next to a pamphlet titled "What You Need to Know About Your Kidneys."

I run back and find the doctor still standing where I left him.

"Sorry," I apologize for the tenth time in thirty minutes.

He opens a plain brown door and shows me into a white room. Laney is covered up on the bed, a pretty brown-haired nurse talking to her.

"Lauren, I'm glad you're here." Laney smiles.

"How is she?" I ask, holding Laney's hand.

The nurse smiles. There has to be a class everyone takes on learning how to smile like that.

"Contractions are coming ten minutes apart."

"How long until they're born?"

"Mmm . . ." She presses her lips together and looks at Laney. "A couple of hours probably."

"Is Adam coming? Did anyone talk to him?" Laney asks.

"He's on his way," I say.

The nurse leaves.

Laney smiles at me ruefully. "We forgot my bag."

"Ryan's bringing it."

Her face creases just as another contraction hits. She grabs my hand. Pain explodes in my fingers, travels up my arm, and clenches my shoulder.

Laney's breath comes faster, whistling through her O-shaped lips.

Adam bangs through the door right then, the same doctor who

escorted me behind him. Laney grabs his hand as he bends over, kisses her forehead, and rubs his hand over their soon-to-be-born babies.

Two minutes later she relaxes slightly, enough to acknowledge him. "Hi, Honey," she says, through her teeth.

"Hey, Babe. D-day, huh? You're early. Again."

She smiles.

I squeeze her hand gently. "I'll be in the waiting room, okay, Laney?"

"You don't want to see the birth?" she says, her eyes twinkling.

I give her a glance and smile at Adam. "I'm glad you're here. I don't think I could have taken it."

He grins. "Thank you, Laurie."

I go back down the hallway and sit again on the lumpy red chair. Flip again through the magazines.

You'd think there'd be at least one *People* in here somewhere.

My phone rings again. This time all the women in the room look at me, annoyed.

"Sorry," I mumble again.

I walk back through the door. "Hello?"

"Where are you?" Ryan asks.

"Ryan. I'm at the hospital."

He chuckles. "I meant where are you in the hospital?"

"Oh. Maternity. You go . . ." I had run back to park the car, but I didn't pay close enough attention to how I came back. "Actually, I'm not sure how we came. An orderly pushed us here."

His voice starts echoing. "Okay, well, I'm following the signs for Maternity." He comes around the corner, sees me, and hangs up.

"Hey." He grins and shrugs his arm around my shoulders. "So girls or boys?"

"Nothing yet. Just contractions." I smile, feeling myself relax a little. I wrap both arms around his waist. "I'm glad you're here."

"Oh, bag." He hands me the navy blue backpack carrying Laney's pajamas, toothbrush, and other necessities.

"Thank you so much, Ryan."

"Hey, anytime." He looks at me. "So what's next?"

"I wait."

"And then?"

"Wait some more."

He grins. "Want company?"

"Depends on the company, I guess."

He sends me a look that makes me grin. "Okay, you can stay. You don't have to work?"

"What time is it?"

I look at my watch. "Almost four."

"Nope. There's a vow of silence out there among construction workers. No work after three thirty."

I smile.

We go back through the doors, and he sits in the lumpy red chair beside mine. We both flip through the magazines.

"Here we go," he whispers, handing me a glossy-covered heavy one. *You and Your Baby.*

The picture on the front is the standard cherubic, blue-eyed, gummy-smile, half-naked baby doctored to make every woman on the planet croon. Well, I can resist temptation.

"Awwww!"

Okay, maybe not.

Ryan rolls his eyes.

I turn to the contents page, pursing my lips, trying to look scholarly. Who knows? I'm still young. Maybe I'll get a career in medicine. I can become an obstetrician.

One of the articles catches my eye.

"Ten Seconds to Live: When Childbirth Goes Bad."

Then again, a PhD will take many years to get, and I don't have that kind of patience.

Ryan elbows me in the ribs. "Hey." He points to his magazine. "This woman in Kentucky had a termite infestation in her *intestine*." He sucks his breath in through his teeth. "Ah. That picture hurts. Oh! Oh, don't look. Man!"

The two remaining pregnant women and the desk lady send Ryan a look.

"Shh," I tell him.

The door bangs open and Brandon comes charging in. "Laurie!" he yells. "Where's Laney? Where's Adam? Has she given birth yet?"

If looks could kill . . .

I grab his bicep and yank him down in the seat next to mine. "Not yet. They're both in the birthing room."

"How far along is she?" he half-whispers.

"She's been in labor three hours."

"What's that mean?"

I shrug. "I've never been through labor."

Ryan hands Brandon his magazine. "Hey, man. Look at page forty-eight."

Brandon does as asked and then double takes. "Oh my gosh," he says slowly and quite loudly.

I smile apologetically yet again at the women.

"Keep it down," I say in a low voice.

Brandon's mouth is open as he stares at the magazine. "That stings," he tells Ryan, mouth still ajar. "Heck, I didn't know that could happen."

"What?" I finally ask.

Brandon gives me the same answer. "Don't look, Laurie."

The same white-coated doctor comes around the corner. "Lauren Holbrook?" he says, looking at me.

I stand and walk over, Brandon and Ryan following.

"What's wrong?"

He smiles that same smile at me. "Laney's doing fine. Terrific, actually. She's coming right along. She's about halfway dilated and feeling good. I think we'll be seeing those babies in less than two hours."

I can't keep the grin off my face. I could hug the Annoying-Smile Doctor. I settle for turning and hugging both Ryan and Brandon at the same time.

"She's doing great!" I grin, one arm around each of their necks. Brandon pushes me off.

"I heard, Laur. Think we can go back there?" He looks to where the doctor disappeared.

The desk lady glares at us. I step meekly back to my chair, yanking Brandon down with me. "Probably not," I whisper.

An hour and a half passes by slowly. I read three articles on liposuction, decide it isn't for me, then look around at the waiting room. Why do they always paint waiting rooms that beige/tan color?

I sigh.

Ryan turns, smiles, and wraps his arm around me. "Bored?" he says in a low voice.

I settle against his shoulder. "To tears."

"Want to play twenty questions?"

"Not particularly, no."

"Hey, look," Brandon whispers, pointing to his magazine. "Doctors in Connecticut are trying to patch ulcers using parts of a cow's stomach."

Ryan makes a face.

"That's gross," I say.

Brandon stares at the page a second longer before turning it. "I think I'd have serious problems eating a hamburger after that."

Dad finally walks in the door and I smile. "He came," I say quietly to Ryan. "Hi, Dad."

"Hi, Sweetie. Ryan. Brandon." Dad sits beside Brandon, looking pale. "What's happened?"

"Nothing, sir," Brandon tells him. "I have now read an entire copy of *Physician's Weekly*. Other than that, nothing at all."

"She was halfway dilated ninety minutes ago," I say to Dad, shifting my weight and leaning harder on Ryan. Whatever adrenaline ran through my system has drained away. I feel exhausted. I yawn.

"Try to relax, Kid," Ryan tells me.

"I'm trying," I mumble, changing positions again.

Suddenly the doctor stands in the waiting room, grinning, a mask pulled down around his chin. "Congratulations, Laney and Adam are the parents of two beautiful babies," he says loudly.

Ryan, Brandon, Dad, and I go ballistic. Even the desk lady doesn't get on the doctor for speaking loudly.

"Boys or girls, Doctor?" I yell.

"One of each," he beams. "Laney did beautifully. She'd like to see you all now."

I run down the hallway and push open Laney's door. She has collapsed back against the pillows, pure exhaustion written on her face. Adam stands beside the bed, stroking her hair.

"Laney, oh my gosh, I'm so excited!" I burst, climbing onto the side of the bed and hugging my sister.

"Careful, Lauren," she cautions and then hugs me back. She pushes me back so I can see her face. "They're beautiful," she whispers, tears pooling in her eyes.

I smooth her hair. "I can't wait to see them." I narrow my eyes at her. "What are their names?"

Her face splits then, half-laughing, half-crying with sheer joy. "Michael Adam Knox and Lauren Alexis Knox." She squeezes my hand. "We'll have to call her Allie, though. I don't think this family can take another Laurie or Lexi."

I laugh through my tears.

Brandon comes in and pumps his big brother's arm. "I heard my middle name. Did I finally get a kid named after me?"

Adam grabs Brandon in a hug. "Good to see you, little brother."

Brandon smacks Adam on the shoulder. "Don't get mushy on me, Adam Knox."

Ryan and Dad walk in, and I scoot off the bed so Dad can see Laney. Ryan squeezes her foot through the covers. "Congratulations, Laney, Adam. I can't wait to see them."

"They named one after me." I grin.

"Hey, you too?" Brandon asks.

I wrap my arms around his neck, laughing and crying, and he leans down close to my ear. "*Five* nieces and nephews," he says, his voice incredulous. "Who would have thought we'd survive that, Laur?"

Chapter Nineteen

I push through the glass door of The Brandon Knox Photography Studio on Wednesday morning, yawning. It is the Fourth of July, so I'm wearing a red shirt.

I am patriotic.

Hannah sits at her desk, squinting at the clock. "You're late," she announces.

"I am now the proud aunt of yet another niece and nephew," I tell her.

Her mouth drops open. "Oh my gosh!" she yells, running around the desk and giving me a hug. "Congratulations! Oh wow! How's Laney?"

"She's good, she's good. Brandon and Adam are helping her, and Lexi's with the other kids."

Lexi and I swapped places early yesterday evening so she could spend some time with Laney and have a break from the extremely rambunctious and excited brothers and sisters.

"What are their names?"

I grin. "Michael Adam and Lauren Alexis."

"Oh, those are great names. Hey, isn't Brandon's middle name Michael?"

"Yep. We both got one named after us."

Hannah waves her hands. "Wait a second. Your family has another Laurie?"

"Not very nice, and no. We're calling her Allie."

"Aww!"

Ruby comes out of Studio One, waves good-bye to a blond-headed couple with a pair of towheaded kids, and gives me a hug. "Ryan told me," she says. "I am so excited for you guys! When can I see them?"

"Hey, me too!" Hannah yells.

"Um, well, they're still in the hospital . . . maybe later this week after they've been released?"

They grin at each other. "Good. We'll hold you to that," Ruby says.

"I love babies." Hannah sighs.

Paul and Rachel Morgan and their two kids come through the door. "Hi, Laurie," he says. "I think we're your nine o'clock. Sorry we're a few minutes late."

By twelve thirty, I've photographed four families, and Ruby has taken pictures of six. I fall against Hannah's desk. She stops typing and grins at me.

"Why ever are you tired, Laurie?" she says, blinking her big eyes in pretend ignorance.

I give her a look and crawl fully on her desk, sprawling on my back.

"Watch the tax forms, Laur."

Brandon comes through the door then, holding a white paper sack from Merson's. He stands over the desk and stares down at me.

"What are you doing?"

"I'm washing my hair. What does it look like?" I smile up at him. "Hey, Uncle Brandon."

"I brought sandwiches," he says, shaking the bag over my face.

I bat it away. "Oh good. I'm hungry." I lay my arm over my eyes, shutting them.

"And coffee," he finishes.

I sit up straight and lunge for the cardboard tray in his hand. "Yay!"

He pulls it out of reach and frowns at me. "Take some advice from a very old friend. Get a life, Laurie."

"Hey." I spread my hands out, palms up. "I am who I am."

"Now that was profound," he says.

Hannah chuckles.

He looks around me to her. "Hey, Hannah."

I hope she catches the way he says her name. Sort of soft and squishy-like. *Hannn-ahhh.* I wrinkle my nose, my stomach rolling. You should never watch your best friend fall in love on an empty stomach.

She smiles, spinning a pen between her fingers, her eyes twinkling. "Hi, Brandon. Congratulations."

He stares at her. "For what?" he says after a few minutes of stare-fest.

I close my eyes, hop off the desk, grab the bag and coffee tray, and smack him upside the head. "'Birth is a life-changing experience for all involved,'" I tell him. "*You and Your Baby*, volume 8."

Hannah starts laughing. Brandon grins self-deprecatingly and nods to the bag. "Part of that is ours. Where's Ruby?"

"In with client number seven. I'm in your office!" I yell, slamming his door Brandon-style.

I climb up on Brandon's desk, find a napkin in the bag, and spread it out on the desk, pulling out what looks like a turkey sandwich and popping the lids off the cups until I find the light tan, sugar-smelling one.

I feel like one of those seagulls in *Finding Nemo*. "Mine! Mine! Mine!"

Ruby sticks her head through the door. "I heard there was lunch," she announces, pushing a strand of curly brown hair behind her ear.

"Yep. Come on in."

She does, closing the door behind her and staring pointedly at me on the desk. "Ever heard of a chair, Laur?"

I finish chewing, my forehead creasing as I think. "Ch-air?" I pronounce slowly.

She chuckles. "Sandwich, please. And black coffee. Good grief, Laurie, I can smell the sugar in yours."

"Exactly the point, my friend."

She sits in the chair in front of me and unwraps her sandwich. "So tell me about Ryan," she starts.

"You don't know him?" I lower my sandwich. "And here this whole time I thought you were siblings!"

"Laurie."

I set my sandwich on the napkin. "What would you like to know?"

"Do you like him?"

"Ruby, if I didn't like him, I wouldn't still be hanging around him."

She shakes her head. "No, I mean *like* him, like him. You know. Little tingly feelings when you're around him."

I look at her. "Is that how you feel about Nick?"

She blushes like a newlywed. "Yeah," she says, drawing the word out sweetly.

"Do you think Hannah feels that way about Brandon?" I ask, voice lowered.

Ruby finishes chewing and swallows. "I don't know. I've never asked her."

"You asked me!"

"Not about Brandon. There is a line somewhere regarding your boss."

"A line?" I question. "Like in literature? Like in a poem?"

She closes her eyes. "No, Laurie, like an invisible boundary. Some things you just don't ask about your boss." She sees the look on my face. "Okay, some things *I* just don't ask about my boss."

"Better."

"So about Ryan . . ." She grins at my distress.

Evil woman.

"I don't know, Ruby," I say. "I mean, he's nice and sweet and he's always there for me. . . ."

She nods, lips pursed. "So far, all of these qualities could also belong to your dog."

"Well, Ryan talks."

She looks at her sandwich for a second before looking back at me. "So you don't like him that way?"

I stare at my hands. "I don't . . . I don't know, Ruby," I stutter. "I never am quite sure where we stand with each other. I mean, we're dating . . . sort of. But mostly it's like we're just . . . just really good friends . . . you know? I just . . ." I look up at her. "I just don't want to get attached to him as a future . . . *whatever* and then hear him tell me he's met someone else he wants to marry. You know?"

Her eyes soften into a smile, and she leans forward and rubs my knee. "Yeah, Laurie," she says quietly. "I know. I felt the same way about Nick, actually."

"You did?" I ask, surprised.

"Sure. When we first started doing things together, I never knew what he was thinking."

"I did."

"Yes, but you're a meddling little creature, and I was his demure possible future wife." She grins. "There is a difference."

"Demure?" I smile. "I don't think I have ever used that word to describe you, Ruby Palmer Avery. Punctual, yes. Pretty, yes. Demure? No."

She squeezes my knee and leans back. "Funny girl. So about Ryan . . ."

"I thought we covered this."

". . . I don't think he'll come in one day with someone else he wants to marry. I think he knows exactly who he wants to marry."

"Really? Who?"

She gives me a look, and I smile, rubbing my eyes. "Listen, Ruby, we'll just have to see, okay? I mean, who knows what will happen in the next few months. He might look at my dad's hypochondria and Lexi's—there's not even a word to describe her!—and think, 'Why in the world would I ever want to marry into that?'"

Ruby shakes her head. "Doubt it. Ryan loves your dad and Lexi."

"Or you know, I might find someone else." I shrug. "Who knows?" I repeat.

She gives me a long look before smiling. "You're right, Laurie. Only God knows right now. But promise me this: No matter what happens with you and Ryan, you and I will always be good friends. Okay?"

I grin. "Deal."

I leave at six o'clock, right after my last client. I race home, kiss my dad hello, run up the stairs to my bedroom, pull out a pair of jeans, keep the red shirt, change pants, run back downstairs, kiss my dad good-bye, and drive the three minutes to Nick and Ruby's new house.

Already cars line the street and fill their driveway. I can see their little neighborhood kids playing with sparklers.

I walk in through the open door, noticing that the group fits very nicely in the humongous living room and huge kitchen.

Ruby and Nick stand by the door like proper hosts. Nick gives me a hug. Ruby squeezes my arm.

"Wow, look at this," I exclaim, waving at the room. "Room to walk! Room to breathe!"

"Great, isn't it?" Ruby grins. "It's the perfect house."

"There's food in the kitchen, Laurie. We'll be making sundaes later," Nick says.

"Hey, find me when you do. I can help."

"Oh no you can't," Ruby says. "You are our guest. You don't work."

I gawk at her. "You are not making sundaes for sixty-eight people by yourselves. We'll be here all night!"

She exchanges a humored glance with Nick and shrugs. "We'll see," she says.

Holly and Luke come in then, and I go into the kitchen to see what food resides there.

Three coffeepots line one countertop, and the island is filled to heaping with brownies, cookies, pies, and cakes, many of them decked out in flag-related colors.

I inhale the scent of the coffee and grin. I know whose coffee this is. I'm peering at the brownies when Shawn comes in, setting three trays down by the other ones.

"Last load," he mumbles.

"You brought all these?" I ask, smiling. "That is so sweet, Shawn."

He shrugs, embarrassed. "Someone had to help with the food. Nick and Ruby couldn't do everything."

"And the coffee?"

He clears his throat and leans down close to my ear. "I've seen the way Ruby makes coffee. It's better if I just bring my own."

I laugh.

Hannah walks in, followed by Becca and Rochelle, two girls I know by name only.

"Did you decide where you two are going for your honeymoon?" Becca asks.

Hannah fiddles with the foil wrapper on a plate of cookies. "We're not engaged!"

"This is so exciting!" Rochelle twitters, obviously not listening. "I can't believe Brandon's getting married! To you! Your kids will be soooo cute!"

Hannah's eyes widen even more than they already are. She sends a desperate look toward me and Shawn.

I glance up at him. "Going to help her?"

He chuckles. "Right. How?"

"Falls to me then, I guess."

"Guess so."

I walk across the kitchen and loop my arm through Hannah's. "Hey, Hannah." I grin.

"Laurie," she says, her voice filled with relief. "Do you know Becca and Rochelle?"

"Kind of," I say, smiling politely. "How are you?"

"I'm fine, wonderful, actually. I can't believe Brandon's engaged!" Rochelle says again.

"Mind if I steal Hannah for a bit?" I ask.

They both shake their heads and start talking to each other about the engagement.

I pull her out of the kitchen and down the hallway. She leans her head back against the wall.

"Laurie, you see? You see what it's like?"

"Look, Hannah, try not to let it get to you. It'll be okay." I smooth her hair, smiling gently. "I promise. It'll be okay."

She manages a small smile and shrugs. "Did Shawn really bring all those desserts?" she asks, changing the subject.

"Most of them."

She sends a grin in the direction of the kitchen. "He is closer to Christianity than he knows."

"I would agree with you, yes."

Brandon walks over to us, covering a yawn. "Hey, girls, why are you in the hall and not socializing?"

"Oh, people were just getting a little too social about your wedding for Hannah's comfort." I grin.

Brandon smiles at Hannah apologetically. "Sorry again."

"It's okay." She smiles shortly. "Really."

Brandon watches her for a minute, The Look crossing his face again. "Hey," he says slowly, his voice deeper than normal, "can I talk to you for a second? There's a fireworks show outside. Want to go watch it?"

She nods. "Sure."

He takes her elbow and leads her toward the door.

I lean up against the wall Hannah just vacated, eyebrows raised in thought.

Granted, it was my idea to try to get the two of them together.

But this is just *weird*. I have known Brandon since the second grade. I have watched him make stupid mistakes and break his arm, and I've built forts with him out of TV trays and blankets.

I take a deep breath and rake a hand through my hair, feeling the aftereffects of yesterday's stress and today's hectic craziness at work.

I love Brandon like a brother.

Here's what I think: It's completely unnerving watching your brother fall in love.

I straighten, walk back into the living room, and find a seat on one of the new pristinely white couches Ruby bought. I look around, not seeing anyone I particularly want to talk to. Come to think of it, I don't really feel like talking at all.

Odd for me.

I glance across the room and see Ryan leaning against the French doors leading to the backyard, holding a cup of coffee in his hand and talking with the male half of Married Couple Number 4.

He sees me watching him and waves.

I smile.

He changed from his typical work outfit to nicer jeans and a not-quite-so-beat-up flannel shirt, and rather than combing his hair, he has a backwards baseball cap on it. I have to grin because it is so typical of him.

He comes over and sits down beside me, balancing his cup on his knee.

"Hey. Happy Fourth of July."

"Hi," I say.

"You look a little down."

I rub my eyes. "I think I'm just tired. I had a really long day at work today, and yesterday with Laney was . . ." My voice trails off.

"Tiring?" Ryan suggests. He hands me his coffee.

I sip it, puckering slightly at the lack of sugar. "Thanks."

"You're welcome." He watches me drain the cup, frowning slightly. "Sure that's all?" he asks.

"Well . . ."

"Aha. Not all."

"I think . . . I think Brandon's . . . I think he's falling in love with Hannah," I mutter, turning the empty cup around and around in my hands.

Ryan's forehead creases. "So? Isn't that what you wanted? Shouldn't you be jumping excitedly?"

"Yeah, yeah. It's just . . ." I wave one hand.

"It's just . . . ?" he prods.

"Weird."

"Got it. Because you grew up with him?"

"He's like my brother," I say.

Ryan grins and slips an arm around my shoulders. "Now you know why I was so freaked out about Ruby and Nick." He pats my arm. "Welcome to the club, Laurie."

"What club?"

"The Siblings Club."

I frown. "But it wasn't like this when Lex and Laney got married. I was really happy for them." I frown, remembering. "I think it was Brandon, actually, who was freaking out."

Ryan laughs. "Yeah, but see, you feel protective of Brandon. You didn't feel protective of Lexi or Laney, did you?"

I narrow my eyes at him. "Sometimes you're too smart."

"Thank you for the compliment."

I rub my eyes again.

"Why don't you go home to bed?" Ryan suggests. "You look like you're about to fall over right now."

"Yeah," I mumble. "That's a good idea."

"Want me to drive you back?"

"No, no, I'm good. The caffeine's starting to kick in." I hand him back the mug. "Thanks again."

I stand.

"Hey," he says.

I turn, and he smiles gently up at me. "Sweet dreams, Laurie-girl."

Impulsively, I bend down, wrap my arms around his neck, and kiss his cheek. "I'm really glad I met you, Ryan," I say, meeting his surprised gaze.

Something shifts in his eyes, and I pull back quickly, wave, and head out the door.

I have one foot outside when every muscle in my body freezes solid like those poor people in *The Day After Tomorrow*.

My mouth is open, my eyes are wide, and my breathing stops totally. My hand grips the door handle like Mr. Incredible.

Brandon and Hannah are sitting on the porch steps. Fireworks are exploding in the dark sky behind them. One of his hands rests lightly on her shoulder, the other gently strokes her face as he kisses her.

Chapter Twenty

I stand there reenacting the "Han Solo Frozen in Carbonite" scene for I don't know how long until one surviving electrical impulse in my brain screams, "SHUT THE DOOR!"

I back carefully into the house and silently close the front door, its *clicking* almost imperceptible.

Turning, I march down the hall and into the first bedroom, which became Nick and Ruby's workout room, and sit on Nick's weight bench.

What on earth just . . .

I blink rapidly, staring at the blank TV across from me.

Brandon kissed Hannah!

I jump up, my blood pumping double-time to make up for the Mr. Freeze back there.

He kissed her! Probably still is!

I swear I can't help it. "OH MY GOSH!" I shriek, jumping up and down, screaming. Any weirdness I formerly felt vanishes like Prince John's gold in the presence of Robin Hood.

Ruby comes running into the room. "Laurie! Lauren Emma Holbrook, what on earth . . . ?"

She grabs my shoulders and tries to hold me still. I laugh, shriek, and grab her in a hug.

"What happened?" she yells.

"Go look out your front door!" I yell.

She whirls and runs for the entry.

"Wait, Ruby!" I scream, running after her. "Don't open it!"

She skids to a halt in front of the door, peeping through the tiny window set in the center.

A few people milling at the edge of the living room give us odd looks.

We ignore them.

She mashes her forehead against the door, squinting. "I can't see anything, Laurie."

"Shh." I shove her out of the way and look through.

All I can see is Ryan's beat-up Chevy parked out front.

"Brandon . . ." I huff, clearing my throat. "Is . . . oh my gosh!" I grin.

Ruby grabs my face in her hands and jerks me a few feet forward, making me look her in the eyes.

"Laurie," she says slowly. "Concentrate. Tell me slowly and clearly what is going on."

I nod, swallow, and take a deep breath. But I can't keep the grin off my face. "Brandon . . . is . . . kissing . . . Hannah." I take short gasps between each word.

Ruby stares at me for a full ten seconds before she drops my face and slaps her hands over her mouth, muffling her screaming. I drag her back to the first bedroom, and she hugs me tightly, both of us screaming and jumping and shrieking and laughing hysterically.

She finally pushes me back to arm's length. "It happened!" she shouts. "Oh, Laurie, it happened!"

"I know! I know!"

She grabs me in a hug again.

Ten minutes later, when we have finally somewhat calmed down, we both collapse on Nick's weight bench.

She giggles. "Oh, Laurie, they'll be so happy together," she whispers.

"Yeah."

She squeezes my hand. "I knew it. I *knew* he'd end up with Hannah."

"Because I told you?"

She laughs.

"Hey, Ruby?" I hear Nick yell.

"In the workout room!" she yells back, both of us wiping tears off our cheeks.

Nick comes in and stares at the two of us crying. "Oh no, who died?"

Ruby dissolves into laughter, stands up, grabs her husband by the neck, and kisses him solidly. "Everything is wonderful, Darling," she sings as he stands there blinking at her. "What did you need?"

"Wha . . . um . . . the sundaes . . ." he stutters.

"Oh right." She sends him a dazzling smile and looks at me. "We'll go start making them. Want to help, Laurie?"

I nod and follow them through the crowd and into the kitchen. Shawn and Hallie are the only ones in there, sitting at the table, quietly talking.

"Laurie?" Ryan comes into the kitchen, looking at me curiously.

"Hi, Ryan."

"You have makeup on your face," he says. I rub at my cheeks, and his nose wrinkles. "No, that's worse."

"Come here, Honey," Ruby says, wetting a paper towel in the sink and brushing it under my eyes.

"Uh, weren't you leaving?" Ryan asks.

"I changed my mind," I say, looking up at the ceiling while Ruby rubs at my mascara.

"All right. That's it," Nick says, pulling the ice cream out of the freezer. "Explain."

I take the paper towel from her. "Well, see, I was going to leave, but then I decided not to."

Nick pops the lid of the carton and stares at me. "What?" he says finally.

"You asked me to explain."

"*Why* did you change your mind?"

I bite the inside of my cheek and look at Ruby, who shrugs. Shawn and Hallie's conversation around the kitchen table ceases.

I watch Nick roll out two scoops of ice cream and clear my throat. "Sundaes." I nod to Ruby. "I'd forgotten about the sundaes."

"Why were you crying in the workout room?" he asks. Ruby squirts chocolate fudge sauce over the ice cream. Then, in keeping with the holiday, she shakes red, white, and blue sprinkles on top.

Ryan touches my shoulder. "You were crying in the workout room?"

I try not to read too hard into the tone he is using.

I go for the classic Will Smith Blow-Your-Breath-Out-and-Deny-Everything move. I shake my head, laughing. "You know me when I get around chocolate." I grin, spreading my hands out.

Shawn raises his hand. "I can attest to that."

"Whoa, whoa. Did I just have a momentary hearing lapse? I never heard anyone ask your opinion, Shawn Merson," I answer back.

He grins.

Ryan's hand is still on my shoulder. "Are you sure, Laurie? I mean, you fizz out sometimes around chocolate, but I've never seen you reduced to tears."

"I had a rough day, Ry. I guess the combination . . ." I let my voice trail off.

He looks worriedly at me. "Want to go talk about it? We can go outside and—"

"No!" I shriek.

Nick jumps and drops the ice cream scoop into the carton. "Dang it, Laurie!" he growls.

"Sorry," I say. I peek at Ryan's face.

He has that determined look again.

"Aha," he says in a low voice. "So you're hiding something, is that it?"

Silence is always the best option. I press my lips together and calmly ignore him.

"Is there something on the front porch, Laurie?" Ryan asks like I'm a little kid caught with cookies. I know the tone because I heard it on a daily basis growing up.

Again, I keep quiet.

"Mm-hmm. Well, thanks for tonight, Sis. Nice seeing you again, Nick. I think I'll head out now. I had a long day."

He leaves the kitchen. I send an agonized look to Ruby and run after him.

"Wait, Ryan, please hold up," I beg, grabbing his arm.

He stops right in front of the door and leans down until he is eye level with me. "Why?"

I try pleading with my eyes like all the heroines do in the movies, but Ryan doesn't break down. I drop my hands from his arm and look down. "Becauseheisser," I mumble under my breath.

Ryan uses his index finger and props my chin up until he is once again burning my pupils with his eyeballs. "What?"

"Because Brandon is kissing her," I say slowly.

He lets go of my chin, his mouth open. "Who's her?"

"Hannah."

His mouth opens farther. I push it closed, and he blinks rapidly, shaking his head.

"Brandon is kissing Hannah?" he whispers in my ear.

I grin.

"On the front porch?"

I laugh.

His face splits in a grin so wide I hear his eardrums pop. "Well, that's very interesting."

He suddenly gets serious and touches my cheek. "Are you okay with this? Is that why you were crying?"

I bat his hand away. "They were good tears, Ry. We were so excited."

"Ruby cried too?"

"She's obviously wearing waterproof mascara."

He slaps his forehead. "Of course Ruby cried. Ruby cries even when she watches *Elf.*"

I frown. "She cries at that?" I ask in disbelief. "That's not a cry movie. That's a funny movie."

Ryan shrugs. "Debate it with her. All I know is she has to have the Kleenex box beside her anytime she watches it."

I push Ryan aside and march back into the kitchen. "You cry watching *Elf*?" I ask her, mouth agape.

She sets the fudge sauce down and gives Ryan a look. "Thanks. Thanks, Ryan. Really helpful."

He grins at her. "What can I say? I do my best, Sis."

~⊕~

Thursday morning I walk through the studio door and smile normally at Hannah.

"Morning, Hannah," I say, half-yawning. I set the cardboard tray of Merson's on the desk.

She looks at the four cups of coffee and smiles. "One for me?" she asks.

"No, Honey, these are all mine."

"You're pitiful."

"I'm kidding." I point to hers, and she wrenches it out of the holder. "So I didn't see you much last night," I say, putting my backpack in the cubbyhole behind her desk.

She sips her coffee and goes back to her computer. "I left early. Headache."

I put on a concerned face. "Are you feeling better?"

She looks over and smiles again. "Yeah. Coffee will help too. I think I was just tired. Yesterday was crazy here."

"You can say that again."

Ruby comes through the door and smiles at both of us. "Hi, girls."

"Hey, Ruby," Hannah says.

"Hi, Ruby. Free coffee." I point to the straight-up black. She pulls it free and sets a box of Krispy Kreme Doughnuts on the desk.

"Yay!" I yell.

Hannah stares at the box. "What's this?"

Ruby shrugs. "My yearly box of doughnuts. It is the first week of July, right?"

Hannah nods.

"See? It has been exactly a year since I had my last doughnut."

I pull a sticky one out of the box and *tsk* at her. "You lead a tragic life, Ruby."

"According to your standards, probably."

Ryan walks in. "Hey, guys."

I smile at him, feeling fuzzy. "Hi, Ryan. What are you doing here?"

He grins, walks over, and kisses my cheek. I blink.

"Just thought I'd say hi," he says. He looks at Ruby and Hannah, who are both grinning like the evil Queen of Hearts in *Alice in Wonderland*. "And I brought these." He pulls a huge bag of assorted chocolates from behind his back and sets it on the desk to join the other offerings.

"You brought us chocolate?" I squeal.

"Why?" Ruby asks.

"I had to go to the grocery store anyway." He gives me a mischievous look. "I was out of Eggo waffles."

I press my lips together.

"These were on sale. And I figured three females and Brandon in the same office? Chocolate is probably much needed."

Hannah smiles curiously at him. "Oh, okay. Great. Thank you."

We all stand there, grinning at her.

"What?" she asks, fiddling with her coffee.

"Nothing. You look really pretty today," I tell her. She wears a knee-length pastel blue fluttery skirt and a powder blue top that makes her eyes pop.

Ryan and Ruby voice their agreement.

She smiles the same curious smile. "Okay. Thanks."

Ryan clears his throat. "Well, I should go . . . I guess. Hey, what's Brandon up to lately? Haven't seen him around much."

Hannah looks back at the computer, again fooling with her cup lid. "Oh, nothing new. Actually, you should ask Laurie. She's closer to Brandon." She takes a long swig.

Here's what I want to say: "Honey, no one has ever been as close to Brandon as you were on the porch last night."

Here's what I do say: "We haven't really talked in a long time." The truth of the statement hits me, and I suddenly feel like crying.

My best friend and I are growing up.

I don't like growing up.

I bite my lip and manage a smile.

"So Brandon's not here?" Ryan asks.

"Nope," Hannah says, typing something.

Ruby gives me a sideways glance. "I didn't even see him last night. Was he there?"

Ryan shakes his head. "I didn't see him."

Hannah looks at us briefly. "He was there."

"Where was he?" Ryan asks.

"He talked to me and Laurie for a little bit." Hannah swallows.

"A tiny bit," I correct. "He must have left after talking to you because I didn't see him again." I cock my head. "Speaking of which, what did you guys talk about?"

"Oh . . ." Hannah says, keeping her eyes on the computer. "Work-related stuff."

"Really? Hey, you didn't happen to talk about the couple thing, did you?" I ask.

She looks up quickly. "The couple thing?"

"Yeah. Some couples are wanting to be photographed before the wedding in their wedding attire, and Brandon thinks there's too much liability as far as the dress goes."

She looks down as quickly as she looked up. "No, we didn't talk about that," she mumbles, taking another long drink.

I look at Ruby and Ryan, who shrug. I am a fervent believer that being subtle is the best way to get someone to confess.

Well, hang subtlety.

"Hey, Ruby, did I tell you I saw a movie last night that I think you'll love?" I say, keeping my eyes on Hannah.

"No. What is it?" Ruby asks.

"It's called *Kissing on the Front Porch*."

Hannah closes her eyes, sets her coffee down, and then looks up to see the three of us standing there, grinning.

"How much did you see?" she demands.

"None," Ruby and Ryan say together, pointing to me.

I smile cheekily. "I saw most of it."

Hannah covers her face. "Is that what this is all about? The coffee, the doughnuts, the chocolate? Why didn't you just ask me?"

"We were trying to be subtle," I say.

She groans, stands, and heads down the hallway toward the bathroom.

"Hey, don't worry. I think it's good!" I yell, running after her.

"That's what I'm worried about!" The bathroom door shuts, and I hear a click.

I go back into the lobby. Ryan is kissing the top of Ruby's head.

"Got to go to work," he says to me.

"Still working at Mrs. Galen's?"

"Yep." He reaches over and squeezes my shoulder. "Walk me out?"

I nod and follow him out the door, squinting in the sunlight as we walk to his truck.

"What are you doing tonight?" he asks, jangling his keys.

"I get off work at six." I shrug. "I'll probably go home."

"Let's get dinner then. I'll pick you up, and you can leave your car here." He is also squinting.

I know neither of us likes sunglasses, which automatically means we're both going to have crow's-feet sunk so deep in our heads we'll someday have to hold our eyes open with toothpicks to see.

"Okay. That sounds good," I answer, smiling.

He returns the smile, leans over, and kisses my cheek again.

There has been a lot of kissing going on. It must be spring.

But wait. It's July. It's summer.

What is with all the kissing?

Hannah leaves the office at noon, claiming she needs a break, and Brandon doesn't get in until twelve thirty, claiming his alarm broke, so the day as far as they are concerned is a total waste. Add to that spilling three pieces of ravioli on my khaki-colored jeans at Vizzini's with Ryan, and my day isn't going very well.

I drive to my house, park in the garage, walk in, pet little Darcy on the head, look up, and freeze, blinking repeatedly.

No wonder the house smells odd.

"Um, Dad?" I yell.

He walks into the entry, a dusting rag over his shoulder. "Hi, Sweetie. Have a good dinner?"

I point wordlessly to the living room.

Dad smiles proudly. "Do you like it? I did that today."

Yesterday the living room was a nice cream color with white trim. We had two couches, a love seat, and my dad's recliner all situated around the fireplace and TV.

Tonight all the living room walls are *green*.

It isn't even a nice green for walls, like a forest green or a muted kelly green. The color? Lime green. So is the trim.

Two new lime green suede couches are on either side of the living room. A darker green love seat sits mostly in the middle of the room. Dad's recliner is unchanged, still rocking by the fireplace.

I swallow and press a hand to my throat like Ariel in *The Little Mermaid*. My voice. My voice is gone. Sucked away by *green*.

Dad looks it all over proudly. "Took me most of this morning to get the paint the right shade. And these are slipcovers on the sofas. See?" He lifts the overhanging fabric on the bottom of the sofa, and I see part of the tan leather underneath, smothering. *I'm sorry*, I tell it silently.

Dad lets the slipcover fall back in place. "Ingenious, whoever thought up slipcovers. Easiest thing I've ever installed." He looks around. "And then I just rearranged the furniture, and that was it. Simple. Now I'm working on the study."

He turns to walk back in there, and I close my eyes, my feet refusing to budge.

I open my eyes, and I'm nearly blinded again.

What terrible color for paint! Lime green is a cute color for capris. But it's a totally different breed on walls.

Dad stops just before he steps through the doorway to the study and smiles. "It's a good color for this room. Joan was right."

My voice comes back in full strength. "Who was right?" I choke.

"Joan. She's coming on Saturday, remember? Her favorite color is lime green. She told me her living room was this color, and, well . . ." He blushes slightly. "I want her to feel at home here."

I step a few feet toward the study and have to slap my hand over my mouth to keep from crying out loud.

The room is like this: ORANGE.

And empty.

"Where's all the furniture?" I ask.

"Oh, I put it in my room while I'm painting. Do you like it? Joan really likes bright colors. She said they invigorate the mind." He looks around, hands on his hips. "And I agree. I feel very invigorated right now. Don't you?"

I feel like throwing up.

I mumble something, smile tightly, and run up the stairs to my room. Thank goodness! He hasn't touched my room.

I close my eyes, press my forehead against the cream-colored wall, and kiss it.

Like I said, kissing is in high season here.

I fall back on my bed and stare at the ceiling, seeing orange dots where the color burned into my eyeballs.

So, Lord, Brandon and Hannah are together.

I tuck one arm behind my head, thinking of the verse I read last night, 1 Corinthians 7:36: "They should get married."

I have to admit, I feel pretty good about this. Not only did I arrange my own sister's wedding, but I also managed to also arrange my basically brother's marriage.

It's all in the family.

Brandon will be happily settled, and I will . . .

I will what, Lord? Half the singles' class is married.

Shawn and Hallie are still single, as of yet, but they've been as easy to get together as accidentally cutting the cord of an electrical hedge trimmer.

With Brandon and Hannah finally at peace, my life outside of my home will get very boring very quickly.

Inside my home is a different story. Life with Dad used to at least masquerade as peaceful, but if Joan Abbot's living room is *lime* green, I'm thinking whatever veneer of tranquility we had will be gone.

Then there's Joan Abbot herself, God.

Saturday could be interesting.

Chapter Twenty-One

I once read that nine out of ten families are dysfunctional. Which begs the question, why haven't they become functional and the other one out of ten become dysfunctional? And why is the *dys* in *dysfunctional* spelled with a *y*?

As the apostle Paul would put it, "What shall we say, then?"

I'm just climbing into the car with my very excited father to pick up Joan Abbot from the airport and thus clench the title "Dysfunctional" for my family when Hannah calls my cell phone.

"You didn't answer at your house," she says, not bothering with common courtesies like "hello" and "how are you?"

"Hello," I say. "How are you?"

"Are you not at your house?"

"Technically? Yes. We're in the garage."

"Stay there!"

"Hannah, I can't. We're going to pick up Joan Abbot."

"I have to talk to someone," she mutters. "And I tried talking to Lucky, but he's no help."

"Dogs usually aren't great at advice, Hannah. What do you need to talk about?"

"Just stuff," she hedges.

I have a feeling stuff includes someone male with a *B* at the beginning of his name.

Dad hops (being very literal here) into the driver's seat, grins at me, opens his mouth to say something, and then sees the cell phone attached to my head.

"Something wrong?" he whispers.

"Hannah needs to talk to someone," I say in a low voice.

"I really do, Laur," she says.

Dad nods. "Stay back then. I can get Joan by myself, Honey."

"Are you sure?"

He nods, giddy.

I'm feeling a little weirded out by all this.

"Joan won't be upset?"

Dad pats my hand. "She rarely gets upset, Laurie-girl."

This from the woman whose living room is lime green. I figure any woman with a lime green living room will have issues of some kind.

"All right, Hannah, I'm staying back."

"Thank you, thank you, thank you!" she gushes. "I'll be there in five."

I climb out of the car and wave as Dad backs out.

I walk back inside, and Darcy quirks his head at me as I let him out of the kennel like, *Hey, didn't I just get shoved in here?*

"Time passes quickly, Buddy," I tell him.

I swear the dog shrugs.

~─◈─~

I make a pot of the hazelnut-cinnamon coffee blend I keep for serious heart-to-heart discussions, and I'm digging out a package of Oreos I hid behind the rock salt at the bottom of the pantry when Hannah rings the doorbell. I have to hide the chocolate in this house to keep my ears from a serious tongue lashing from my dad about nutritious eating habits.

Don't believe me? I'll prove it. There is an entire bag of Hershey's Kisses in the pocket of my robe. Hiding chocolate in sock drawers is for wimps.

I open the front door, and Darcy and I grimace together.

Hannah's long blonde hair is twisted back in a tangled heap that I assume is an attempt at a ponytail gone bad. Her eyes are red-rimmed and puffy, and she's wearing ratty pink fleece pants and a T-shirt that says, "STAY ALIVE IN '05. GET ME COFFEE FAST. PHILLIPS 66."

"You look awful," I greet her.

She sniffles. "Yeah." She comes in, grabs the Oreo bag from my hands, and does a double take.

"Whoa, what happened to your living room?"

"Joan Abbot. Coffee?"

She schlumps onto one of the couches. "Looks like a fruit stand exploded all over your house." She digs out a handful of the cookies and frowns. "I thought you said you were going to pick her up. How did she do this if she's not here?"

I bring in two cups of highly caffeinated, highly sugared and creamed, highly dangerous coffee and set one on the table in front of her. "Her living room is lime, and Dad wanted her to feel at home."

She swallows, brushing crumbs off her face. "Oh."

I watch her devour the Oreos, worried. Hannah does not eat Oreos like this. Hannah is the Queen of Exercise. She has one piece of chocolate a day for her mental health, and that's it. Then she goes and jogs ten miles.

I grab the bag the moment she lets go to pick up her coffee.

"Hey!"

"You've had enough," I tell her in no uncertain terms. "What is going on?"

She drains half the mug.

"Hannah?"

She sets the cup down with a bang. "Brandon asked me out."

I blink at her. "Okay."

"He asked me out *to dinner*," she annunciates.

"Okay."

"To dinner, just the two of us. Alone!"

I still don't see the problem. "That's generally how dating takes place, Hannah."

"Not with Brandon!"

I frown. "Why?"

She waves her hands. "Because," she blurts finally, "it's Brandon!"

I look at her like she has sponges growing out her ears. "So?"

"So he's my *boss*."

"So?"

"So you don't go out with your boss."

"Says who?"

She again goes through the whole wave-hands motion. "Everyone! Dr. Laura. Dr. Phil. Even my vet says that."

I give her a look. "You asked your vet if you should go out with Brandon?"

She sighs. "No, Laurie."

"Then how do you know what your vet thinks?"

She covers her face.

"Why does it even matter what your vet thinks? It doesn't matter to me what my vet thinks. Unless it regards Darcy, of course, but that's—"

"Laurie, that was just a figure of speech. An example."

I pull an Oreo out of the bag and watch her for a minute. "Look, Hannah," I say softly, leaning forward. "I've known Brandon since second grade."

She nods, her eyes bleak. "I know."

"And I've watched him grow up and meet girls, and he's never gotten emotionally attached."

She stares at me, her eyes tearing.

"And then he met you, and things started changing. I mean, this is the first time he's ever really shown interest in a girl. You know?"

She nods, swiping at her cheeks.

"So I think ultimately it doesn't matter what Dr. Laura thinks. It matters what God has designed and what Brandon thinks and what you think."

She sniffs. "Thanks, Laur."

"So what do you think?"

She looks away. "I think . . . I think I might . . ." she stutters, looking at her hands. "When he kissed me I . . ."

Ding-dong.

I just about crush the bag of Oreos.

"Hold that thought," I command, stalking to the door and preparing to lambaste whatever poor salesperson or Jehovah's Witness is here.

I rip open the door.

"Hey, Laur. I was hoping you were home."

Ryan stands there, grinning adorably and holding two paper sacks from Merson's.

The kid is cute, but he has the worst timing on the planet.

I clench my hands and manage a terse smile. "Hi, Ryan."

"Hey, is Hannah here? I noticed her car." He steps in and almost steps back out. "Holy cow!" he yells. "What happened to your living room?"

"Long story."

He sees Hannah then and does another double take. "Wow, Hannah . . . you look terrible."

She sniffs again. "Ryan." She looks at me. "I'm going to go wash my face," she mutters and goes into the guest bath.

"What happened to her?" Ryan asks, staring after her.

I shove him back outside and close the front door behind us. Hannah has been known to listen at doors.

"Brandon asked her out."

He looks at me the same way I looked at Hannah. "So?"

"So she's freaking out because he's her boss."

"Well, that's stupid."

I have to smile at his maleness. "You should have been a shrink," I tell him. "You're so understanding."

He grins at me. "Okay, sorry. But it is stupid. They're perfect for each other. Want me to tell her that?"

I put a hand on his arm. "She knows. She was getting ready to tell me when you rang the doorbell."

"Oh. Sorry," he says again. "I was going to ask you to lunch."

"Is that what's in the bag?"

He nods. "Yep." He frowns at me. "Didn't he kiss her?"

"Hannah?"

"Yeah. She let Brandon kiss her. And she freaks out because he asks her out after that?" He shakes his head. "I will never understand women."

"Yes, well, such is life."

"I'm glad you're not like that."

"Not like what?"

"Like that. *Emotional.* I mean, sure, you have your moments, but for the most part you're okay."

I squint at him. "For the most part?"

"Yes, Laurie, sometimes you are very hormonal." He sees my look. "But not all the time. See? Not all the time."

"Do you want a shovel?"

"Excuse me?"

"So you can dig the hole you're in a little faster?"

He tips his head at me. "That wasn't an insult, Laur."

"Mm-hmm."

"Okay, tell me the truth. If I kissed you and then asked you out, would you go into a panic attack?"

I stare at him, hands on my hips. That weird squishy feeling hits my stomach, and I bite my lip.

"Umm . . . probably not." I clear my throat. "But we're dating. That's the difference." I make an excuse to get away. "I need to go check on Hannah."

He doesn't buy it. "Mm-hmm. Good try, Laurie Holbrook." He follows me into the house.

The bathroom door is still closed.

"She's taking a long time on her face."

"Into the kitchen," I command, shoving him in that direction. I push him into a kitchen chair and hold up my index finger. "Not a word."

"Yes, ma'am." He grins.

I go back through the living room and tap on the bathroom door. "Hannah?"

She opens the door, sniffling, her face looking worse than before. *Eek.*

"Did Ryan leave?"

"He brought lunch. Let's talk in here," I say, walking into the bathroom and sitting down on the bath mat, leaning my back against the tub. She sits beside me and cradles her splotchy face in her hands.

"You were saying about Brandon?"

She sniffs and backhands her eyes, smearing a long line of mascara across her temple.

"I don't know, Laurie," she says softly. "I don't know!" she repeats, this time moaning. "He's so . . . sweet."

"Yeah, he is."

"And thoughtful. You know? And he's such a great example of a Christian guy. I mean, he loves the Lord."

I nod. "Always has, actually."

"He's so wise in that area too. I mean, when I'm having a bad day and stuff, he's always got a Bible verse for me and he always prays with me." She starts tearing up again. "Then there was his witnessing that really paved the way for my salvation."

"Hannah?" I squeeze her knee. "I'm not understanding the problem."

She rips off a couple of sheets of toilet paper and blows her nose. "What if I'm falling in love with him and he's just trying to be nice?" she says, wiping at the tears on her cheeks with the toilet paper.

Yes. The used toilet paper.

I lean over her, dig through the cabinet under the sink, and come out with a box of Kleenex.

"Thank you."

"Hannah, that's ridiculous."

"What?" she blubbers.

"That he's just trying to be nice. Honey, all you have to do is notice the way he looks at you or how he's different when you walk into the room to see that it's more than being nice."

She blows her nose again. "Really?"

"Really." I pat her shoulder. "Now. When did he ask you out?"

"Today."

"No, I mean, for when?"

"Oh. Tonight."

"For dinner?"

"And a movie." She swipes at her cheeks. "You think I should go?"

I stare at her, taking in her swollen, red-rimmed, bloodshot eyes, her splotchy cheeks, her beet red nose, her wreck of a ponytail . . .

I pat her shoulder again. "I think you should let me help you get ready."

The old Hannah is returning. "That bad, huh?"

"Worse."

"Don't tell me. I don't even want to know."

"Just don't look in the mirror when you stand up."

She smiles and leans her head against my shoulder. "Thanks, Laur. I love you."

"I know." I stroke back a few escapees from her hair band.

"I should go."

"You don't have to."

"Ryan's here."

"I know."

She lifts her head, gives me a look, and stands, carefully averting her gaze from the mirror.

"My mother taught me you should never keep Prince Charming waiting," she lectures, marching out of the bathroom.

The old Hannah is back with a vengeance.

"Yes, but . . ." I say, trailing after her like a little lost dog with my ears cut short and my tail cut long.

She stops at the front door and turns on me. "But you've kept him waiting! And not only that, you've kept him waiting with lunch!"

"But it's *Ryan*, Hannah, and he—"

"No!" she says, holding up a hand. "Not another word. I'm going home to put cucumbers on my eyes and a cold rag on my face." She massages her forehead. "And to take some ibuprofen."

I watch her walk down the steps and to her car. "Drive carefully."

"Go eat, Laurie."

I shut the door and go into the kitchen.

Ryan munches a chip, leaning his arms against the table, grinning cocklly. "So," he drawls, "you've kept Prince Charming waiting?" He widens his eyes. "Where?"

I flounce into the chair catty-corner from him and glare.

"Oh, but wait!" he shouts dramatically. "Could she have meant me?"

"Stuff it, funny boy."

He about doubles over laughing. "I'm trying, Laur. I'm trying. You should have seen me in here when she went off!"

I can't help the smile. I poke his arm. "Thanks for lunch. What is it?"

"Sandwiches and chips. How's Hannah?"

"Better."

He hands me one of the bags and a three-inch stack of napkins.

Ryan has been around me too long. He knows what a klutz I am.

"What'd you say to her?" he asks, pulling out his sandwich.

"I told her she was being ridiculous. Anyone who sees Brandon when Hannah's in the room can tell he's nuts about her."

Ryan goes to the fridge and grabs two Dr. Peppers, bringing them back to the table. "Well, females anyway."

"You don't notice how he gets all jittery when she's around?"

He shrugs. "Could be a number of things, Laur."

"Simpleton," I accuse him.

He pops the lid on his soda. "There's nothing worse in dating than being verbally abused by your girlfriend in nineteenth-century English."

We are just cleaning up lunch when I hear the garage door go up. I latch onto Ryan's arm.

"Oh my gosh, they're home," I shriek, pure terror washing down the back of my spine.

"Whoa, Laur. I have a half-full can in my hands." He switches the drink to the other hand and sets it on the counter, looking at me curiously.

"I'm scared to death," I mutter, clenching his flannel shirt in my fist.

He puts a hand over mine, his expression worried. "You're shaking. You really are scared!"

"I wouldn't lie to you."

The door between the laundry room and the garage opens, and I hear Dad's voice. "This is the unattractive way to come in to the house," he says, chuckling.

"No, I like it. It makes me feel right at home," a female voice I recognize from the phone answers.

I look at Ryan. He bends down and kisses my forehead. "It'll be okay," he whispers. "Buck up, Private." He rips my hand off his sleeve and holds it steadily in his.

Dad comes into the kitchen, his eyes lit up, a huge smile on his face. A petite, brown-haired woman with sparkly blue eyes and a pretty face is behind him.

"Oh good, Ryan, you're here too." Dad smiles.

"Yes, sir. Good to see you."

"Laurie-girl, Ryan, this is Joan. Joan, this is my daughter, Laurie, and her boyfriend, Ryan."

Double shock. This is the first time my father has ever referred to Ryan as my boyfriend.

Ryan pinches the back of my left hand and I jump, forcing a smile and stretching out my right hand. "Hi. Nice to meet you."

She takes my hand in both of hers, understanding in her blue eyes. "It's wonderful to finally meet you, Laurie."

I like the way she says my name. *Laurie*. Warmly. Like it means something.

I smile more genuinely. "Can I get you something to drink?"

"No, no thank you." She looks curiously at Ryan's heavy-duty construction boots.

"I'm in construction," he says before she can ask.

Her eyebrows raise. "Really? So is my son. What kind?"

"Mostly residential. Houses. I work for a builder."

Joan nods. "My son is in commercial."

Ryan smiles easily. "There are pros and cons to both." He squeezes my hand, and I'm suddenly very glad he is here.

"Coffee?" I ask, even though I already offered drinks.

"You'll learn this quickly about Laurie," Ryan says. "She breathes caffeine like most people do oxygen."

Joan laughs. A nice laugh, actually. Not twittery like an airhead cheerleader, but deep and comfortable, like she laughs a lot.

I pull my hand out of Ryan's and start making another pot of the hazelnut coffee. He and Joan chat about construction and buildings, and Dad leans over and squeezes my shoulder.

"Thanks, Laurie-girl," he whispers.

I smile. The water starts heating, and Dad moves the two others toward the living room.

"Oh, what a beautiful room." Joan smiles. "This is my favorite color."

Dad beams.

I balance my elbows on the counter and watch the coffee dribble through the lid of the pot.

I hear the three of them talk about Laney and the new twins and Lexi's idiosyncrasies. Finally the coffee is done.

I make Ryan's black and mine tan and stick a mug of water in the microwave to make Dad's lemongrass tea.

"Joan, how do you take your coffee?" I ask, walking into the living room. Ryan lounges on one of the couches, Joan sits pristinely on the other. My dad?

Good guess. In his chair. Like usual.

Joan looks over the back of the couch at me. "Oh, Honey, I don't drink coffee anymore."

"Tea, then?"

"Tea would be lovely."

And suddenly I'm entertaining Julie Andrews.

I nod. "What flavor?"

"What do you have?"

I let my breath out. "Blackberry, raspberry, peach, plain black, green, chamomile, peppermint—"

Dad interrupts me. "Or there's my favorite. Lemongrass."

Joan smiles sweetly at him. I give Ryan a wide-eyed stare. This is the first time I have ever seen anyone flirt with my dad.

Ryan's dimple appears.

"Lemongrass? Sounds wonderful."

I clear my throat and lean down close to Joan's ear. "It's very strong," I caution her.

"The stronger the better," she says, waving her hand. "Thank you for offering, Dear."

I go back into the kitchen and pour another mug of water. The microwave is beeping, and I pull Dad's out.

This is the worst part of making lemongrass tea.

I rip open the container, yank out a tea bag, snap the lid shut, throw the bag in the water, and slap a napkin over the mug, not breathing the entire time.

Anytime you open the lemongrass tea tin, a big cloud of choking yellow granules floats up and clogs the atmosphere with its eye-watering scent.

Joan Abbot calls from the living room, "Oh, that tea smells delicious!"

I wipe my face with a wet paper towel and can't help the sigh.

Ryan gives me a smile as I bring in the two mugs of waxy sludge for my father and Joan.

"This looks fabulous," Joan croons.

Sure, if you like drinking melted-down Tupperware.

I hand Ryan his cup and sit down next to him with mine. He takes a drink and nudges my shoulder. "Good coffee."

"Thanks."

Joan sips her tea. "Wonderful. Laurie, tell me about yourself."

"Me?"

She nods, smiling.

"Okay, well, um," I stutter. "I'm a photographer at a friend's studio. I'm pretty involved in a singles' Bible study."

Ryan snickers.

I continue. "During the school year I help teach a junior high girls' Bible study." I shake my head. "Other than that, not much. I hang out with friends."

Joan nods, still smiling. A miracle, considering what she is drinking. "Sounds like a full life."

"And she didn't even get into her hobbies," Ryan says.

I elbow him hard in the ribs while smiling angelically at Joan. He almost drops his coffee.

"Hobbies?" Joan prods.

"Nothing interesting. I collected jawbreakers for a while."

"Jawbreakers?" Joan asks.

"The candy."

"Ah." She nods.

"Laurie-girl, you were eight when you collected those," Dad says.

Ryan wisely sets his coffee down before speaking. "Now she just collects wedding invitations." He sucks his breath in as my elbow again connects with his rib cage.

Joan apparently doesn't see any of the physical contact and plods forward. "Wedding invitations?"

"Of the people she—"

I calmly grab Ryan's bicep and pinch. "Of the people I know." I smile while Ryan grimaces. I bat my eyes at him. "Right, Darling?"

"Of course, *Sweetheart.*"

Joan blinks confusedly at Ryan's tone but doesn't comment on it. "I know what it's like, believe me," she says to me.

"What what's like?"

"Being single while everyone else is getting married." She looks at her mug, a gentle smile on her face. "I was twenty-five before I met Gene."

"Gene?" I ask.

"My late husband. By that time all the girls in my circle of friends were married, some with children." She looks up at me, a mischievous glint in her eyes. She doesn't explain it though. "You have time, Laurie. Lots of time."

"We know," Ryan says.

I give him a sideways glance. *"We?"*

Dad pipes in then. "Tell us about your kids, Joan."

Joan smiles maternally. "Josh is twenty-six, and he and his wife, Kerrianne, live in southern Colorado. My daughter, Ruthie, is twenty-five, and she lives with me in the northern area of New Mexico."

"She still lives at home?" Ryan asks.

"No, no. She got married about four months ago to a wonderful young man named Steve. They live a few blocks away." Joan smiles at me. "Actually, you remind me of Ruthie."

"Really?"

"Yes. The hair, the eyes. The way you smile. You two look very similar."

Ryan leans down next to my ear. "Scary thought," he whispers while Dad asks Joan about her neighborhood.

"What?"

"That Joan has a daughter similar to you." He wrinkles his forehead. "I don't think your family can take another Laurie."

Dad finishes his tea and smiles at Joan. "Would you like to meet Laney and Lexi now?"

"I would love to."

They stand. Dad looks at me and Ryan. "Do you want to come with us?"

I squint at the clock above the TV. "You know, Dad, I think we'll stay behind because someone has to pick up the barbecue in half an hour."

He nods, smiling. "Good thinking, Laurie-girl. Whenever you're ready, Joan."

She picks up her purse from the floor and smiles at me. "Laurie, it was such a pleasure to meet you."

"Same here," I say, smiling from the couch.

They leave, Darcy nosing after them.

Ryan keeps sipping his coffee. "So are Laney and Lex coming over for dinner?"

"Yep. And Adam and Nate and Brandon and all the kids."

Ryan raises his eyebrows. "Full house."

"That could be a great name for a TV show." I grin at him. "Want to stay?"

He gives me a look. "Would you like me to?"

"Yes."

"Then, yeah, I'll stay."

"Don't tell Dad, but I'm picking up a cheesecake from Merson's for dessert."

"Evil child."

"Thank you."

He wraps an arm around my shoulders. "So admit it."

"What?"

"Joan Abbot isn't as bad as you imagined."

I shrug. "She's nice. She did like the lemongrass tea though."

Ryan laughs.

"This is bad, Ryan. I will never be able to eat chocolate in my house again."

"Unless you're all by yourself."

I stand and mimic Celine Dion. "Alllll byyyyyy myyyyyself . . ."

"You can be quiet now."

Chapter Twenty-Two

The doorbell rings at 5:20, just as I slide the aluminum container chock-full of barbecue into the oven to stay warm. Ryan goes to answer it, and I hear the unmistakable sound of Jack and Jess.

"Hi, Ryan!" they yell.

"Hey, boys." I can sense Ryan's grin, and a warm, sticky feeling slithers through my chest.

Dorie, my five-year-old niece, comes skipping into the kitchen. "Hi, Auntie Lauren," she sings out. "Look, I got a new dress. Where's Miss Joan?"

"Upstairs unpacking," I tell her, kissing the top of her head.

"Want me to help with dinner, Auntie Lauren?"

I grin at her. Dorie barely comes halfway up on the cabinets.

"Sure," I tell her. "Want to wash some dishes?"

"Okay," she singsongs.

I drag a step stool out of the pantry and set it up in front of the sink, which is littered with our mugs from earlier and a few utensils.

Dorie gets right to work, and Laney comes into the kitchen a minute later, hefting baby Allie in her baby carrier.

"Hey, Lauren," she says, setting the baby on the kitchen table and coming over to kiss my check. "Smells wonderful."

"I slaughtered the cow this morning, so it's good and fresh."

Dorie looks up from the sink. "Mommy, what's slaughtered?"

Laney sends me a look. "Good going," she tells me. She looks at Dorie. "Nothing, Sweetheart. Auntie Lauren's just joking."

Dorie wrinkles her nose. "Auntie Lauren jokes a lot."

"Yes, well, we all have our failings." I smile, unlatching Allie's seat belt and picking up the wide-eyed baby.

There's nothing in life that makes me melt more than holding a newborn baby. They're so soft and warm and look at you so trustingly.

I hold her closer. Allie is the prettiest baby ever, with sweet little cheeks, big, dark blue eyes, and soft, wispy blonde hair.

"Hi, Precious," I whisper softly, brushing my lips against her warm forehead. She blinks at me, staring at my face. "You're beautiful." I kiss her cheek.

The doorbell rings again, and I look up to see Ryan's back disappearing for the door. Laney leans against the counter, grinning. "That boy is falling hard," she declares in a low voice. "He just stood there staring dumbly at you."

I blush.

Lexi comes into the kitchen and sets a big bowl filled with salad on the counter.

"Hey, everyone," she says, running a hand through her hair and yawning.

"Auntie Lexi!" Dorie yells.

"Hey, Kid." Lexi grins, ruffling Dorie's hair. "Your Auntie Laurie's already put you to work?"

Dorie nods solemnly.

I shake my head. "That's it, Dorie. You can no longer hang out with me."

She grins impishly.

Joan comes down the stairs and smiles at us girls. "Kitchen is for girls only?"

"Trust me, you don't want any of the guys in here," Lexi says.

Laney bursts into laughter. "Hey, remember that time when Nate and Adam decided they'd fix us dinner?"

I gag. "They even messed up Mac 'n Cheese. The boxed kind. I have never seen anyone mess up instant macaroni and cheese before."

"It was terrible," Lexi tells Joan.

"What can I do to help?" Joan asks.

"Well," I say, shifting Allie. "Dorie's washing the dishes, the barbecue's ready when we are, I mixed up coleslaw, Lexi brought salad, and there are baked beans in the oven, so . . . nothing, I guess."

Laney smiles at me and Allie. "I think my daughter likes you."

"Well, she's named after me."

"And me," Lexi says, coming over and smoothing Allie's wisps. "My turn," she says.

"I don't think so," I counter, turning slightly away. "You look good, Laney." I change the subject.

She rubs a hand down her flatter stomach. "Thank you. It's nice to be able to fit through doorways."

"Brandon here yet?" I ask.

Lexi shakes her head. "No, but Ryan is." She grins evilly at me.

I stick my tongue out at her.

"Mommy, why did Auntie Lauren stick her tongue out at Auntie Lexi?" Dorie pipes up.

I close my eyes. "I'm never having children." Then I remember. "Hey! I think Brandon's taking Hannah out tonight. He may not even come."

Laney snorts. "Brandon? Miss a family gathering? With barbecue? Get real, Honey. He'll probably just bring Hannah here."

"Hannah is your coworker, right?" Joan says.

"Right." I nod.

Ryan walks into the kitchen, comes over, and calmly takes Allie from me.

"Hey!" I yell. "That's *my* niece."

He lays her casually over his shoulder like he handles babies every day. "Well, it's my turn," he says.

"Sorry, mister, I was here first," Lexi says.

Ryan smiles at her. "Sorry." He rubs Allie's back and kisses her head. "She's beautiful, Laney."

"Thanks, Ryan. You can hold her as long as you want. Lexi held her all day today."

"What about Mikey?" I ask, referring to the nickname we gave Allie's twin brother.

"Adam hasn't set him down yet."

Ryan chuckles.

I hear the front door open.

"Uncle Brandon!" Jack and Jess yell. "Will you play wif us and Uncle Nate?"

"Sure," Brandon says, coming into the kitchen, Hannah behind him.

Ryan smiles at me.

"Hey, guys," Brandon says. He walks over and sticks his hand out to Joan. "Ma'am." He grins. "I'm Brandon, Adam's brother. This is my girlfriend, Hannah."

Suddenly I'm very glad I'm not holding Allie. I would have dropped her at that statement. I sag against the kitchen table.

Joan shakes his hand, smiling. "Nice to meet you, Brandon, Hannah."

Hannah shakes her hand as well. "Hi." She comes and takes Allie from Ryan.

"Hey!" Ryan protests.

"Go play with the other boys," Hannah tells him, cuddling the baby close.

I still stare slack-jawed at Hannah.

Ryan narrows his eyes at her, grins at me, and leaves.

"That boy's in love," Lexi states loudly.

"What boy?" Brandon turns.

"Dinner's ready!" I yell, interrupting Lexi's response.

She rolls her eyes at me. "You can run, but you cannot hide," she warns.

I pull the baked beans and the barbecue from the oven while Joan finds the coleslaw in the fridge.

"Spoons?" she asks.

"Second drawer on the left."

Hannah kisses Allie's brow. "Laney, can I keep her?"

"Sure," Laney says.

"But, Mommy, I thought she was going to be my sister," Dorie protests.

Joan puts serving spoons in the bowls and looks around at everyone talking at once, her gaze finally landing on me. "Are family gatherings always this loud and confusing?" she asks.

I peel the aluminum lid off the barbecue and grin. "You'll get used to it."

She blinks and her face softens, interpreting the message I just sent her: *You're welcome here.* Coming over, she gives me a gentle hug and smoothes my hair like my mother used to. "Thank you, Laurie."

After dinner is eaten and cleaned up, Dorie, Jess, and Jack scuttle to the guest room to play with the stash of toys Dad has there, and all the rest of us go into the living room.

Ryan drops to the floor beside me and leans back against the fire place hearth. "Thanks for feeding me, Laur."

"You're welcome, Ry." I smile at the baby twins, fast asleep in their carriers. Laney sits down beside Adam on the love seat. Dad takes his chair, Lexi and Nate sit on one couch, and Brandon, Hannah, and Joan take the other.

Laney pulls her knees to her chest. "I love not being pregnant."

Adam chuckles. "Good. Because we're never getting pregnant again. Five kids is all one man can stand, I think."

She grins.

"I don't know, man," Nate says, loud as ever, one arm around his wife. "My cousin Abner and his wife have eleven kids."

"Your cousin's name is Abner?" Hannah asks, forehead creased.

"Would that be Fern's son?" I ask.

Nate nods. "Yep. One and the same."

Joan is laughing. "You guys definitely have the prize for the oddest family I've ever come in contact with."

Brandon grins proudly. "Why, thank you."

Lexi pats Nate's leg. "Which is why we've decided against reproducing."

Brandon nods. "Good, good."

I shake my head and lean back, half against the fireplace and half against Ryan. "You guys will have kids," I predict. "You like babies too much not to."

"But see, Laurie," Nate says. "Between Laney's kids, your kids, and Brandon's kids, we'll have our fill of babies."

"Maybe you haven't noticed this, Nate, but I'm not married."

He gives Ryan a glance, and Ryan grins.

A change in topic is needed here. Quickly!

Hannah sees my distress and takes charge. "What's your favorite movie, Joan?"

"I guess I'll admit it. *Pride and Prejudice.*"

Hannah and I both gasp.

"You've heard of it?" Joan smiles.

"Heard of it?" I say.

"We love it," Hannah gushes. "Love it, love it."

"You're kidding," Joan says.

I shake my head. "Not at all."

"I remember reading the book as a child. When they released the BBC/A&E version, I fell in love with it. They released it right after my husband died." She smiles whimsically. "My daughter and I would watch it together to escape."

"So how old were you when the book came out?" Nate asks.

Lexi hits Nate on the head. "That came out in the nineteenth century," she chastises.

"Don't mind me, Joan. I'm clueless," he says.

"What's your favorite scene in the movie?" Hannah asks.

Joan lets her breath out. "That's a tough one, but I'm going to have to go with the lakeside scene at Pemberley when Mr. Darcy finds Elizabeth at his house."

"That's my favorite scene too!" I shout.

"Listen, Laur, if you're going to lean against me, you'll to have to cut the jumping," Ryan says.

I grin at Joan. "We'll watch it then. The three of us," I say to Hannah.

Darcy flops into the room then, coming from the guest room.

"Kids wear you out?" Dad asks my dog, rubbing his ears. I swear Darcy nods, then turns and falls to the floor next to me.

"So your dog is named after Jane Austen's character?" Joan asks. "I wondered."

"Fitzwilliam Darcy." I nod.

Joan grins, and the conversation solidifies my earlier feelings.

I like this woman!

———⊕———

By eleven forty-five everyone is gone. Joan is already asleep in the guest room upstairs beside my bedroom; Dad's in his room down the hall from the living room.

I flick the TV off, yawning. I just found out from Stacy and Clinton on *What Not to Wear* that I'm not wearing the right clothes. No new information. Lexi tells me this all the time.

I climb the stairs, brush my teeth, and fall into bed ten minutes later. I pull my Bible over, rubbing a hand through my hair.

I'm remembering the day's events and smiling. *Thanks, Lord. Joan's pretty special, actually.* I bite my bottom lip. *Will they get married? I know You are sovereign and all, but, God, that's a little scary. A new mom? I don't know if I can handle that.*

I look down at Psalm 100. "Know that the Lord is God. It is he who made us, and we are his; we are his people, the sheep of his pasture."

Okay, Lord. I get that You're in charge. But seriously, this is starting to freak me out.

"For the Lord is good and his love endures forever; his faithfulness continues through all generations."

I smile and let my breath out. *Wow. How quickly I forget that You are not just sovereign; You are also a God of love.*

I turn off the light and fall asleep.

———⊕———

Monday afternoon I go through the door at Merson's and grin at Hallie as I step up to the counter.

"Hey, Laurie," she greets, holding an order pad.

"Hi, Hallie." I look around. "Where's Shawn?"

"He's home sick."

"He's *sick*? Shawn's never sick!"

She shrugs, fiddling with the pen. "He sounded really congested on the phone. I told him to stay home. It could be a cold."

I frown. "In the middle of summer? This is terrible! Poor guy."

"I took him some chicken soup earlier, and he didn't look too bad." She pauses and swallows. "Anyway, what did you want to eat?"

"Wait a second. Hold on," I say, waving my hands. "You took him soup?"

She nods once.

"To his house?"

She sighs now. "Yes, Laurie."

I purse my lips as I think. Soup, empty house, sickly man . . . it all sounds vaguely like a movie I've seen, but I can't remember the title.

"Okay, Florence. I'd like a cup of coffee and a brownie, please."

She scribbles the order down. "Florence?"

"Nightingale."

"Aren't you supposed to be at work?"

I sip the coffee. "Nope. I have the next two days off because my future stepmother is in town."

Hallie brightens immediately. "Joan Abbot is in town? How come I haven't met her yet? Where is she?"

"She's out on a tour of the town with Dad. Don't worry, they're meeting me here. You'll get to meet her."

Her eyes squinch in a grin. "Shawn will be so disappointed that he didn't get to meet her."

"You look happy about that."

She hands me the brownie. "Well, now I have something to rub in his face."

"Evil girl."

"Chocoholic."

"Good. We're even."

She grins, and I find a table near the windows so I can watch for Dad and Joan.

Joan has been here two days. Yesterday morning she made us cinnamon rolls before church. Homemade! From scratch! With sugar!

I decided she and Dad can get married next month in a small backyard wedding. Her colors will be blue and white, and she can carry pink roses.

Dad pulls into the parking lot and stops. Joan climbs out the passenger side and laughs at something Dad says.

Dad looks different. Happy. Relaxed. He even had a cup of *blackberry* tea today instead of lemongrass.

They open the door and I wave.

"Beautiful town," Joan says, sitting next to me. She smiles. "Okay, Laurie, I hear this is your favorite place to eat. What's good?"

"Everything." I lift my coffee mug. "Coffee's excellent, and the desserts are fabulous."

She watches me bite into the massive brownie. "There goes my diet."

"Did you decide what you want, Joan?" Dad asks, waving to Hallie.

Joan squints at the menu, strung up above the cash register. "Do they have tea?"

Dad nods. "Any kind you can imagine."

"Black tea and a brownie, please."

Dad's eyes crinkle in a smile. "Sure." He leaves to order and Joan turns to me, smoothing her khakis.

"You like brownies?" I ask, in shock.

"No," she says. "I *love* brownies. My daughter, Ruthie, had to clean out my pantry for me after I decided to start dieting. I would have eaten the chocolate if I'd found it."

"I'd like to meet your daughter."

"I'm sure you will. Eventually."

I study her expression as she watches Dad order.

"Hey, Joan?"

"Yes, Dear?"

I take another swallow of my coffee and lean down, lowering my voice. "Do you like my dad?"

She smiles, her eyes twinkling, laugh wrinkles appearing by her mouth. "Yes, Laurie, I do."

I nod. "I think he likes you."

She pats my hand. "He's very concerned about you."

I frown. "Me?"

"He said you didn't take the singles' conference idea well."

"Because it was *weird*."

She laughs.

Dad comes back to the table holding two cups of tea. Hallie is right behind him with a brownie.

"There you go, Joan," Dad says, handing her the mug.

"Oh, painted ceramic mugs. How unique!"

Hallie gives her the brownie, smiling. "Thanks. Shawn had some of the kids at the elementary school paint them."

I chew my brownie, noting the way Hallie says Shawn's name.

Sweetly.

I grin.

Hallie sees my look, shoots me a "Shut up" glare, and smiles at Joan. "I'm Hallie," she introduces herself.

"Joan Abbot. Nice to meet you. Shawn is your husband?"

Hallie starts coughing. "Uh, no, no. He's not . . . that is to say, we're not . . . he's . . ." She wrings her hands together. "No."

"He owns this place," I say, swallowing.

Needless to say, I'm relishing this.

Joan is good at getting this Confession of Love!

Joan's eyes twinkle mischievously. "Then you are his sister? Hallie Merson? I like that name."

"No, no, no," Hallie corrects, blushing. "Hallie Forbes. I just work here with him."

"Well, it's good to meet you, Dear. This tea smells lovely."

"Thanks. I'll just be behind the counter." She makes a run for it.

The moment she is out of earshot, Joan leans toward me and says, "That girl's in love."

"I put them together," I whisper.

Joan nods. "Good job. Is this one of those hobbies Ryan was talking about?"

I grin sheepishly. "Um, yeah."

Dad sets down his lemongrass tea.

Blegh.

"I really wish she wouldn't do it," he tells Joan. "Nothing good can come from meddling."

Joan nods. "Oh, I absolutely agree."

I shrink down in my chair.

We finish eating, and Joan asks if she can ride back with me. Dad grins proudly.

"Sure." I smile.

She closes the passenger door and turns to me. "Okay, tell me everything," she says, buckling up.

"Everything?"

"Shawn and Hallie? Did you introduce them?"

I turn the ignition and stare at her. "I thought you didn't approve of matchmaking."

"If anyone asks, I don't. I don't approve of it or practice it. But if anyone looked hard enough, they'd see that I not only introduced both of my children to their future spouses, but I've also basically arranged three other weddings."

I start laughing.

"So tell me about Shawn and Hallie."

"They're perfect for each other."

Joan smiles. "Hallie seems like a nice girl."

"She is."

"Her hair is beautiful."

"Yeah, it is."

"She makes a good cup of tea too."

"I bet."

"So how much do you like Ryan?"

I blink. "I'm sorry?"

"Sweetheart, anyone can tell that he really likes you. I'm just curious about how you feel," Joan says.

I look at her, narrowing my gaze. "You arranged both of your kids' weddings?"

"Yes, I did," Joan says proudly.

I stop at a red light and stare at her.

"So?" she asks.

"So what?"

"Tell me about Ryan. He's such a sweet boy. Seems to love the Lord too. Which is very important."

"Well, he, uh . . . yeah, um . . ."

The light turns green and I press the gas, trying not to read too much into that *mm-hmm* expression on Joan's face.

What is going on here? I am the matchmaker of this family, yes?

I pull into our driveway and hop out. Lexi's car is parked in my place in the garage. This is Lexi's way of driving me insane.

"Lex!" I yell, going into the house, Joan following me.

"Kitchen!" she yells back.

I walk into the kitchen and find her measuring coffee into the coffeepot. She looks up. "Hey, Baby."

"You're in my spot."

Her eyes widen. "No, really?"

Joan chuckles and sits down at the kitchen table. "Hi, Lexi."

"Hi, Joan, how are you?"

"Fine, thank you."

Lexi keeps counting the scoops. "Put some in there for me," I tell her, slinging my backpack on the counter.

"You just had coffee and you're having more?" Joan asks.

Lexi finishes and grins at Joan. "You'll learn this about Laurie, Joan. There is no amount of coffee that is too much."

"So what are you doing here, Sis?" I ask, sitting on the counter.

"Nate took today off, and he and Ryan are out buying peat moss. I got bored sitting at my house, so I decided to see what you were up to."

"You went to Laney's first, didn't you?" I ask.

Lexi sighs. "They weren't home."

I have to laugh. "Poor little Lexi."

"What? I have yet to hold Mikey. I would like at some point to be introduced to my nephew."

Joan smiles a little self-satisfied smile and folds her hands together on the table. Lexi and I exchange a look, then attack.

"You got to hold him?" Lexi shouts.

"When?" I ask.

"Yes and Saturday night," Joan replies smugly.

"I don't believe this!" Lexi yells. "Who let you hold him?"

"Adam."

"What?" I shriek. "He hasn't set him down yet!"

Joan nods, calm despite our rising volume. "I gave the man three glasses of iced tea and stood around waiting."

Lexi and I both start shaking our heads.

"When he decided he needed to take care of business, I told him I could hold the baby while he was in there."

Lexi clicks her tongue. "Joan Abbot, you are too smart for this family."

I bow from the waist, hands outstretched. "You are good," I tell her.

Joan watches, one eyebrow raised. "I can't imagine raising even the two of you alone," she remarks.

Lexi hits the power button on the coffeemaker and shrugs. "It wasn't boring."

Joan chuckles. "No, I would guess not."

Chapter Twenty-Three

Brandon opens the glass door of his studio on Wednesday morning, marches over to Hannah's empty desk, upon which I sit, and takes my face in his hands.

"Who am I?" he demands.

I blink at him. "Is this a trick question?"

"Laurie. No. Who am I?"

I mash my lips together before answering. "Brandon?"

"What am I?"

"Human?"

He sighs, lets go of my face, and leans against Hannah's desk. "I meant on a deeper level, Nutsy."

I frown at him. His hair is a disheveled mess, he hasn't shaved this morning, and I swear those khakis aren't clean.

"Um, Brandon?"

He looks up at me. "Yeah?"

"What's going on?"

"What do you mean?"

I grab his face. "Who am I?" I ask, deepening my voice.

He smiles.

"See?"

He pulls away. "Do you think I'm husband material?"

I snort. Not very becoming, I know, but it carries the appropriate message. "Nope," I say cheerfully.

He gives me a look.

"I mean, yes. Absolutely. I think you'll be the best husband in the nation, and the president himself will give you a badge that says—"

"Laurie!"

"What, Brandon?"

He covers his eyes, grinning. "To think I've put up with this for sixteen years."

I smile at him.

He pushes himself off the desk and faces me. "Okay. I need an honest answer now. Do you think I'll make a good husband?"

"To the right person? Yes."

His face crumples. "Well, how do I know if she's the right person?"

"She is." I pat his shoulder.

"You don't even know who I'm talking about."

"Brandon, please."

One corner of his mouth curls. "Okay, maybe you do."

"Trust God, Brandon." I hop off the desk and give him a hug. "You're going to be a great husband," I tell his shirt. "Know how I know?"

"How?"

"Because you're a great best friend."

He pushes me back to arm's length and looks at me. "It'll be weird having another person hanging out with us."

"Not weird. Just different." I manage a smile.

"Our classic debates will have another voice."

I laugh, but tears are stinging my eyelids. "Honey, I don't think another person could be heard during one of our debates."

He smiles gently at me and pulls me back into the hug. "I love you, Kid. You know that, right?"

I sniff a response.

This is my basically brother here. Thinking *marriage.*

It is one of those "I'm glad this day came but not" moments.

"Then I have your blessing?" Brandon asks after a minute.

"Do you need my blessing?"

"No. But I'd like to have it anyway."

I blink, my mouth drops open, and I push him away. "We just quoted *Pride and Prejudice!*"

Brandon gives me a look. "Not possible, Nutsy. I've never seen the movie."

"But we did! We were almost word for word!"

He grins. "Guess you've rubbed off on me."

"Guess so."

"So?

"So what?"

"Do we have to do this all over again?"

"Oh! Yes, yes. Marry Hannah. Please."

His grin widens. "You think we can handle having her around?"

"I think the question would be, do you two think you can handle having me around?"

"Oh, right."

I pat his cheek. "I'm happy, Brandon, really. My best friend and my almost-best friend getting hitched."

"What more could you ask for?" he drolls, rolling his eyes dramatically.

"What more? How about a Mustang convertible with beige leather interior and metallic blue—"

"I was being sarcastic," he interrupts.

I grin.

"So you really think she's the right one?" he asks again.

"Goodness, Brandon!"

"Sorry. It's just I've been praying about this, and I think . . ."

The door opens and Hannah walks in, yawning.

"Morn-mpgh," she mumbles. "Sorry I'm late." She sets her purse on the desk and rubs her eyes. "Lucky chewed the cord to my alarm clock."

"Sure, blame it on the dog," I say, waving a hand. "I'm in Studio Two today. I think Newton has Studio Three. Let me know when the Morrises get here."

"Hey, Laur, did Joan get off okay?" Brandon calls after me.

"Yeah, she called last night to let us know she's at her house." I smile. "I like her." I point my finger at Brandon. "And I know you'll be a very good friend and not say—"

"Told you so," Brandon interrupts.

I roll my eyes and go into the studio, closing the door until it's open just a crack.

Call me Eavesdropper.

"Did I tell you good morning?" Brandon asks Hannah.

She smiles tiredly. "No."

He leans down and kisses her.

I close the door with a barely perceptible *click*. I walk over to the sofa and sit, grinning.

That display, folks, is a good six months of heavy-duty work, lots of prayer, long hours, and poor pay. From the moment I met Hannah (okay, well, not *the* moment), I knew the fates of her and Brandon were designed by God to be together.

I pull my cell phone from my pocket and dial Ryan.

"Score!" I yell when he answers.

He is quiet for a minute. "Okay, knowing you," he starts, "this could be good or bad."

"Brandon and Hannah are kissing."

"Again?"

"And today, strictly off the record, Brandon asked me if I thought he'd be a good husband."

"Really?" Ryan asks, and I can hear the smile in his voice.

"Really."

"So what did you say?"

"I told him no."

"No? Why not? I think he'll be great."

"I'm kidding, Ry. So what are you up to?"

"Today, Lauren Emma Holbrook, I am finishing at Mrs. Galen's house."

"Yay!"

"Exactly."

"Are you there now?"

"I was getting ready to get out of the truck when you called. Why?"

"Call me Curious."

I am beginning to sound very *Moby Dick* here.

He laughs. "Would Curious like to join me for lunch?"

"Curious would, thank you."

"Pick you up at one-ish?"

"Sounds good."

"Later, Laur."

I hang up and peek through the door again. Hannah sits at her desk alone, sipping from a thermos.

I open the door. "Morrises still aren't here?"

"Nope."

I walk over and hop on her desk. "When I get married . . . well, if I get married," I start, staring out the window, "I want to walk down the aisle carrying a basket filled with coffee beans and Hershey bars."

Hannah just about spits out her coffee.

"Don't you think that would be romantic?" I am gushing.

She wipes her mouth and blinks away tears. "Laurie, warn me before you say stuff like that."

"What? I think it would be fun. It'd be different."

She nods, one eyebrow raised. "Yes, it would."

"Fine, Miss Traditional, what do you want to carry? Roses?"

Hannah cups her chin in her hands and leans her elbows on the desk. "Mmm. My favorite flowers are tulips. I'd carry tulips."

I raise my hands, palms up. "Good and boring, no offense. At least say they aren't pink."

She shakes her head. "Not pink. I like the ones that are that dark orange with the yellow at the tips."

I smile. "Well, see? That's different."

"Am I still boring?"

"Of course not." I angle my head at her. "You're not having your bridesmaids wear orange, are you?"

She grins.

"Hannah . . . *Darling*, perhaps I'm being presumptuous. . . ."

"About what, Laurie Dear?"

"But as one of your best friends . . ."

She holds up a hand. "Make that *the* best friend," she says.

"Okay. As your best friend, I have to tell you that I look similar to that lady who played Miracle Max's wife when I wear orange."

Hannah starts laughing.

I grin at her. Now that she has caffeine in her system, her eyes are perking up, and she looks a little less than half-dead.

Her long hair shimmers down her back, her blue eyes are set off by the baby blue tank top she wears, and I decide she is the prettiest girl I've ever seen.

"What?" she asks, watching me stare.

I shake my head. "Nothing."

—◦❖◦—

At twelve thirty I escort my twelve o'clock out the door, and Brandon pounces on me. "I need you in my office," he whispers.

I look around. "Where's Hannah?"

"Bathroom. Get in my office quickly."

"Brandon, I have to meet Ryan in—"

"Shut up and get in my office!"

I sprint down the hall.

He closes the door behind me. "Okay," he says, going around his desk and flopping into his chair. "I need your help."

I crawl up on his desk. "Help with what?"

He steeples his fingers and purses his lips at me. "You're female."

"Thank you for noticing."

"So you know more about this kind of stuff."

"Like what? PMS? Periods?"

He flushes a deeper red than I've ever seen on him. "No, no, no." He waves his hand.

I grin.

"Diamonds," he whispers, leaning closer.

I mimic him and lean closer as well. "Diamonds," I copy.

He blows out a breath and nods. "Like engagement rings."

My grin grows.

"Could this be for a certain secretary I know?"

He blushes again. "Possibly."

"When do you need this diamond?"

He looks at me, his eyes twinkling, a huge smile on his face. "The last Saturday of the month."

"Why the last Saturday of the month?"

"That gives me two and a half weeks to plan it."

I nod. "Okay."

"Can you come shopping with me this Saturday?"

"Words I've never heard you utter."

He grins again. "There's a first time for everything, Nutsy. Please?"

I pat his cheek and climb off the desk. "Sure can. Oh, and something I learned this morning. Tulips are her favorite flower."

"Tulips," Brandon repeats slowly. "Which ones are those?"

I stare at him for a minute before opening the door. "Listen, I'll take care of the flowers, okay?"

He sighs with relief. "Thanks, Laur."

"Anytime, Kid."

Ryan stands in the lobby, chatting with Hannah. "So it was okay," he is saying. "I just wouldn't recommend it." He smiles at me. "Hey, Laur."

"Hi, Ry. You wouldn't recommend what?"

Hannah answers. "*Cheaper by the Dozen*. I'm trying to come up with movies for Brandon and me to rent tonight."

"How about *Emma*?" I grin, digging my backpack out of the cubbyhole.

"Tried that one before. It didn't work."

Ryan makes a face. "And who can blame him?"

"Hey!" I say. "That's a good movie."

"Mm-hmm. See you later, Hannah." Ryan smiles, opening the door.

"Bye, guys. Have a good lunch."

Ryan drives to Vizzini's and comes around and opens my door. "Why, thank you," I say, sliding out.

"You're welcome."

We get seated right away, and a blonde waitress I haven't seen before takes our drink orders.

After she leaves, Ryan puts his menu down and grins widely at me.

"What?" I say.

He doesn't answer, just keeps grinning.

"Ryan? What is it?"

His dimples are showing.

This is getting annoying.

"I know something you don't know," he singsongs.

Arrg. The classic "I like to annoy you" maneuver.

I retaliate with disinterest. "Oh really?" I say mildly, unfolding my napkin on my lap. "That's nice."

He smirks.

"She sure is taking a long time with the drinks," I say, mentally going over everything it could possibly be. I'm the one who told him about Hannah and Brandon, so it's not that. It could be something about Lexi, since Ryan sees my sister more than I do. Or it could be about Nick and Ruby.

"I . . . hope they bring . . . bread . . ." I mumble, thinking.

Ryan starts laughing. "Go ahead and admit it."

I sigh dejectedly. "I . . ."

"Keep going."

"Would like . . ."

"Mm-hmm."

"To know!" I cover my face with my hands.

He grins. "That was hard for you, wasn't it?" he taunts.

"You're mean."

"I know."

I narrow my eyes at him and he laughs again.

"Okay, okay," he says.

"What is it?" I bounce in my seat and lean forward.

He leans forward as well. "I can't tell."

"What?" I shriek.

He laughs harder.

"That's so mean!"

"Again, I know."

"Cruel, cruel, cruel!"

He holds up his hands. "But I know you'll find out tonight."

I glare at him.

Wait a second. Tonight is Wednesday night. Bible study. I fold my hands together, thinking.

Someone is either getting married or pregnant. Those are generally the big announcements at the singles' Bible study.

Ironic, huh?

"Who's getting married or pregnant?" I ask.

His mouth curls in a grin.

"Please tell me, Ryan." I blink big Bambi eyes at him.

"I can't, Honey. I promised I'd let them tell you."

"Then why'd you torture me like this?"

He frowns, thinking. "Because it's fun?"

"ARRG!"

Blondie shows up with the drinks. "Ready to order?" she croons to Ryan, batting her eyelashes at him.

It takes a very secure woman to flirt with a man on a date with someone else.

Ryan doesn't even blink in her direction. "The number four, please."

"My favorite," she murmurs.

"Sweetheart?" he drawls. "What do you want?" He reaches over and picks up my hand.

"The number twelve." I smile at Blondie.

She doesn't answer me, writes it down, and leaves.

I turn to Ryan. "I think you just broke her heart."

He squeezes my hand. "She'll probably get over it."

I smile, a thousand little Smurfs running around in my stomach.

Ryan is hard to stay mad at.

Of course.

"So tell me your latest verse on delight. Go," Ryan commands.

I nod. "'When your words came, I ate them; they were my joy and my heart's delight, for I bear your name, O Lord God Almighty.' Jeremiah 15:16."

Ryan grins. "Good one."

"Thank you." I balance my chin on my fists. "Want to know why I like that word so much?"

"What word?"

"Delight."

He's still smiling. "Sure."

"Because it means to be greatly pleased or experiencing a lot of pleasure."

He nods. "And?"

I grin. "And it sounds Jane-Austen-y."

"I knew it!"

I shake my head. "You know me way too well."

⌒~⊕~⌒

I dig through my closet later that night, yank out a bright red T-shirt, and replace my semi-nice sleeveless sweater with it. One does not wear work attire around single guys holding drinks that stain . . . unless one doesn't like the work attire.

In this case, though, I like the sweater.

I redo my mascara, try to smooth the ends of my hair, give up, run downstairs, and plow directly into Dad.

"Laurie-girl!"

"Sorry, Dad. Are you okay?"

He nods, mouth tight. "Have a good time tonight."

"You too, Dad. Your turn to call?"

He grins. "Mm-hmm."

I smile back. He and Joan decided to take turns calling each other every night.

I think it is sweet, in a sort of disturbing way.

"Okay, well, I need to go, Dad."

He gives me a hug. "Don't speed."

I gape. "But, Dad, how else am I supposed to meet Keanu Reeves?"

"Good-bye, Laurie," Dad says, walking away.

"Bye."

~…◈…~

I drive to Nick and Ruby's house and park behind Holly and Luke's little red sedan. I open the front door without knocking. Knocking or ringing the doorbell is a sign of a newcomer.

"Hey, Laur," Nick says, smiling pastorally.

"Hey. Where's Ruby?"

"Fixing her hair."

I nod and go down the hallway to the master bedroom, through the impossibly neat room, and knock on the open bathroom door.

Ruby looks over, holding a curling iron. "Hi, Laurie."

"Hey."

I sit on the edge of the whirlpool tub behind her and smile.

She smiles back and curls another strand of hair before turning around and asking, "Are you okay?"

"Are you?"

"Should I not be?"

She curls another piece of hair.

I study the reflection of her face in the mirror. If she is glowing, she's covered it up with makeup.

Her eyes meet mine in the mirror and she laughs. "Okay, Laurie, whatever it is, just ask."

"Okay." I take a deep breath. "Are you pregnant?"

I expect her mouth to drop open, then laugh, then deny it, then go on curling.

Instead, she sets the curling iron down and turns around. "What?"

"Are you pregnant?" I ask again.

She looks at me for a long minute before her mouth curves in a smile. "Ryan?"

"Ryan what?"

"Ryan said something, didn't he? He couldn't keep a secret if his life depended on it."

"Ryan didn't tell me you were pregnant."

"He didn't?"

"Are you?" I ask, blinking.

She smiles and sits down beside me, a sweet look on her pretty face. "I'm four weeks along."

"Did . . . you . . . oh my gosh!" I yell, throwing my arms around her. "You are? Really? You're pregnant? With a baby?" I shriek.

She laughs and hugs me. "Most pregnant people typically are." She grins.

"Four weeks?"

She watches me and laughs. "You can stop counting. I got pregnant on our honeymoon."

I grin. "Wow."

She nods.

"That's kids really fast, Ruby."

"Trust me, Honey, I know."

"Can you handle that?"

"Guess God thinks I can, right?"

I stare at her waistline, knowing that inside there is a little person God placed there.

Weird feeling.

Ruby keeps talking. "But then I figure both Nick and I are in our thirties. I'd rather have kids now than wait until it's harder to get pregnant."

I nod.

She puts a hand on my arm. "But you can't tell anyone, okay? I don't want the group to know until I'm farther along." She bites her lip. "When you're in your thirties, miscarriages are more frequent."

"Yeah, sure, keep it quiet. I can do that. Unlike your brother, I can keep a secret."

She smiles, her eyes twinkling. "I know. That's why I decided I could tell you."

"Baby, we're starting!" Nick yells from the hallway.

Ruby stands and flicks a hand through her hair. "Remember?"

"Quiet." I grin.

"Wipe that smirk off your face, Laur, or everyone will know."

I mash my lips together.

We walk into the living room, the usual crowd there, most of the kids sprawling on beanbag chairs. Ryan pats a seat beside him on the sofa.

I sit down and he leans close to my ear, wrapping an arm around me. "So she told you?" he asks.

"I didn't say anything," I whisper back.

"You didn't have to. Stop smiling."

I grin wider. "I can't."

Nick shoos a guy about twenty-two with straggly, college-kid hair off the couch and helps Ruby sit down.

I look at Ryan. "Well, that right there gave it away."

He frowns. "Why? He was just being polite."

"At the party last week Ruby sat on one of the beanbag chairs."

"So?"

"So this week that's not good enough. Talk has started." I point to a legion of girls on one sofa who all start twittering.

Ryan shakes his head.

Nick takes his place in front of the group and opens his Bible. "All right, today we're continuing our short break from the life of Christ to look at Psalm 127."

I open my Bible, find the passage, and clamp a hand over my mouth. Ryan sees it and closes his eyes.

Nick starts, "'Unless the Lord builds the house, its builders labor in vain. Unless the Lord watches over the city, the watchmen stand guard in vain. In vain you rise early and stay up late, toiling for food to eat—for he grants sleep to those he loves.'"

The girls on the sofa start snickering as they read ahead of him.

"'Sons are a heritage from the Lord, children a reward from him. Like arrows in the hands of a warrior are sons born in one's youth. Blessed is the man whose quiver is full of them. They will not be put to shame when they contend with their enemies in the gate.'"

I look over at Ruby, who is shaking her head, a half-annoyed, half-amused expression on her face.

Beside me, Ryan is shuddering with silent laughter, one hand over his face.

The moment Bible study is over, a crowd of girls descend on Ruby like a pack of overly giddy, perfumed wolves.

Ryan watches them. "I feel for her," he says after a minute.

"Not enough, I guess, because you're still sitting here."

He grins.

Hannah comes over, wearing a frown. "Maybe I'm reading too much into this," she starts. "But Nick helped Ruby sit down, taught on a passage about parenthood, and prayed for all the unborn children." She cocks her head. "Is Ruby pregnant?"

I just laugh.

Chapter Twenty-Four

Saturday morning the front door opens at ten thirty on the dot. Brandon comes in, whistling and swinging his keys around his finger.

"You could try knocking," I tell him, slightly irritated.

"You could try locking the door if you care that much," he returns easily. He notices my pajamas and frowns. "You're not ready?"

"No, I'm not ready. You said eleven thirty, Brandon!"

"I did?"

"Yes! Like three times! And then I clarified. Like three times!" I throw my hands up.

He shrugs. "Ah, well. So I'm early. It's not like I've never seen you in your pj's before, Nutsy."

I cover my face. "Go sit in the living room and watch cartoons or something. I'll go get dressed."

Dad comes in from the kitchen, sipping a cup of tea. "Brandon," he says and smiles.

"Hello, sir."

"What are you doing here?"

"Laurie and I are going shopping."

I climb the stairs, and their conversation fades out. I change into jeans and a T-shirt and go into the bathroom to fix my hair.

Bless his heart, Brandon's so excited.

I grin evilly at myself in the mirror. He obviously has never been jewelry shopping before.

Thirty-five minutes later, my hair looks as good as it will without a haircut, and I go back downstairs.

Brandon and Dad are still talking.

"The business is growing, so I'm looking into investing some of the profits," Brandon says.

Dad nods and sips his tea. "Wise idea."

"What did you invest in with your Internet company?"

"Mutual funds."

"Really?"

"Sure."

"Could you . . . do you think we could set up a meeting and you could coach me through some of this?" Brandon asks.

Dad nods, smiling. "Of course, Son. Any time that works for you."

Brandon looks up and sees me. "I'll give you a call Monday when I'm looking at my calendar."

"Sounds good. You two have fun."

"We will, Dad." I kiss his cheek and open the front door.

Brandon backs out of the driveway. "Okay, so we're looking for a ring."

"We are?"

"Funny, Laur. Where do I go?"

"How about the mall?"

He makes a face. "The mall? I hope she's worth this."

"I hope that comment was a joke."

He grins. "Did you find out what kind she wants?"

I smile and cross my arms over my chest proudly. "First tell me I'm good."

"You're good."

"Thank you. And, yes. Ruby, Hannah, and I went to lunch, and I told Ruby I liked her ring." I shrug. "The rest was simple."

Brandon frowns. "It was?"

"Sure. Ruby's ring is the standard gold band with a round-cut diamond."

The frown hasn't left. "So?"

"So I said I liked it because it was simple, and Hannah said she liked it but she wants a white-gold band with one diamond on the engagement ring and diamonds around the wedding ring."

He smiles at me. "You're good."

I grin.

He parks, and I drag him into the mall and over to Hayley's, a local jewelry store.

I point through the glass. "There's one like she wants."

Brandon glances at it. "Okay. Let's get it."

"Brandon!"

"Sorry, sorry, sorry." He leans down and squints at the diamond. "How many carats?"

"In the set? One-half," a male voice says from behind the display case. I smile nicely at the suited, slicked-hair salesman.

Brandon straightens. "Hi," he says.

The salesman smiles at us. "A beautiful couple," he croons.

Brandon gives me a look and then turns back to the salesman. "This is my sister-in-law," he tells him.

"Oh!" the salesman says. "Oh, I'm sorry."

"Happens all the time," I say. "We're looking for a ring for Brandon's girlfriend."

The salesman, potential-sale hopes restored, smiles again. "Ahhh," he says. "The wedding set here is a beautiful choice."

He pulls it out of the display case. I have to agree.

"It's pretty," I tell Brandon.

Brandon fingers the rings. "How much?"

"It's very affordable," the salesman says. "Note the excellent craftsmanship."

"Yes, it's nice," Brandon says. "How much?"

"The diamond on the engagement ring is a full carat; the diamonds inlaid on the wedding band combine to make another carat."

I nod, eyebrows raised. "Who can put a price on something this exquisite?" I ask seriously.

The salesman's smile grows wider. "Such an eye!" he praises me.

"Thank you."

Brandon shoots me a look that could've shut any other person up.

Sad for him, I'm not any other person.

"Diamonds are forever, right?" I ask the salesman.

"They are indeed!" he replies, wringing his hands giddily.

"How much?" Brandon asks again.

"The gold is fourteen carat," the salesman tells me.

"I would have guessed that," I tell him.

"Have you worked in jewelry before?" he asks.

I shake my head. "No, I just like it."

He laughs.

"My sister's wedding ring is a bit like this one," I say, rubbing my finger over the silvery gold. "Her husband bought it here."

"A referred customer!" the salesman exults.

I nod. "You gave him a great price."

"That's Hayley's motto."

Brandon stares open-mouthed at me.

I nod again, smiling. "Such a beautiful ring," I murmur. "It does look like my sister's." I smile whimsically. "She now has five children,"

"Five!" the salesman revels.

"Two sets of twins."

"Oh my!"

"And through all those kids . . ."

"Her ring has lasted." The salesman nods proprietarily. He surveys me and Brandon. "And she recommended her siblings to come here?"

"Yes, she did."

The salesman sighs, smiling. "What a testimony. Just for that, I'll take twenty percent off the price."

We leave a few minutes later, bag in hand.

Brandon shakes his head, holding the door for me. "You're good," he says.

I bow.

He starts his car, handing me the bag carefully and rolling the windows down.

"So tulips," I say.

He nods.

"When do you want those?"

"The Friday before, I guess."

"Where are you taking her?"

He opens his mouth to answer and then stops. "Oh no you don't," he says. "If I tell you, you'll come watch."

"I will not!"

"You did with Nick and Ruby."

"Yes, well—"

"You did with Lexi and Nate too."

"But—"

He grins at me. "Sorry, Nutsy. I would like privacy when I propose."

"Spoilsport," I pout.

"I think you'll live."

I smile. "Oh well. Hannah will tell me what happened."

He moans.

I pat his shoulder. "Can I at least give you some pointers?"

"No."

"You have to get on one knee. And don't just hand her the box like Nick did. Get creative. And Hannah loves when guys in mushy movies say something really heartfelt and sappy when they're proposing."

"Didn't I say no pointers?"

"Say something about when you first met her. That will go over well. And when you ask her to marry you, say, 'Will you marry me?' not something like, 'Will you be my wife?'"

He frowns. "What's the difference?"

I wave my hand. "The second one sounds corny."

He stops in my driveway and covers his face.

"And don't do that. You need to maintain eye contact."

He groans again.

"And make sure you don't forget to—"

"Hey, Laurie," Ryan says, climbing out of his truck.

"Hey, Ryan, what are you doing here?"

He smiles and shakes a bag labeled Merson's.

"Lunch!" I yell and hop out of the truck.

"Wait, Laur, what am I not supposed to forget?" Brandon shouts, climbing out as well.

I shrug. "I don't remember." I turn to Ryan. "Did you get coffee? Please say you brought coffee!"

He grins, leans down, and kisses my cheek. "On the passenger seat." He straightens and smiles at Brandon. "There's plenty, if you want to stay."

Brandon shakes his head bleakly. "She's all yours," he mutters.

I wave at Brandon, then pick up the tray of coffees and follow Ryan up the front steps.

"Thanks for lunch, Ry." I smile, gesturing with the coffee.

"You're pitiful," he replies.

"If you think I'm so pitiful, why do you keep bringing me coffee?"

"Because at least you're predictable then."

I roll my eyes and go inside.

Dad is on the phone in the orange study. Laughing.

I peek in. He sits in one of the swivel chairs, his back to the doorway. "That's very funny, Joan," he chuckles. "What did she do then?"

I go into the kitchen, where Ryan is pulling out sandwiches.

"I got a couple extra because I wasn't sure if your dad wanted to eat with us."

"He's on the phone with Joan," I say, sitting at the table.

Ryan raises his eyebrows. "Joan?" He brings the sandwiches to the table. "How often do they talk?"

"Since she left? Seems like every couple hours."

"Hi, kids," Dad says, coming into the kitchen, holding the cordless phone.

"Hey, Mr. Holbrook." Ryan smiles.

"Who was on the phone, Dad?" I ask innocently, unwrapping a turkey sandwich.

"Joan. She said to tell you hello." Dad puts the phone in the charger and keeps smiling.

"There's a sandwich here for you, sir," Ryan says.

"Oh, thanks." Dad sits in his usual seat at the table, *humming*.

My father *never* hums. He thinks it strains your vocal cords and leads to laryngitis, sore throats, and ultimately tonsillitis.

Don't ask me how.

Ryan shoots a glance at Dad and then grins knowingly at me.

"When's Joan coming back, Dad?" I ask.

Dad blinks. "What, Dear?"

I smirk. "When's she coming back?"

"Two weeks from now."

Ryan grins wider and bites into his sandwich.

Dad chews his, staring thoughtfully at something just above my right shoulder. I turn around. Nothing but plain walls.

I smile and shake my head at Ryan. "How's Ruby?"

"Good."

"Still pregnant?"

Dad blinks at that and clears his throat. "Please don't use that word, Laurie."

I frown. "What word?"

He blushes and squirms slightly. "The word you just said."

"Pregnant?"

His red deepens. "When I was growing up, I wasn't allowed to say that word."

"So what did you call a pregnant woman?"

"With child."

I chew my sandwich and then look back at Ryan, who is trying very unsuccessfully to hide a grin. "Is Ruby still with child?"

"As far as I know," he replies, eyes sparkling in that cute little-kid grin.

I look back at Dad, who is once again in Never-Never Land.

"Hopeless," I mutter to Ryan, who grins again.

"What, Dear?" Dad asks.

"Copeland's, Dad."

He frowns. "The video store?"

"We're going there next."

"What are you renting?" Dad asks.

I shrug at Ryan. "How about *Smitten with No Return*?"

Ryan nods, playing along. "Sure."

Dad cocks his head. "I haven't heard of that one."

"I think you have," I say after I swallow. *Too late.*

He is already back in La-La Ville.

Chapter Twenty-Five

Nick grabs my arm on Wednesday night.

"Mmm-ch!" I growl around the cookie in my mouth. I swallow. "Watch it, Nicky. Hot coffee."

He frowns at the cup in my hand and shakes his head. "Laur, I really need a decision," he says, without explaining.

I purse my lips. "Personally? I like the name Riley. It's a little close to Ryan, but I think we could manage."

He stares at me for a long moment. "What?"

"I just gave you a name."

"For what?"

"Your kid."

He ignores my response. "I need a decision about the junior high girls, Laurie. Are you going to teach again next month, or do I need to find a replacement?"

"Yes, I'm teaching." I glare at him. "I'm very offended that you would consider replacing me."

"Well, you haven't told me yes or no yet."

"You didn't ask."

He smiles, rubbing his hands together pastorally. "So you're in?

Good, good. I'm very happy. The returning girls will be glad."

He walks over to his wife, who lounges on one of the beanbag chairs, fending off questions about the authenticity of her being with child.

Hannah and Brandon are sitting on the couch next to each other, his right arm around her shoulders, conversing quietly. I amble that way, shielding my coffee.

"Anyway, want to go out next Saturday?" Brandon asks her.

She studies him for a minute, apparently sees the same thing I do, and nods. "Okay."

Ask where you're going! I plead silently.

"Hi, Laurie." She smiles, looking up at me.

Here's the thing about Hannah: She's too polite. If I were on the verge of engagement, I would not interrupt that pivotal conversation with my future husband to say hi to one of my friends.

"Hey," I say. I sit down in front of them as Nick takes his place.

"Well, guys, we've now been without music on Wednesday nights for two weeks since our beloved Stephen Weatherby left us for med school, and so it is a great relief to introduce you to my new friend, Keller Stone."

A very good-looking guy holding a guitar stands up from one of the beanbag chairs.

Make that a *very* good-looking guy.

I peek around the room. It doesn't matter if she is single, dating, married, or pregnant, every female in the room has her eyebrows raised.

Keller takes the seat vacated by Dr. America and gives us a perfect smile, tinged with a little nervousness.

I can hear the thoughts of every girl: *Awww.*

"Hello. I'm Keller."

I have to cover my mouth to keep from bursting.

Our new guitarist has an English accent!

Hannah kicks me hard in the pants.

Now I cover my mouth to keep from yelping.

There is the nervous smile again. "I can see your expressions, and, yes, I'm from England. I moved here with my family about a year ago to help my father start his own business."

A good-looking, English-accented, family-oriented guy.

The word *perfect* keeps ringing in my fuddled brain.

"So with that introduction, we'll start with the music. Join me in worship?"

He rakes a guitar pick down the strings, his fingers moving deftly through the chord progressions.

"Before the throne of God above . . . I have a strong, a perfect plea . . ."

A good-looking, English-accented, family-oriented, God-centered guy who can *sing*!

He's got to have a flaw somewhere.

He sits back in the beanbag after playing four songs, and Nick stands, whistling. "Thanks, man, that was . . . wow, that was amazing. Good to have music here again."

Keller smiles modestly.

Rats. Humble too.

I sneak a look around the room again. There has to be a perfect, unattached female around here for him.

Nick flips open his Bible and I catch myself.

Bad Laurie!

I've barely laid eyes on the guy, and I'm already setting him up.

There will be—to use an Old Testament phrase—ramifications for this. Probably from Ryan.

I feel eyes skewering the back of my brain, turn, and bite the inside of my cheek.

Yep. Most definitely from Ryan.

"Turn to Mark 1:14, please," Nick says. "We're going to continue our study on the life of Christ."

Thirty minutes later he concludes. "Note the immediacy of the disciples' decision to follow Christ. When we're making the same kind of decision—whether for the first time or in a new direction—do we listen and drop everything immediately? Or do we hesitate?" He looks around the room. "Let's pray."

After he says amen, the loud din starts. Brandon and Hannah start discussing the various points of the teaching. About half the females in the room gather around Keller, chattering obnoxiously. Ruby smiles at her husband.

Ryan taps my shoulder, eyebrows raised in a question.

I grimace.

"Lauren Emma Holbrook . . ." he starts.

"Yes, actually, I am a little hungry. I'm going to go get a snack," I say, speed-closing my Bible and hightailing it for the kitchen.

"Laurie!" Ryan yells after me.

I dive into the kitchen, around the counters, and cower by the chocolate chip cookies Isabel Walters brought.

Ryan comes in a second later.

"I can't believe you!" he growls.

My only consolation is the tiny smirk hiding on his face.

"You were looking around the room for future wives, weren't you?"

"No, I was not *looking*. I was glancing."

"Same thing," he says, stopping in front of me.

"It is not. *Looking* implies an interest. *Glancing* is looking without interest." I cross my arms. "So there."

The smirk wins over, and he grins. "I swear, Laurie. . . ."

"What? You saw him same as I did."

He chuckles. "I highly doubt that."

"That what?"

"That we saw him the same way."

"Surely you jest." I smile, batting my eyelashes as I try out my English accent.

Keller Stone himself scoots into the kitchen just then, flinching. He sees us and pushes a half smile on his face. "Hi," he says, peeking back into the entryway.

"Hey. Are you okay?" Ryan says.

Keller looks at Ryan and frowns. "Are the girls here always like this?"

"Pushy?" Ryan asks, sending a glance my way. I stick my tongue out at him and Keller laughs.

A nice laugh, actually.

Shoot. Where is this guy's flaw?

"No." Keller smiles. "Um . . . overbearing."

Ryan pauses for a second and then nods. "Yep. I would say so."

"Funny, Ryan." I lean over the counter and stick my hand out. "Hi, I'm Laurie. This is Ryan."

He shakes it, smiling. "Keller. Nice to meet you."

"Same here. What business is your father in?" I ask.

"Landscaping."

Ryan brightens. "Really? That's pretty coincidental, I'd say. Listen, Keller, I'm working on Laurie's sister's backyard, and we're having some trouble establishing a retaining wall."

Keller listens carefully, eyebrows cocked intelligently. "Yes, I've noticed that the soil here is very sandy."

"What do you suggest?"

"Use cement to plant the wall down. Then you can cover the concrete with sand or plants or something a little more decorative."

Ryan nods. "Good idea. Thanks, Keller. Hey, you don't play basketball, do you?"

Ah, male bonding. I pull a cookie out and lean against the counter, half-listening, half-thinking.

The only perfect female I've ever met is now married and pregnant at nineteen. Tina.

Maybe . . . if the Opposites Attract Theory falls into place here, Keller will go for someone absolutely imperfect.

I have experience with imperfection, and, speaking personally here, I would have serious problems being married to a perfect man. I think mental institutions would have to be called.

"What do you think, Sweetheart?" Ryan says, grinning evilly, obviously knowing I was not paying attention.

Then again, there are problems with marrying imperfect people too. Such as living with a sadistic, evil child like Ryan.

"About what, *Darling*?" I ask, enunciating the endearment.

Keller blinks in confusion.

Ding! Ding! Ding! We have an imperfection! The man is not quick-witted!

"About us introducing Keller to Smith Valley Barbeque." Ryan shoots me a look that says, *Be nice, the man is new here.*

I need a guy who can't read my thoughts so easily.

"Sounds good. When?"

"Today's Wednesday," Ryan says. "How about Sunday? After church? We can introduce you to the group then."

Keller smiles, nodding. "That would be great."

I smile at both guys. I will need to begin hunting for a girl for Keller.

As easy as clothes-pinning an itsy-bitsy, teeny-weeny, yellow polka-dot bikini to a clothesline.

I'm flipping to Psalms in bed that night when Jeremiah 31:3 jumps off the page and grips my eyeballs. "'I have loved you with an everlasting love; I have drawn you with loving-kindness.'"

Everlasting love.

I grin. *Thank You, God.*

⎯⟋⎯❖⎯⟍⎯

I walk into The Brandon Knox Photography Studio early Thursday morning and yawn into the dark, dismal space.

Apparently I'm the first one here.

I flip on the lights, turn on Hannah's computer, crank the AC, and shove my backpack in my cubbyhole.

Hannah comes in then, also yawning. "Morning, Laur. You're here early."

"I've got the Tennysons. They're always here right at nine."

"Ruby probably loves them."

I laugh.

She sits at her desk and covers another yawn.

"Hey, Hannah?"

"Yeah?"

"Was Hallie there last night? I didn't see her."

Hannah leans her head on her fist. "Um, no. I don't think so. Shawn was."

"I saw him." I grin. "My, my, my."

She returns the smile. "Why do you ask about Hallie?"

"Well, I was thinking. . . ."

"Not good already."

I ignore her. "Maybe, if we're very good and subtle, we could get Shawn and Hallie a bit more serious, if you know what I mean."

Hannah frowns at me. "And just how do you intend to do that?"

"You saw Keller, right?"

"Yeah, and let me say this — and Laurie Holbrook, you can't breathe a word of this to anyone—if I wasn't nearly engaged to Brandon, I would have been in that pack of girls who assaulted him last night."

I laugh. "Hannah, I'm shocked." I grin. "Nearly engaged?" I question innocently.

She blushes prettily and fiddles with a pen. "We've talked marriage."

"You've talked marriage? As in like, 'We could get married'?"

"As in like."

"And this was a serious conversation?"

"It was."

I lean over the desk and hug her. "Hannah, my pretty, I will like having you for a sister-in-law."

"What?"

"Well, Brandon's my basically brother, so that would make you my basically sister-in-law. Yes?"

Her forehead wrinkles. "Then again, I might have to give the whole marriage issue more thought."

"Very funny."

Her eyes sparkle at me. "Yes, Laurie, I figured that out. And it will be fun."

"Yeah, it will."

"However, it will be more fun when you and Ryan tie the knot."

I shoot her a look and clear my throat. "Think what you will."

"Thank you for your permission. Now. Tell me why we're discussing Keller in relation to Hallie and Shawn." She steeples her fingers on her desk.

I drop into one of the chairs in front of her desk and lean forward, lowering my voice.

"What if . . ." I start. "What if we introduced Keller to Merson's coffee?"

Hannah's eyes narrow as she follows my train of thought. "Where Shawn and Hallie work."

"And Keller is . . . how do you say it? . . . *very* good-looking," I say, waving my hands.

"That is how you say it." Hannah grins.

"You said it yourself: If you weren't nearly engaged, you would have been there fawning, right?"

"Right."

"Hallie is not nearly engaged."

"No, she is not."

"Therefore, I submit that Hallie will be taken aback by his . . . shall we say beauty? Shawn will be wildly jealous, declare his love, and all will be well."

"I accept that submission." Hannah nods. "Excellent strategizing, Sherlock."

I raise my finger. "The question is when."

Hannah fixes a thoughtful expression on her face and tips her head toward the ceiling. "In times such as these, I have a saying."

"Do tell, dear Watson."

"Why wait?"

I grin. "Hannah, my dear, you and I are kindred spirits." I stand, lean over her, and grab her phone, dialing quickly.

"Don't tell me you memorized his number," Hannah says.

"Of course I have," I say, batting my eyes.

"Hello?"

"Hey, Ry."

Hannah rolls her eyes.

"Hi, Laur. What's up?"

"Can I have Keller's phone number?"

"Laurie, shouldn't you be at work?"

"I am at work."

"Okay, wrong question. Shouldn't you be working?"

"I am working."

"Again, wrong question. Shouldn't you be photographing?"

"I could, but the only person here to photograph is Hannah. Not that she wouldn't be a beautiful subject . . ."

Hannah nods her thanks.

"Wait a second, wait a second," Ryan says. "The only other person there is Hannah? And you want Keller's number?"

"Please?"

"Where's Ruby? Where's Brandon? Where's Ty? Where's Newton? Where's someone who can save Keller from whatever evil you've planned?" Ryan rants.

"It's a necessary evil, if that helps."

"It doesn't help."

"And it doesn't involve Keller and a girl." I frown and look at Hannah, who shrugs. "Well, not technically anyway."

Ryan sighs. "What are you going to do to him?"

I try pulling an Ethel Mertz. "Well . . ."

"Nice try."

"We just want Shawn to get jealous."

"Of Keller."

"Right."

"Why?"

"So he'll step up to the bat as far as Hallie's concerned."

He pauses. "Good sports analogy."

"Thanks!" I grin.

"You've been waiting to use that on me, haven't you?"

"Yep."

He laughs. "All right, okay. Got paper?"

I write in the air to Hannah, and she passes me a yellow sticky-note pad and a pen.

"Go ahead."

He reads me the number. "No emotional damage, Lauren Emma

Holbrook."

"If that was a question, then, no thanks. I don't have any."

"That was a command, Laurie."

"Oh. All right."

"I can't believe I'm encouraging this."

"I always knew you'd come around," I say sweetly. "Bye."

I hang up and turn to Hannah. "Got it."

She raises her hands, palms up. "What can I say? You're a genius."

"Thank you, thank you."

"When are we meeting him?"

I glance at her calendar. "We can see about this afternoon."

"That works." She waves at Newton as he comes in.

I dial the number and wait. Three rings later, his accented voice answers.

"Hi, Keller, this is Laurie Holbrook. We met last night."

"Oh, Laurie, hi. It was very good meeting you last night. I enjoyed talking to you and Ryan."

I bite my lip, suddenly not liking the plan. Why in Tarzan's nation am I tossing this guy to Hallie when I can have him?

No, no, Laurie. Stick to the plan.

"Uh, right," I fumble. "Listen, I'd like to introduce you to the local watering hole."

"The local watering hole," Keller repeats.

"Right. Merson's. It's a little café here. You like coffee?"

"I do."

"They have the best coffee. And desserts."

"Really? This would be a good place to know."

"Yes, it would. A friend and I will meet you there. Say two-ish?"

I hear him flipping papers around. "Two works."

"Great!" I grin. I rattle off the directions and hang up, schlumping into the chair, shoulders easing from their tension.

Hannah watches me, shaking her head. She opens her mouth to tell me something just as the Tennysons run in.

"We're nine minutes late!" Mrs. Tennyson moans.

Perfectionists. I know there is a reason they're on this planet, but for the life of me, I can't think of why.

"It's fine, Mrs. Tennyson. Come on back."

~◈~

At one forty-five I dig my backpack out of the cubbyhole and follow Hannah to her car.

"You do realize it takes us five minutes to get there," Hannah says.

"Better to be early and get a good seat."

She parks in front of Merson's, and I watch, mouth open, as Keller steps from his car beside us and opens my door.

"Hi." He smiles perfectly. "I see we both had the same idea about getting here early."

I watch his eyes widen as he catches sight of Hannah.

"This is my best friend, Hannah," I introduce.

She smiles a friendly smile. "Hi, Keller. I was at the Bible study last night; I just didn't get a chance to introduce myself."

Keller holds the door for us. "It's a pleasure to meet you," he tells her.

Shawn sees us come in and waves from behind the counter. "Hey, Laur, Hannah," he calls. Then he sees our Handsome Guest, and his eyebrows go up in confusion.

I step up to the counter and introduce them.

"Shawn, this is Keller. He just moved here from England. Keller, this is Shawn Merson, the maker of the coffee."

Shawn shakes Keller's hand, still obviously confused. "Hi," he says politely. "Actually, I heard you play last night. It was good."

"Thanks. It's nice to meet you," Keller returns.

"What can I get you?" he asks, sending a look toward me that says, *Why are you here with him?*

I smile. "Coffee, please. And one of those chocolate chip cookies."

"Make it two," Hannah says.

Keller smiles. "Three."

Shawn totals it up. "Six bucks, fifteen cents."

I pay him and turn to follow Hannah and Keller, who are looking for a seat.

Shawn grabs my sleeve. "Why are you here with him?" he asks in a whisper.

Good grief, I nailed that look.

"What do you mean?" I ask.

"I mean, I thought you and Ryan . . . well, I just thought you two were—"

"Were what?"

"An item, I guess."

"Oh," I say and start to follow them again. He grabs my sleeve again.

"You're not?"

"I'm not what?"

"You and Ryan aren't dating anymore?"

"Sure we are!"

"Then why are you here with him?" Shawn asks, exasperated.

"I think you should ask Hannah that question," I say.

I am mean.

Shawn gasps. "What? Brandon told me last week he was going to *propose* to her!"

This is getting interesting.

"Did he say where, by any chance?" I ask.

"No. Why is she here with Keller?" He practically spits the name.

I smile. "She's not. We're just showing him the best local coffee-house. We're being kind to one another."

He shakes his head and half-smiles. "Laurie, my life will be shorter because of you."

I pat his shoulder. "Better get right with God then. Excuse me, I need to go. The plan is not for Keller to fall in love with Hannah."

"Better run. That girl's cuter than ears on a chipmunk."

I grin. "Nice analogy."

"Thanks."

I sit next to Hannah, who found a nice corner table and is busy chatting about . . . who else? Brandon.

"So anyway, we've been dating for about . . ." She looks at me. "How long would you say, Laur?"

I shrug. "Not sure."

"Oh well." She smiles. "I've liked him for a long time."

I watch Keller's expression fall and feel sorry for him.

Hallie comes from around the back with our coffees and cookies and just about drops the tray when she sees Keller.

Aha. Plan is in progress.

"Hi . . . Laurie, Hannah . . ." she stutters, staring and then trying not to stare at our quite attractive guest.

"Hallie, this is Keller Stone. Moved here from England. He's our new guitar player at Bible study, which you would have known had you been there," I accuse.

She gives me a look. "I was helping my dad set up a pool table, Laur."

"Oh. In that case, you're forgiven."

She smiles kindly at Keller. "How'd you end up with these two?"

"I don't like that tone," Hannah says from behind me.

Hallie grins. "Three coffees, three cookies." She sets the tray on the table.

Keller's eyes warm as he watches her. "Hallie, right?"

She holds out her hand. "Right. Hallie Forbes."

He shakes it, standing. "I hope to see you again."

"Come back and you will. Let me know if you need anything else."

I sneak a look at Shawn as Hallie dives for the back room and Keller resumes his seat.

Shawn's eyes are cool as he appraises Keller and then follows Hallie into the back.

I smile at Hannah and then grab my spoon and coffee. "Need to go to the doctor's station, excuse me," I say, standing and going back to the counter where Shawn keeps his sugar and milk.

I open the milk canister, lean over the counter, grab a cup, pour the remaining milk into the cup, hand it to Hannah, and then pick up the empty canister and head around the counter to the back, where I can now hear Shawn and Hallie's conversation.

"You weren't there last night," Shawn is saying.

"No. I helped my dad put together a pool table."

"You should've called me. I could have come and helped."

"I thought about it, but I really wanted you to go to the Bible study. A new Christian needs to grow, Shawn."

My chin hits the milk canister as my mouth drops open.

"What was that?" Shawn asks.

Hallie shifts to the left and sees me standing there. "Hi, Laurie."

"Shawn! Oh my gosh!" I yell.

He closes his eyes in annoyance, but can't stop the grin.

"You're a Christian?" I shriek. "You believe?" I skip over and grab him in a hug. "I am so happy!"

He rubs my back and then hugs me too. "Yes, Laurie. Now that you know, can you calm down? The whole restaurant can hear you."

I pull away and hug Hallie. "You!" I laugh. "I knew it! I knew it the whole time!"

She steps back, grinning. "Knew what?"

Ooo. Need to tread carefully here.

"That you would be a great witness. I am so excited," I gush, while mentally going *whew!*

"Why are you behind the counter, Laurie?" Shawn says, gruff exterior back in place.

"You're out of milk." I hand him the canister. "That is . . . wow . . . I'm really, really happy for you, Shawn." I grin. "Now you get to spend all of eternity with me. Aren't you happy?"

"Ecstatic." He rolls his eyes, but smiles. "It's cool, Laur. It's so cool." His voice has a softness I've never heard before, his eyes twinkling. "Hallie helped me. She walked me through all these verses about God's holiness and love and my sinfulness. I just . . ." His voice trails off and he shakes his head. "It was so cool," he says again.

I'm smiling so wide, tears are building in my eyes. Or maybe I'm crying. I half-laugh and swipe my bottom eyelids. *Wow, God! You are amazing!*

Shawn refills the canister, grins at Hallie, and escorts me out of the back room and in front of the counter.

I pour the milk into my mug while he watches.

"The whole concept of milk in coffee really grosses me out," he says. "Sorry."

I stir the coffee and turn to go back to the table when he grabs my sleeve again.

"Laurie," he whispers.

I look at him, waiting.

"Look, you're really good at matchmaking. . . ."

"Thanks." I smile.

"Keep your voice down. Listen, I want to ask Hallie out. How . . . that is to say, what do I do?" he says slowly.

"What do you mean?"

"I mean, how do I do it?"

"How do you ask her out?" I whisper.

"Right."

I shake my head. "Shawn . . . you can't tell me you've never asked a girl on a date."

"Laurie, I've never asked a girl on a date."

I stare at him. "Why? You're nice, you're a good-looking guy, and you can cook!"

"Keep your voice down!"

"Sorry. Look, all you do is say, 'Will you go out with me?'" I sip my coffee. "See? Easy as nothing."

He studies me for a second, then nods. "Okay, okay. I can do that. When?"

"When what?"

"When should I ask her?"

"Well, based on Keller's reaction to your pretty waitress, I would say as soon as possible."

He nods slowly. "When?"

"Um, Shawn, I just—"

"No, I mean, when should we go out?"

"I don't know, Shawn! Be creative! Take her out for barbeque tomorrow night."

"Barbeque. Tomorrow night."

I smile and pat his arm. "Trust me, it's not that hard."

"What's not that hard?" Ryan says from behind me.

I whirl and bite my lip. "Uh, hi."

"Hi." He smiles knowingly.

Ick. I am in major trouble here.

Shawn leans closer, keeping his voice low. "How did you ask Laurie out?" he asks Ryan.

Ryan looks at me, brow furrowed. I shrug.

"I have no idea," Ryan says.

"Glad I mean that much to you, Honey," I say.

"Do you remember?"

"Nope."

"Why do you need to know?" Ryan asks Shawn.

"He's going to ask Hallie out," I whisper.

"Ah." Ryan nods and claps Shawn on the shoulder. "Good luck."

"He's a Christian," I tell him.

Ryan pauses, midclap. "Who is?"

I grin, and suddenly the tears are back.

Ryan's face lights up, and that adorable smile spreads across his face. "Holy cow!" he shouts, grabbing Shawn in a hug across the counter. "Wow, man!" He claps his shoulder harder. "We've been praying"—he looks at me—"how long?"

"Since we met you," I tell Shawn.

"Yeah," Ryan says.

Shawn smiles at Ryan. "Thanks, guys."

"Wow. Well, I'd say your chances with—"

"Shush!" I put my finger to my lips.

"—her just went up," Ryan whispers.

Shawn takes a deep breath just as Hallie comes out of the back room. She sees Ryan and smiles. "Hi, Ryan. How are you?"

"Great, thanks. Awesome news about Shawn!"

She's laughing. "I know, I know!"

Shawn's green eyes soften considerably as he watches Hallie's excitement.

I hum as I stir my coffee, *"Goin' to the chapel of love."*

Hallie's mouth falls open. "I love that song!"

Chapter Twenty-Six

A week and a half later my cell phone rings as I go downstairs. It's Saturday and a gorgeous, sunshiny day. A perfect day for an engagement. "This is Vizzini," I answer.

"Inigo. Position?"

"Still at the Farmhouse."

Hallie groans. "Laurie—"

"Vizzini," I interrupt.

"Whatever. I thought we were tailing them from nine on."

"We are. I didn't set my alarm right. I'm there in ten."

"Fine. Inigo out." There's a click.

I hang up and Joan laughs, stirring a cup of raspberry tea at the kitchen table.

"You're using code names why?" she asks, her eyes sparkling.

I shrug. "It's fun."

"How long are you going to follow Brandon and Hannah?"

"As long as it takes."

She sips her tea and watches me for a second. "I guess the thought of just letting them have their moment in privacy didn't occur to you."

"Nope," I say cheerfully.

Joan drove here this time, arriving late yesterday afternoon. Dad was so excited, he nearly did another coat of lime paint on the walls.

I talked him out of it.

I smile at Joan, noticing how comfortable she seems in our house. She makes her own tea; she helps with dinner; she watches movies with me. . . .

Come to think of it, I'm comfortable with her in our house. It is actually kind of nice having another female around.

Darcy skitters through the kitchen barking, and I let him out back.

"Are you wearing that?" Joan asks.

I look down at my jeans and tank top. "Yep."

"What if he takes her to a fancy restaurant?"

I shake my head. "Not Brandon's style."

She grins. "Have fun."

I take two steps toward the door before turning around, leaning down, and kissing Joan's cheek lightly. "I'm glad God put you and my dad together," I tell her.

Her eyes fill. "Oh, Laur. Thank you, Honey."

She squeezes my hand, and I leave.

I drive to Brandon's apartment building and park down the street, dialing Hallie.

"Inigo," she answers.

"This is Vizzini. I'm at the Pit of Despair. Repeat, I'm at the—"

"Heard you the first time, Viz. Loud and clear."

"Have we touched base with Miracle Max yet?"

Hallie pauses. "Who's Miracle Max again?"

"Shawn, Hallie."

"Oh, right!"

"Sheesh. Forget your own boyfriend."

I can hear the irritation in her voice. "We've had three dates, Laur. I'd hardly call him my boyfriend."

"The name is Vizzini, and I would call him your boyfriend." I grin and settle back in my seat, watching the door to Brandon's place. "Okay. What about Fezzik?"

"Ryan?"

"Hallie!"

"Sorry, sorry, sorry," she mutters. "Yeah. Fezzik is down a few blocks from you. Max is between Main and Parkway." Hallie pauses. "So, Laur, if Shawn is my boyfriend, does that make me his girlfriend?"

I try my best to keep the smile out of my voice. "So I've always been told, Hallie."

"Hmm." Another pause. "It does have a nice ring to it."

"What does?"

"My boyfriend." She giggles, and I let my smile spread across my face.

Movement catches my eye and I sit up straight, squinting. Brandon opens his front door, walks out, closes it behind him, swings his keys around his finger, and unlocks his car.

"Inigo?"

"Here."

"I've got Westley in sight. He's getting into his car. He's turned the car on."

Hallie giggles. "This is so much fun!"

I grin. "Alert Max. I'll give Fezzik a call."

"Aye, aye. This is Inigo, over and out."

I hang up and dial Ryan.

I hear him swallow. "This is . . . Fezzik. I think."

"Vizzini here. Are you eating on the job?"

"Yes, ma'am. Finished, ma'am." I can tell he's smiling.

"Westley's backing out of his driveway." I turn the ignition and wait a few minutes before following. "He's driving toward Main."

"Um . . . Miracle Max, right? He's there."

"Inigo is alerting him."

"I'm right behind you, Vizzini."

I look in my rearview mirror. Ryan lifts a few fingers off his steering wheel in a wave.

"I see you, Fezzik."

Brandon turns right on Main.

"Inigo's calling me," Ryan says. "I'm switching over."

He hangs up. I dial Shawn.

"Max? Vizzini here," I say.

"Hey, Vizzini."

"Westley's headed your way."

A moment later, Shawn says, "Ah. Got him, Vizzini. I see you too."

"Who's at Buttercup's house?"

"Inigo was heading there." I wave at Shawn as I pass him. "Hey, Vizzini?" he says.

"Yes, Max?"

"What's Ryan's name again?"

"Fezzik," I answer.

"Right. Fezzik's right behind you."

"I know."

"I'm getting behind Fezzik."

I smile. "We're going to look like a funeral procession."

"Keep Brandon a couple cars ahead of you."

"Westley, Max. His name is Westley."

"Right." Shawn sighs. "Why am I doing this again?"

"Because it's fun."

"It's nosy. We should leave the man alone."

"It's interesting and I'm curious."

He sighs again.

My call-waiting beeps, and I glance at the phone. "Got to go, Max. Inigo's calling me."

I switch over. "Hey, Inigo."

"Hi, Viz," Hallie says. "Westley just turned on Buttercup's street."

"Got him. Stay back so he doesn't see you."

"I'm four buildings down, parked under one of those group carports."

"Good."

I drive past Hannah's apartment building and spot Hallie's car. "I see you. I'm parking next to you."

She rolls down her passenger window, and I roll my driver's window down. "Hey, I'm thinking we should go in one car," she yells at me. "Less obvious."

I nod. "Okay."

Ryan pulls in beside me, and Shawn pulls to the other side of Hallie.

"Everyone in my car," Hallie says.

"Wait until they're driving out," I caution. I turn around, watching.

A few minutes later, Brandon and Hannah come down the stairs from her apartment. He opens the passenger door for her, and she slides in.

He starts the engine and turns around.

"Ready . . . go!" I shout.

We all slam out of the cars and dive into Hallie's baby sedan, Shawn and Ryan knocking heads in the backseat.

They both let out a cry.

"Sorry, boys," Hallie says, looking at them in the rearview mirror as she follows Brandon. "Hazards of a little car."

I grin back at Ryan, and he squeezes my shoulder. "You're pathetic."

"I hear you there, Inigo," Shawn says, stretching.

Hallie looks back at him. "I didn't say anything."

"Wait a second," Shawn says. "Who are you?" he asks Ryan.

"Fezzik."

"Oh, right. Sorry, wrong name."

Brandon turns down a side street and stops in front of a park.

"Careful, Inigo. Go slow," I say.

Brandon gets out carrying a cooler, goes around, opens Hannah's door, helps her out, and then kisses her solidly.

Hallie and I smile tearfully at each other.

"I wonder what's in the cooler?" Ryan says, wistfully.

"Shut up!" Hallie and I whisper together.

Hallie parks on the other side of the street. She pulls a pair of binoculars out of the glove compartment and hands them to me, grinning.

Shawn grins cockily. "Guess your name shouldn't have been Vizzini; it should've been Spy Girl," he drawls.

"My name is Inigo!" She laughs. "Good grief, Shawn!"

I train the binoculars on Brandon and Hannah and watch as he spreads out a blanket and sets the cooler on it. They sit.

"Shh," I whisper. "Don't be loud; the windows are open."

Brandon pops the cooler open and pulls out two sandwiches and two Cokes.

"What are they eating?" Ryan asks.

"Sandwiches."

"Mmm," Ryan and Shawn say together.

Hallie shushes them.

"What? It's lunchtime and we're hungry," Shawn defends. "What do you say, Ry? My place afterward?"

"It's a date." Ryan grins.

I glance at Hallie, whose eyes slit before she bursts into laughter. "So much for the sweet comfort of having boyfriends, Laur. I think we just lost them."

"It's okay, girls," Ryan says, patting each of our shoulders. "Shawn and I are just lunch buddies."

"Wait, wait, wait!" I stare through the binoculars.

"What?" Hallie whispers.

Brandon props himself up on one knee and is reaching into his pocket. His back is to me, so I can't see what he says, but it must be nice because Hannah is crying.

"She's crying," I whisper to Hallie.

"Aww." She coos.

"He's handing her something," I whisper.

Hallie starts getting teary.

"Oh gee whiz," Shawn says.

Hannah backhands her face and starts nodding vigorously.

"She's nodding!" I shriek.

"She said yes?" Ryan asks.

"They're kissing!" I yell.

The boys start grinning. Hallie's face splits in a smile.

I can't see anymore. Tears are filling my eyes, giving my contacts a good swimming pool.

Ryan leans forward and wraps his arms around me and my seat. "It happened, Kiddo." He grins, kissing my cheek.

I sniff and wipe a tear off my cheek. "Yeah," I say, smiling. *Thanks, Lord! This is such an answer to a lot of prayer!*

Hallie grabs me in a hug, laughing loudly. "We did it! We did it!"

In our excitement, we aren't exactly being quiet. My door is suddenly yanked open, and someone drags me out of the car by my arm.

"Ow." I gasp, sniffling, and then smile at Brandon. "Hi, Brandon."

He shakes his head, closing his eyes. Hannah bites back a smile.

"Lauren Emma Holbrook . . ." he starts.

I look up at him and wipe another tear away.

His face softens. "Oh good grief," he says finally. "I'll let you off the hook. For now."

I grin, give him a huge hug, then pull Hannah into it as well.

"I love you guys," I sniffle.

Brandon kisses the top of my head. "Love you too, Nutsy."

Hannah and I start crying all over again, and Hallie joins us in the tear-fest.

Shawn and Ryan climb out and clap Brandon on the back. "Congrats, Brandon," Ryan says. "Just for the record, none of this spying stuff was our idea."

"None of it at all," Shawn echoes.

I sniff and wipe my eyes, smiling at my basically brother and his sweet fiancée. Our sovereign God created those two for each other before time began. It makes me wonder. . . .

I look over at Ryan, who grins at me and then turns to Brandon.

"What kind of sandwiches did you bring?"

About the Author

ERYNN MANGUM is a twentysomething single who still lives at home and has no immediate plans to leave. She has been published in *Teenage Christian Magazine*, has completed the two-year apprenticeship course given by the Christian Writers Guild, and recently finished the one-year Journeyman course. This is her second novel. To learn more about Erynn, visit her website at www.erynnmangum.com.

CHECK OUT THESE OTHER GREAT TITLES FROM NAVPRESS!

Miss Match

Erynn Mangum

ISBN-13: 978-1-60006-095-3

ISBN-10: 1-60006-095-1

Lauren Holbrook's calling is matchmaking the romantically challenged. She sets out to introduce Nick, her carefree singles' pastor, to Ruby, her neurotic coworker. When Lauren's foolproof plan begins to unravel, she learns that a simple introduction between friends can bring about complicated results.

On the Loose

Jenny B. Jones

ISBN-13: 978-1-60006-115-8

ISBN-10: 1-60006-115-X

Life is looking up for Katie Parker as she adjusts to her foster family. But things turn chaotic when she's accused of stealing and she loses the lead in the school play, as well as her shot with a real-life Prince Charming. Then her foster mom is diagnosed with cancer, and she begins to doubt if God really does care.

Hollywood Nobody

Lisa Samson

ISBN-13: 978-1-60006-091-5

ISBN-10: 1-60006-091-9

Fifteen-year-old Scotty Dawn has spent her young life on the road. Scotty is wise beyond her years, but she struggles to find her identity. Complicating matters is a mother who offers no guidance and a father she's never met. She documents her journey on a "Hollywood Nobody" blog, but as she begins to find dark answers to tough questions, will her story have a happy ending?

To order copies, call NavPress at 1-800-366-7788
or log on to www.navpress.com.